"How badly will they suffer?"

"Charming of you to be so considerate of your intended victims, Baron," Magus said. "If we used the liquid lewisite instead of sarin, their agony would be much prolonged. The blister agent causes immediate burning pain in the chest and eyes, temporary blindness, and after a latency period of a few hours causes severe inflammation of the lungs, leading to death. On the other hand, high doses of sarin gas chill relatively quickly, if not painlessly. The nerve agent disrupts the normal functioning of the body's muscles. They go into spasm or cease to operate altogether. Unlike lewisite, its victims, once poisoned, don't move very far. They collapse, go into convulsions, then total paralysis sets in, which causes suffocation. Salting the earth and water around Sunspot with liquid sarin will make it uninhabitable for many years to come. A permanent solution to your quandary is what you wanted. That's what you've got."

"Yes, so it would appear."

"And you're ready to pay the price?"

Other titles in the Deathlands saga:

JAMES AXLER

DEATH LANDS®

Sunspot

A GOLD EAGLE BOOK FROM

W💥RLDWIDE®

TORONTO • NEW YORK • LONDON
AMSTERDAM • PARIS • SYDNEY • HAMBURG
STOCKHOLM • ATHENS • TOKYO • MILAN
MADRID • WARSAW • BUDAPEST • AUCKLAND

First edition December 2007

ISBN-13: 978-0-373-62590-1
ISBN-10:   0-373-62590-1

SUNSPOT

Oh for a lodge in some vast wilderness,
Some boundless contiguity of shade,
Where rumor of oppression and deceit,
Of unsuccessful or successful war,
Might never reach me more.
                    —William Cowper
                       The Task [1785], Book II:
                       "The Timepiece"

THE DEATHLANDS SAGA

This world is their legacy, a world born in the violent nuclear spasm of 2001 that was the bitter outcome of a struggle for global dominance.

There is no real escape from this shockscape where life always hangs in the balance, vulnerable to newly demonic nature, barbarism, lawlessness.

But they are the warrior survivalists, and they endure—in the way of the lion, the hawk and the tiger, true to nature's heart despite its ruination.

Ryan Cawdor: The privileged son of an East Coast baron. Acquainted with betrayal from a tender age, he is a master of the hard realities.

Krysty Wroth: Harmony ville's own Titian-haired beauty, a woman with the strength of tempered steel. Her premonitions and Gaia powers have been fostered by her Mother Sonja.

J. B. Dix, the Armorer: Weapons master and Ryan's close ally, he, too, honed his skills traversing the Deathlands with the legendary Trader.

Doctor Theophilus Tanner: Torn from his family and a gentler life in 1896, Doc has been thrown into a future he couldn't have imagined.

Dr. Mildred Wyeth: Her father was killed by the Ku Klux Klan, but her fate is not much lighter. Restored from predark cryogenic suspension, she brings twentieth-century healing skills to a nightmare.

Jak Lauren: A true child of the wastelands, reared on adversity, loss and danger, the albino teenager is a fierce fighter and loyal friend.

Dean Cawdor: Ryan's young son by Sharona accepts the only world he knows, and yet he is the seedling bearing the promise of tomorrow.

In a world where all was lost, they are humanity's last hope....

Chapter One

Ryan Cawdor stood out of the line of fire, his back pressed against a mud-brick wall. The ground was partially frozen underfoot, the early morning sky streaked with scudding low clouds. Gusts of wind shrieked through the ramshackle hilltop maze of Redbone ville, drowning out the screams of the dying.

A makeshift barricade of rocks and dirt and tree limbs stood less than one hundred feet from Ryan's position. It blocked the entrance to a narrow path that was the ville's only remaining escape route. The blueless sights and muzzles of three AK-47s poked out through firing ports, gaps in the layers of piled debris.

From the opposite direction, near the center of the pesthole ville, a frantic flurry of gunshots rang out. With black powder revolvers and remade single-shot 12-gauges, Redbone's trapped residents fought off a superior force. The resistance was answered by short, efficient bursts of heavy-caliber autofire.

Time was running out, for all concerned.

Ryan stepped from cover, his scoped Steyr SSG-70 longblaster slung over his shoulder, a SIG-Sauer P226 semiautomatic blaster securely holstered under his left armpit. With empty hands in plain view, he advanced up the rutted path, past a rude stock pen on his right, toward the waist-high, twelve-foot-long barricade. A blast of wind scoured the frosty earth, whipping up the stench of pig manure. The pigs themselves were nowhere to be seen, but mounds of loose droppings lay scattered over the track.

The worn AK sights held steady on his chest as he closed the distance, walking straight into the maw of a firing squad. Fifty feet. Forty feet. The adrenaline coursing through his veins made his fingertips tingle and his scalp crawl. The empty socket of his left eye began to itch like a rad bastard under its black patch. The sensation spread along the jagged welt of scar that split his brow and cheek. Ryan didn't scratch. He kept his hands in sight, well away from his body.

"Stop there!" someone shouted from behind the barrier.

Ryan kept walking, spreading his arms wide, displaying open palms in a gesture of surrender.

"Stop or you're dead!"

Ryan was betting they wouldn't shoot unless he made a move for his blasters. Baron Malosh paid his press gangs by the head. The live head. This crew's job was to capture or to turn back any ville folk trying to escape conscription into the baron's army. To Malosh even a one-eyed man had value, if only as cannon fodder.

"Stop!"

"I give up," Ryan said as he continued forward. "You win. Take my weapons…"

"Get on your belly! Now!"

"No way am I going to lie facedown in pig shit," Ryan shouted back. Though his words and tone were defiant, as he advanced he raised his hands even higher. "I said you could take my blasters."

Ryan was five yards from the barricade when the baron's men realized they had a problem. The man was tall and broad across the shoulders, and the closer he came to the narrow path entrance with arms spread, the more he blocked their view—and their ability to control the entire kill zone. To see around him, to see what was coming directly behind him, they had to move to the side and stand from cover. This they did more or less in unison.

As the men jumped up, Ryan dived to the dirt in front of the barrier, leaving them exposed to incoming fire.

At once, tightly clustered blaster shots and the canvas-ripping clatter of an Uzi rang out from behind him. The volley of slugs whined a yard above his head, thudding into wood, ricocheting off rock and smacking flesh.

The burst of blasterfire lasted no more than three seconds. Ryan pushed up from the ground and, drawing his SIG from shoulder leather, vaulted the barricade, leaping into the tight, shanty-lined lane.

All three of Malosh's men were down.

Over the sights of his SIG, Ryan quickly checked the fallen for signs of life. Overlapping layers of worn duct tape held the soles and tops of their boots together. They wore no insignia or badge of rank. Their bearded faces and gloveless hands were encrusted with layers of grime. Only one was moving, his legs mule-kicking spastically. His skull had been cratered by multiple bullet hits, front and side; gobs of steaming brain matter clung to the coarse mud wall.

No follow-up shots required.

Ryan raised his weapon in a two-handed grip and surveyed the alley. The tight passage was like a wind tunnel; he squinted his good right eye as grit peppered his face. On either side of the dirt lane, a dozen one-room shanties shared common earthen walls and corrugated metal roofs. The crooked, doorless entryways faced one another, raising the possibility of a nasty, close-range cross fire. Two-thirds of the way down the path, a huge dead hog lay on its side in a pool of blood. Through the gap at the far end of the alley, Ryan saw distant blue mountains bathed in bright sunlight, beyond the edge of the coming storm. Because of the elevation and the angle of view, he couldn't see the cultivated fields around the hilltop's base, or the border where they gave way to desert scrubland. For generations, the area's farmers had retreated to higher ground for their common defense. The fortified ville had easily held off bands of predatory muties and coldheart robbers. Against a large, well-trained and equipped military force, however, Redbone was a sitting duck.

Ryan took a quick glance over his shoulder to check on his companions, who were charging toward him.

Jak Lauren ran in front in long, loping strides, his .357 Magnum Colt Python in his fist. Jak's face was bloodlessly white, his long, lank, platinum hair streamed back from his head. As the albino ran, his ruby-red eyes scanned the doorways and rooftops of the wall-to-wall huts for enemy snipers. Following hard on his heels, puffing from the effort, was John Barrymore Dix. The bespectacled Armorer gripped his Uzi machine pistol in both hands, his shoulder-slung, Smith

& Wesson M-4000 12-gauge pump slapped wildly against his back. His prized fedora was screwed down on his head to keep it from blowing off.

Behind J.B. were two women with revolvers drawn, running shoulder-to-shoulder. In a shaggy fur coat and Western-style boots was tall, red-haired Krysty Wroth, Ryan's longtime lover and soul mate. By her side, the short black woman in a patched, milspec parka was Dr. Mildred Wyeth, whom Ryan and the others had awakened from a hundred-year cryosleep. Both women carried .38-caliber weapons. Krysty's blaster of choice was a Smith & Wesson 640. Mildred's was a Czech-made ZKR 551, the same make and model of firearm she had used to take a silver medal in the last-ever summer Olympic Games.

The world of big-time international sport had ended along with everything else more than a century before, on January 20, 2001. The true causes of Armageddon were lost in the seething, global hellfire of the all-out Soviet-U.S. nuclear exchanges that had occurred on that fateful day. On January 21, 2001 there was no one left to spin the blame for the ultimate catastrophe, to fume and sputter over whose half-trillion dollars' worth of missile defense equipment had malfunctioned first, over who was the aggressor and who the victim. A handful of scattered human survivors had inherited a ruined earth, a disrupted and lethal ecology, an utterly destroyed civilization. With no political entity left to blame for their tragic circumstances, they turned on science, itself. Those who had once proudly worn the uniform of that discipline, the whitecoats, were the target of their deepest and most abiding hatred.

Bringing up the rear of the formation, the tails of his waistcoat flapping as he sprinted in cracked knee boots, was Dr. Theophilus Algernon Tanner. Of the six companions, the tall, scarecrow-like Tanner had the most cause to despise the scientists. Whitecoats from ultra-secret Operation Chronos had trawled him forward from the year 1896 to 1998, ripping him from his life in Omaha, Nebraska, from his wife Emily and his children, Rachel and little Jolyon. In isolated laboratories, researchers had experimented on him for long months, and then they had hurled him blindly into the future; this to rid themselves of his truculent Victorian carcass and as payback for his lack of cooperation. That the hurling had happened only weeks before nukeday was just more of Doc's bad luck. Instead of dying in the conflagration of January 20th, and reuniting with his loved ones in heaven, he had been transported ninety-some years forward in time.

To hell.

In his left hand Doc carried a silver-handled, ebony swordstick, which counterbalanced the considerable mass and weight of the firearm he held in his other hand. The black powder LeMat was a relic. Its short, .63-caliber underbarrel was designed for "blue whistler" scattershot and close-range mayhem—the Civil War's version of a "room broom." The LeMat's five-and-a-half-inch top barrel fired .44-caliber lead balls from its revolver cylinder.

Behind Doc, Ryan saw black smoke begin to pour from the roofs of the jumble of low buildings at the center of the ville. The baron's press gangs were burning out Redbone ville's draft resisters.

As he turned back to the alley, a short man leaned out of a doorway on the right, AK shouldered and ready to rip. Ryan didn't pause to verify allegiance or intent. He opened fire first, punching four 9 mm slugs into the chest and neck of the would-be shooter. The man groaned and fell back through the doorway, dropping the AK across the threshold as he went down. His boots stuck out over the threshold, their silver-tape-wrapped toes pointing skyward.

"Help! Please!" someone called from the shanty.

Others inside took up the desperate cry. "Help! Help us!"

Ryan stood his ground, covering the lane until his companions had jumped the barrier and joined him. On his signal, they advanced quickly and quietly, leapfrogging and clearing the doors on either side as they went. The closer they got to the shanty where the dead man lay, the louder and more frantic the shouting became.

Ryan signaled for Jak, Krysty and Doc to continue sweeping the alley for more of Malosh's crew. Then he stepped over the body and entered the hut, with J.B. and Mildred behind him. The low-ceilinged gloom reeked of fear-sweat and pig muck. Five people sat on the earthen floor, their hands tied behind their backs, their knees drawn up, ankles bound together. Two of the men and the sole female were in their late teens or early twenties, dressed in homespun cloth. One of the men had a crusted-over, bloody head wound; the other had a badly bruised left eye. There was straw and dried dung in the woman's long, coarse blond hair, and her lower lip was split and swollen.

The other two male captives were trussed back to

back. Their clothes were layers of filthy rags. One was in his late fifties with a deeply weather-seamed and pitted face, and wild salt-and-pepper hair and whiskers. The man tied to him was less than half his age and half again his size, bootless, barrel-chested, his pattern-bald hair shaved to stubble, with an oddly smooth and doughy baby face.

"Cut us free," the woman said to Ryan. When he made no immediate move to do so, she shrilled at him, "We're Redbone folk, born and bred. We're on the same side as you. Otherwise we wouldn't be tied up like this."

"If you don't let us go," the man with the bruised eye pitched in, "Baron Malosh will force us to fight his stinking wars. Free us and we'll fight against him, here and now."

"We'll take back our ville," the woman declared.

Ryan gave her a dubious look, but unsheathed his panga and with deft strokes severed all their bonds.

"You know you can't possibly win," Mildred told the quintet as they rose to their feet. "Come with us, away from here."

"We won't abandon our land," the man with the head wound said. "Our kin have been here since nukeday."

"We don't have time to argue with you," Ryan said. "You can do as you please."

The young woman snatched up the AK from the threshold. "If you fight alongside us," she said, "we have a chance."

J.B. succinctly stated the companions' position on the matter. "Not our ville," he told her.

"There are three more AKs outside," Ryan said. "You

can hold off the baron's gang from behind the barricade. Wait until they get close before you open fire…"

Ryan spoke the last words to the trio's backs as they rushed out the door.

"What about you two?" Mildred asked the remaining men. "Are you staying to fight?"

"The fight's already lost," the older one said. "If we stay, the baron's men will catch us. We'll take our chances with you."

"What are your names?" Mildred asked.

"He's Young Crad and I'm called Bezoar."

"This is going to be a foot race," Ryan warned them. "No telling how far we're going to have to run to get clear of Malosh. If you can't keep up with us, you'll get left behind. We won't let you slow us down, and we won't risk our lives to save yours. Do you understand?"

Bezoar nodded, grimacing at the news. Young Crad stared back. Not sullen. Not fearful. Not shell-shocked. If anything, he seemed mildly tickled by Ryan's little speech. The grizzle-bearded man pushed his large friend out into the alley, ahead of Ryan and the others.

When Young Crad saw the dead black-and-white hog lying in the lane, he broke free of the smaller man's grip. He raced to the side of the gutshot animal, dropped to his knees and unleashed a piercing cry of anguish.

Bezoar ran to catch him, limping hard on a right leg that didn't bend at all at the knee. "She's gone, boy," he said. "It's a nukin' pity and a rad-blasted waste but there's nothing more we can do for the old girl. Buck up, now, we've got to go…"

"Move!" J.B. growled.

Young Crad looked up, his eyes streaming tears.

"Piggie dear, piggie dear," he moaned. His chin quivered uncontrollably as he stroked the bullet-riddled hide.

Bezoar grabbed his friend by the shoulders and gently but firmly dragged him from the corpse and pulled him up the lane.

"A gimp and a triple-stupe droolie," J.B. said, shaking his head. "They aren't gonna last half a mile, Ryan."

Such was the harsh reality of Deathlands. It was a place where the bloody bones of the weak nourished the strong. That these swineherds had lived as long as they had was a minor miracle.

Soon to end.

"I reckon it's their choice where they want to die," Cawdor said.

Jak, Krysty and Doc waited at the far end of the lane. The Redbone folk they'd rescued were already manning the barricade, covering their rear with the captured predark assault rifles.

The other hovels were deserted. Mebbe the residents had made it out. Mebbe not. Just beyond the last of the tumbledown dwellings, the alley ended abruptly at the edge of a nearly sheer, three-hundred-foot cliff. Redbone ville was laid out like a medieval castle town. The ville's buildings clung to and jutted up from the hilltop, extensions of the vertical bedrock. From the alley's terminus, a rough zigzag path led down the cliff face to the gridwork of cultivated fields below—beyond them a bleak desert panorama stretched to the blue mountains on the horizon. There was no sign of a rear guard on the plain. Malosh had apparently committed his entire force to a surprise attack.

Krysty took in the unarmed swineherds, then looked at Ryan with concern. Her prehensile mutie hair had already drawn into tight curls, an automatic response to the mortal danger they faced.

He anticipated her question. "They know they're excess baggage," he said. "Let's get out of here."

Jak jumped onto the trail and led the rapid descent. As the companions skidded single file to the bottom, thunder rumbled in the distance. Bolts of lightning shot through the northwestern sky that had turned black as night. It was at least twenty degrees warmer down on the plain, and the wind had acquired a strange, unpleasantly humid edge.

"Could be a chem storm," Krysty said. "A bad one."

"It's going to come down on us hard," Mildred said.

"And shortly, it would appear…" Doc added. "Perhaps we should consider seeking shelter until it passes?"

"No time for that, now," Ryan said. "We have to get out of longblaster range before the baron's men spot us and pin us down. You take the point, Jak. Cut through the fields, then follow cover to the southeast, away from the storm front. Double-time it. No stops."

With the albino wild child in the lead, they broke from the base of the hill and ran into the rows of Cradding cabbages and knee-high potato plants. There were no farmers' bodies lying about. Malosh's army had closed in during the night and had attacked at first light.

As they neared the edge of the fields, autofire roared from the hilltop behind them. The mad clattering sawed back and forth. It sounded as though the folks manning the barrier were giving as good as they were getting.

The companions were about seven hundred yards from the base of the hill when they heard a string of sharp booms—multiple gren detonations, not thunderclaps. As the echoes of the explosions faded, blasterfire ceased.

The barricaded alley had fallen, and with it, Redbone ville.

Jak picked up the pace and Ryan and the others matched it. The desert hardpan was much easier to run on than soft, cultivated earth. A warm tailwind, now driving and steady, pushed against their backs.

The albino led them down into a shallow gully and they followed it, running as low to the ground as they could. The ditch wasn't deep enough to completely conceal them, but the chaparral and scrub along its lip broke up and blurred their silhouettes. They drew no sniper fire from the ville, either because they hadn't been seen or because they were already out of range.

The discomforts of the forced march were all too familiar to them—the bonfires burning in lungs and legs, the jarring impacts on hip joints and knees, the rhythmic rasp of breath in the ears. The two swineherds had managed to keep up so far. Bezoar hip-hopped along, red-faced, his hair matted with sweat, arms flailing for balance. Barefooted Young Crad moved easily beside him with a powerful, lumbering gait.

Fourteen hours ago, on the previous evening, the companions had arrived in Redbone after a long trek south. They had planned on trading part of their stock of centerfire bullets for food and water this morning; instead they had had to expend them making their escape. The breakout was nothing Ryan and the others were ashamed of. Hard-bitten realists, they knew there were things they could fight and things they could not.

None of them had any firsthand knowledge of Baron Malosh. What little information they possessed came from tales they'd heard in gaudy houses and around communal campfires along their route. In Deathlands, stories of barbarism and savagery were taken in along with mother's milk, this to prepare the young for the inescapable facts of life. Exaggerations, misconceptions, distortions and outright lies were expected—even honored—in a dark, misbegotten place where ignorance and chaos ruled. If a tenth of the gossip the companions had heard about Malosh was true, he was an utterly ruthless marauder, and a formidable adversary.

It was said that he had carved a kingdom out of nothing. His own homeland was shit poor, with little water and fertile soil, barely able to support its population. He made up the difference with hit-and-run campaigns against the unprotected borders of richer neighboring barons. Malosh kept his ragtag army in constant motion, resupplying it through looting and pillage, replacing dead fighters with conscripts—norms and muties, male and female. He enforced military discipline with an iron hand. The only way a person left Malosh's service was on the last train west. When he conquered a ville like Redbone, he took away most of the food and most of the able-bodied residents. According to the campfire tales, he always left behind a little to eat and a few breeders; and of course, the old folk and very young children useless in battle. He left sufficient living souls and resources for the ville to eventually recover, albeit with terrible hardship, this so he could prey on it again when the need arose.

The gully widened as it emptied into a much broader channel. The dry riverbed was cut with deep rills and dotted with scrub-covered islands. Jak took them along the near bank, an undercut bluff six feet high.

Ryan brought up the rear, running in grim silence, conserving his energy. Sweat peeled in a steady trickle down the middle of his back. He could sense the storm front rapidly overtaking them. The static charge in the air made the hair on his arms and neck stand erect, the smell of ozone grew thicker and thicker. They were about a mile from the ville when he shouted to Jak, calling a halt to the column's advance.

The company stopped, but Bezoar was the only one to actually sit down, and he did so hard, on top of a boulder.

"Time for a quick recce to check for pursuit," Ryan said. He waved for J.B. to follow, then started to climb up the side of the bluff, using exposed roots and embedded rocks as hand- and footholds.

"Mebbe they won't come after us?" Bezoar suggested.

"If they saw us running away, they're coming," Krysty told him. "Eight live recruits are worth plenty to Malosh. Not to mention him wanting payback for the men we chilled."

As Ryan and J.B. topped the bluff, puffs of dust started kicking up around them. Not from incoming longblaster bullets. From a spitting, widely spaced rain. The drops falling on Ryan's face and hands felt tepid and slightly greasy, but they didn't burn like holy nukefire. It wasn't the caustic, flesh-melting variety of chem rain.

J.B. pulled out a battered pair of compact binocs and looked back toward Redbone. "Men on horseback, coming down the cliff trail," he said. "Pack of dogs running with them."

"Let me have a look-see," Ryan said, taking the binocs.

"I counted a half-dozen horsemen," the Armorer told the others.

"There's twice that many dogs," Ryan said. "Damned big ones."

"By the Three Kennedys, it's a foxhunt!" Doc exclaimed. "The dogs will pick up our scent and the horses will run us to ground in no time."

Ryan turned the binocs to the northwest horizon, where chain lightning flashed again and again through a curtain of black. Below the cloud bank, a torrential downpour obscured his view of the plain.

"Bastard heavy rain is bearing down," he said. "It'll cover our footprints and wash away our scent."

"Baron's men can see that, too," Krysty said. "They're going to come at a dead gallop."

"We're in a flood plain here," Mildred reminded everyone. "We need to find ourselves some higher ground."

As Ryan and J.B. scrambled from the bluff, Jak waved the others after him and headed down-channel.

Bezoar was the only one who didn't move to follow. The old swineherd sat slumped on the rock, his bad leg sticking out straight, his face still beet-red. Young Crad turned back to help him get to his feet.

"It's no use, boy," Bezoar said, impatiently waving

him off. "This old gimp can't run anymore. You go on without me, boy. Save yourself."

Young Crad wouldn't hear of it. "I go, you go," he said. He bent and picked up his comrade, piggyback. Then, as if the added burden was nothing, he broke into a trot, chasing after Jak.

"That one's something special," Mildred commented as she, too, started to jog.

"Short on words and brains mebbe, but long on heart," Krysty said.

"Droolie sure can run," J.B. admitted.

"Better catch them," Ryan said, again bringing up the rear.

As the companions tightened ranks, winding past a maze of dry channel braids, the raindrops got bigger and closer together. The wind whipped the branches of the scrub brush and sent chest-high tumbleweeds bounding and rolling down the riverbed past them. No matter how hard the rain came down, Ryan knew they couldn't stop to wait out the storm, even if the trail they left behind was obscured. The only thing that was going to save them from the pursuit was distance. Only if the dogs and horses couldn't recover the lost trail were they home free.

In a couple of minutes Ryan's clothes were completely soaked through. Falling raindrops hit the earth with such force that they jumped two feet in the air. Daylight began to fade. He looked over his shoulder, squinting into the wind and the looming darkness. In a strobe flash of lightning he saw the approaching squall line, like a vast waterfall stretching across the plain from edge to edge. Amid the wind's howl and the thunder's boom, he could hear dogs baying, not far behind.

As the storm closed on them, it rained even harder. So hard it came down in rattling roar. So hard that it hurt as it hammered upon unprotected heads and shoulders. So hard it was difficult to breathe with all the water vapor in the air. The parched desert earth couldn't soak it up. The ground turned to cooked oatmeal underfoot, boot prints filled with water as fast as they were made. A section of saturated bluff to their right collapsed, sliding partway across the channel. Ryan veered and jumped the barrier, splashing down knee-deep in a muddy, coffee-and-cream-colored pool. The runoff was funneling from high ground to low. Ahead, shallow stream channels filled and overflowed, coalescing into broad stretches of shin-high rapids.

The muffled baying grew suddenly louder. When Ryan looked back again, through the shifting downpour, he saw the dogs—drop-jawed, with lolling tongues, legs driving, splashing through the stream. Behind the hellhounds, torrents of water sheeted over the backs of charging horses and riders.

"Up!" he bellowed at Jak through a cupped hand.

The albino was already doing just that. Because the crumbling bank on the right would never have held the companions' weight, he led them in the opposite direction, to the crest of a teardrop-shaped, scrub-covered island, high ground where they could make a stand.

As Ryan high-stepped through the boot-sucking muck of the island's beach, he heard a growing rumble like an earthquake and half turned. Surging up behind the dogs and horses was a foaming wall of milky-brown water ten feet high.

"Hang on to something!" Krysty cried out to him.

As Ryan grabbed hold of the branches of a low bush, the flash flood slammed into the mounted pursuit. The force of the wave and its load of debris bowled over the horses and riders. It swept away the dogs in an instant. For a split second Ryan glimpsed the head of a horse as it bobbed up, rushing past, its eyes wild with fear, then it disappeared under the churning surface.

The one-eyed man used the scrub limbs to pull himself to higher ground where his companions stood braced, their legs sinking deep into the soggy soil, their miserable, streaming faces lit by lightning. Ryan jammed his boots against the roots of the brush to help hold his position.

"What happened to the pursuit?" Krysty asked.

"Long gone," Ryan told her.

"The water level is still rising," Doc said. "It appears we've departed the frying pan only to land squarely in the fire."

There was no doubt about that. Their little mound of safety was growing smaller and smaller by the minute; the river flowed around their knees. Ryan could feel the ground eroding from underfoot.

"What are we going to do?" Mildred said.

Krysty looked across the mocha-colored river. "Too strong a current to swim through," she said. "We'd never make it to the bank."

"Only thing we can do is wait it out," Ryan said. "Hang on and hope we don't get washed loose before the river starts to fall."

After a while the torrential rain stopped, but the river continued to come up; soon it even submerged most of the brush on the island's crest. Clustered together, the companions grasped the ends of the branches, half swimming at times, their legs dangling back in the flow.

It was looking worse and worse.

When Jak shouted a warning, Ryan looked up to see a row of weak yellow lights bobbing toward them along the bank.

"Surrender or be swept away!" someone shouted over the roar of the torrent.

There was little question who had come to their rescue.

And under the circumstances, the companions couldn't reach for or raise their weapons.

"We could let the current take us downstream," Krysty said. "Mebbe get past them."

"The odds of running those rapids and surviving to tell the tale are slim at best, my dear," Doc said.

"Too many downed trees in the flow," Ryan said. "We'd get snagged and never come up."

"Drowning doesn't suit me," J.B. said.

"J.B., you're half drowned already," Mildred said.

"That's how I know."

"We can die now, without firing a shot," Ryan said, "or we can try to live long enough to fight at a time and place of our choosing."

"Proposed in that way, it is an easy decision to make," Doc said. "There is only one acceptable course of action."

Ryan looked from face to face. "Are we all agreed, then? Is anyone opposed?"·

But for the sounds of the river, there was silence.

"We give up!" Ryan bellowed, though this genuine surrender stuck mightily in his craw.

"We'll throw you a rope," someone shouted back. "Make it fast at your end."

J.B. managed to trap and tie off the line, lashing it around the submerged trunk of a stunted but sturdily rooted tree. One by one the companions used the rope to pull themselves, hand over hand, through the chest-high current to the light of the lanterns.

Ryan was the last to ford the swollen river. As he climbed out of the water, a horseman approached. Black-gloved hands held the reins of the towering chestnut stallion. The rider was dressed in a gleaming black rain cape. Covering the lower half of his face, nose to chin, cheek to cheek, was a matching leather mask. An oval of metal mesh in front of his mouth allowed him to speak unmuffled. There were angry boils and sores on his high, pale forehead. The eyes above the mask were black and wide-set; his shoulder-length, wavy black hair lay plastered to his head by the rain.

There was no mistaking who it was.

Malosh the Impaler.

Chapter Two

A tall, broad figure in an olive-drab trench coat and size-14 patched tennis shoes climbed the steep, barren approach to the base of the Rabbit Ear Spires. The gusting wind beat his BDU pants hard against his legs. His head was shaved except for a fringe of dirty blond hair that fell from the back of his neck to between his shoulder blades. A wide, black-tattooed garland encircled his deeply suntanned skull.

The permanent crown symbolized his authority.

Kendrick Haldane had been declared baron-for-life by a grateful populace.

At a switchback halfway up the trail of loose volcanic scree, Haldane paused to catch his breath. In the valley far below, the Grandee glistened in the slanting sun like a fat green snake. The world-shattering, nuclear exchange of 2001 had freed the great river. Shock waves from ground-burst missile strikes had ruptured the Elephant Butte Reservoir dam some fifty miles upstream, spilling three hundred billion gallons of water and a vast, scouring sediment load into the ancient riverbed. Like falling dominoes, the Caballo, Percha and Leasburg dams had given way under the power of the unleashed torrent.

The once again wild Grandee was the lifeline of

Haldane's small, prosperous fiefdom; and not just because of the water it supplied for agriculture and live-stock. Old Interstate Highway 25, which paralleled the river and connected the cities of Albuquerque and El Paso, was also a casualty of Armageddon. Most of its overpasses and bridges had collapsed, many of its road-beds either washed away by nukeday's flood or eroded to sand by decades of chem rain. With the highway mostly gone, the river had become the prime north-south trade route. It was also a defensive barrier to attack from the west.

Between the still-lethal ground zeros of Albuquerque and El Paso, a narrow habitable strip along the Grandee supported a dozen thriving villes. Baron Haldane con-trolled nearly one hundred miles of riverbank with watchtowers and small fortifications set on cliffs above the stream, and from bankside caves. Based in these strategic squeeze points, his sec men intercepted and dispatched coldheart robbers and bands of marauding muties. In return for a guarantee of safety, every farmer, every traveler, every trader paid the baron a fair toll, either in jack or in a percentage of goods.

Haldane's seat of baronial power lay beside the river in the valley below him. It had been built on the ruins of the city of Las Cruces, north and west of the El Paso–Fort Bliss nukeglass crater, about forty miles north of what once was the New Mexico–Chihuahua-Mexico border. Earth-shaker warheads had rubbleized the predark town; cataclysmic dam failures had swept away most of the debris. Its university, museums, shopping centers and the grid work of residential streets were gone. On the outskirts of the redrawn flood plain, a few of the original industrial sites and warehouses still stood, but they were skeletal relics, with sagging roofs and breached walls. Nueva Las Cruces, or Nuevaville for short, had been constructed well back from the Grandee's new shoreline. Amid groves of trees and green cultivated fields were clusters of immobile mobile homes, dilapidated RVs propped on cinder blocks, and tractor trailers with crude windows cut in their sheet-metal sides. Scattered among the predark-vintage structures were one-story huts and longhouses built with recycled materials, walls made of piled chunks of broken concrete, and of dried river mud reinforced with mats of willow sticks.

Two-thirds of the barony's population tilled the land, processed surplus food for storage and sale, or worked on a fleet of transport barges. The rest of Haldane's subjects were full-time men-at-arms. From the towering height of the Rabbit Ear Plateau, his capital looked bucolic and peaceful, as if time had been reversed. As if Armageddon had never happened.

It was an illusion, he knew.

In the hellscape, safety and stability were the products of a bloody endless fight. Deathland's hardship and brutality reduced everything to the lowest common denominator: simple survival.

Us versus them.

Played out over and over again.

A war of attrition, until there was no "us" or "them" left, and the last, faint hope of humanity's rising from the ashes of Armageddon winked out forever.

As Haldane resumed the climb, struggling up a slope that constantly shifted underfoot, he leaned into the wind. From the belly of a line of black clouds to the northwest, lightning licked down at distant mountaintops. Thunder rumbled. In perhaps two hours, three at most, the storm would be hard upon them, turning Nuevaville's dirt roads to mire and spilling the river over its banks.

Looming above him were the snaggle-tooth pinnacles of the Organ Mountains. With the wind to his back, he followed a well-worn path along the base of the spires. It led to a broad cave in the bedrock, about ten feet high at its tallest, and five times that wide across. Inside the low opening were crude structures built of mud-and-straw bricks. From glassless windows and doorless doorways, rows of faces peered out at him, luminously pale, as round as full moons. He smelled burning excrement, which the cave dwellers dried and used as fuel for heat and for cooking. The filthy hands of three generations of inbred doomies directed him toward the stone hut that stood a few hundred feet downslope.

As was the custom, Baron Haldane left his blaster outside the rude sanctuary. He unslung his Remington Model 1100 12-gauge autoloader. Its barrel and magazine were chopped down to the end of the forestock, its rearstock cut off behind the pistol grip. After he carefully set the truncated, hellacious scattergun on the ground, he pushed aside the brown polyester blanket that covered the hut's doorway, ducking his head to enter. As he did, he was greeted by an explosion of snorting laughter.

Dim light streamed into the structure through uncountable cracks in the walls. There was no fire laid on

the floor, nor candles lit for fear of igniting the dizzy-
ingly sweet, flammable vapors concentrated therein.
As his eyes adjusted to the dark, over the wind sighing
through holes in the masonry, the baron heard a gurgling
sound. It was from the spring that welled up from a deep
fissure in the bedrock.

On a tripod chair positioned directly over the stone
vent, enveloped in lighter-than-air petrochemical
perfume, sat the oracle. The eighty-five-pound doomie's
sole garment was a diaper made of a once-white
T-shirt. He sat with eyes tightly closed, a halo of wispy
white hair crowned his knobby skull. Pale skin like
parchment hung in folds from under chin and arms.
Drooped down his belly were flapjack mammalia,
circlets of white hair sprouted around the wrinkled
aureolas. The doomie's chest heaved as he sucked in
and held lungfuls of the strange gases, dosing himself
for the foretelling.

There was no seat for visitors in the close confines
of the hut. Haldane stood slightly bent over to keep the
top of his head from bumping into the crust of chemical
deposits on the wooden rafters.

"You know why I have come?" the baron asked.

The doomie stifled a giggle by clamping a hand hard
over his mouth. He snorted and honked as he tried to
control himself. The battle lasted only a second or two.
Unable to maintain his composure, he fell into a fit of
laughter that set his pendulous dugs flip-flopping.

When the soothsayer opened his eyes, they were
alarmingly bloodshot. "A dark deed looms," he said
merrily.

"Yes, it does," Haldane said.

"The darkest of dark-dark deeds," the oracle stated. "The noble baron's hands will drip with the blood of slaughtered innocents."

Haldane nodded at the grinning doomie.

"You want to know if there's a less brutal way to accomplish the end you desire," the soothsayer said. "Some other possible strategy, some sequence of events you may have overlooked."

"That's what I want you to tell me," Haldane said. "Do I have to use the terrible weapon I've been offered?"

The doomie shut his eyes and screwed up his face, huffing in and out to force down more of the fumes.

Though all members of the doomie race had the power to see into the future, the rock spring's sweet gas greatly stimulated and focused their mutie supersense. It also made them very, very happy. Too much perfume and they swallowed their own tongues and strangled to death.

Most of Haldane's norm subjects believed that the Creator spoke to them through the oracles of the hut. They believed that true future sight, unknown before nukeday, was a kind of compensatory gift, God's way of saying "I'm sorry for rogering your world so soundly." Ironically, these chosen vessels of the Supreme Being were judged unfit to reside in Nuevaville proper. When not engaged in unraveling the mysteries of the future, they were seen as filthy, moronic creatures of unspeakable habits. They were kept apart from those they served so tirelessly, in what amounted to a mountaintop doomie zoo.

The soothsayer huffed until his scrunched-up face

turned dark and his limbs began to jerk spasmodically. After many minutes passed he opened his eyes and said, "I have looked into your future, Baron. I have seen the struggles ahead. For you there is no other path."

It was not the answer Haldane wanted to hear.

No baron of the hellscape could be shy about chilling, about ordering others to do it, or doing the deed personally, if it came to that. In Haldane's case, chilling had always been in the service of freedom or the dispensation of justice. The bands of coldhearts and muties that threatened his people and their livelihood deserved and received the ultimate punishment. Haldane had always seen himself—and had been seen by his subjects—as a defender and a shepherd, both wise and fair.

The course of action that lay before him was wise, but hardly fair.

In target, in scale and scope, in moral consequences, this chilling was different. Even by Deathlands's standards it was the act of a depraved, unfeeling butcher.

"There will be so much death," he said.

"You alone have the power to put an end to the cycle of terror," the oracle countered. "You can prevent the deaths of those you hold dear, for decades to come."

"I am not a mass chiller," Haldane said. "I am not a monster. I am a protector. I fight monsters."

"I have been shown what will be, Baron. You have no choice in the matter. You will put your beliefs aside to advance the greater good. You will become what you hate to achieve lasting peace and security for your people. And after you do this vile deed, I guarantee that history will understand, and forgive you for the excess. History is written by the survivors, and rewritten by their offspring. They will call you a military genius and hail you as the glorious saviour of your lands. A leader with the courage and the vision to decisively act, and thereby change the fate of this barony forever."

When the baron said nothing in reply, the oracle twisted the metaphysical dagger he held, the dagger of premonition. "If you do not act, Baron Haldane, be assured that Malosh will," he said. "What you so dread doing to others will be done to you and yours. Nueva-ville will become a graveyard. This barony will be turned to dust and scattered to the winds."

With those awful words ringing in his ears, Haldane staggered out of the hut. Though fumble-fingered from the fumes he'd inhaled, he managed to scoop up the Remington 1100. He caught himself as he reached out to push aside the holed-out blanket. At that moment he wanted nothing more than to blow the oracle apart with high-brass buckshot. But in his heart he knew that chilling the messenger wouldn't do any good.

An oracle had predicted the fall of his predecessor, Baron Clagg, who had responded to the bad news by dragging the helpless doomie to the nearest cliff and throwing him off, headfirst. Clagg had then tried to change his fate by all means possible, but everything he had done only served to speed the grisly end that had been described to him. Old Clagg had been a typical Deathlands baron: shortsighted, cruel, despotic. His in-satiable greed had started the conflict with Malosh, setting the stage for this most regrettable day.

Haldane slung the Remington sawed-off and, bracing himself against the wind, started to retrace his steps down the mountain. Knowing that the evil he was about to unleash was preordained and couldn't be avoided did nothing to lighten the weight that lay upon his heart.

Chapter Three

While Ryan stood dripping on the edge of the riverbank, Malosh the Impaler leaned over in the saddle to give his prisoner a closer inspection. On either side of the masked baron, a dozen swampies dug in their heels, fighting to restrain more of the massive, growling dogs by their choke chains. Fanned out behind the stumpy muties were normal-size sec men carrying lanterns and predark Combloc autorifles. Pristine predark weapons were often unearthed from stockpiles and were traded across the Deathlands. Usually the wealthiest barons bought them.

Ryan knew just how quickly he could clear his SIG P226 from shoulder leather. If its action and barrel weren't clogged with muck, he knew he could get off a shot or two before the swampies released the dog pack and the men opened fire. But the one-eyed man wasn't a big fan of suicide, even if there was a bit of justifiable homicide thrown in the mix. His thought, first and foremost, was getting his companions and himself out of this predicament alive. To have any hope of success against such long odds, they had to wait for their chance and work as a team.

At that moment it was unclear whether Malosh was going to let the companions live long enough to do that;

after all, they had taken out a number of his valuable fighters. Slaughtering the guilty parties where they stood would have certainly evened the score. Ryan decided to play a hunch. He figured the baron wasn't just looking for cannon fodder. To win battles he needed hard-nosed, seasoned warriors. Courage in the face of death was the only hole card Ryan held.

"Didn't your mama teach you it's rude to stare?" he demanded of the baron.

Malosh glared down at him and said nothing.

For a second Ryan thought he had made the big mistake that was going to get them all chilled. He prepared himself to quick draw the SIG, determined to angle the first two rounds up through the baron's chin and out the top of his head. Sensing the sudden increase in tension, the dogs' hackles bristled, and they started snapping and snarling, scrabbling in the mud with all fours, dragging their struggling handlers forward.

"My mama was a gaudy house slut," Malosh told Ryan, his black eyes glittering above the leather mask. "To my knowledge she never refused service to man or woman, norm or mutie. She took on her customers three at a time and gave every one his or her money's worth. The only thing my sainted whore of a mother ever taught me was to get the jack up front."

"Sound advice," Ryan said.

Malosh leaned over in the saddle again, gloved hands resting on the pommel. "You know, I was just about to let my hunting dogs tear you limb from limb," he said, "but now I see they'd choke on those brass balls of yours. A man like you will serve me much better in one piece."

The baron waved his sec men forward. "Take them all back to the ville," he said, then he wheeled his horse and spurred it in the direction of Redbone.

As the lanterns closed in, Ryan got a better look at the fighters' faces. They were an odd collection of humanity and near-humanity. The norm men and women were wolf-lean, mostly in their late teens to late twenties. The swampies weren't the only nuke-spawned horrors in the crowd, but the other muties weren't from distinct subhuman species. Some carried prominent, angry tumorous growths on their heads and necks. Some had withered and clawlike extra appendages sprouting from their shoulders. Ryan saw no stickies among the ranks, but that was no surprise. Stickies didn't do well in a military setting. Unlike swampies, they were creatures of uncontrollable urges. They had their own hardwired, homicidal agenda.

Sandwiched between norms, muties and dogs, the companions and the pair of swineherds trudged back along the high bank. It was soggy going; at times they struggled through knee-deep mud. By the time they crossed the farm fields and started back up the zigzag trail, the rain had stopped and the sky had lightened considerably. The sec men put out their lanterns and hung them from their belts.

As the companions reentered the ville, shafts of warm sunlight speared through gaps in the churning gray clouds overhead. They were marched down the same narrow alley they had exited, past the dead pig, past the human corpse in the doorway. There was no sign of the trio they had left at the barricade. The makeshift barrier had been breached in the middle, its rocks and tree limbs dragged aside, and there were scorch marks from gren blasts on the bracketing mud walls.

Ryan had carefully measured their escorts over the course of the return trip. Malosh's sec men were professionals. He saw no evidence of wandering attention despite the long slog, and the fact that they outnumbered their captives a comfortable ten-to-one. Even though they could have, no one slacked off. Their weapons came up at the right moments, without the need of shouted commands. They anticipated the potential for trouble well in advance, and efficiently closed the door on it.

That didn't bode well for a future escape.

The sec men led them to the ville's puddled central square where the air hung heavy with the sour smell of drowned woodsmoke and the sweet scent of burned flesh.

All of Redbone's shell-shocked survivors had been assembled there at blasterpoint. About sixty men and women and twenty children stood before three, fifteen-foot-high posts that had been raised in front of the ville's stone-rimmed well. Threaded onto the tops of each of the debarked, peckerpole tree trunks were two naked men and a naked woman.

All dead.

Ryan recognized them as the defenders of the fallen barricade. They were slumped over at the waist, with chins resting on their chests, their legs and feet smeared with blood. The sharpened stakes had been rammed up their backsides, then they had been hoisted into a vertical position. The weight of their own bodies and their desperate struggles had driven the shaved poles deep into their torsos.

"Dark night!" J.B. exclaimed, tipping back his fedora. "That's a nasty way to go."

"Barbarous," Doc agreed, his long, seamed face twisting into a scowl of disgust. "It would appear that we have been tossed back into the Dark Ages."

"What makes you think we ever left them?" Mildred said.

Baron Malosh paced his chestnut horse back and forth in front of the displayed corpses. When the last of his men had entered the square, he reined in the stallion. Reaching down behind his knee, he unscabbarded a Kalashnikov assault rifle, aimed it at the sky and fired off a full-auto burst. A handful of Redbone's survivors looked up at the baron with desperate dread, the rest looked only at their boot tops.

"I'm offering you Redbone folk a choice," Malosh shouted. "Join my army and fight beside me. It's a hard and dangerous life, but it's profitable, too. There's booty to be had and plenty of food to eat." He pointed the autorifle at a heap of skinny, sharpened poles on the ground behind him. "Join me willingly and share in the spoils of war, or I will keep stretching buttholes until I run out of stakes."

An easy decision for the defeated, a bullet or a saber thrust at some future date being preferable to imminent skewering.

"Form a line, then!" the baron cried. "Do it now!" As his mercies jabbed and shoved the outnumbered captives into a ragged column, he dismounted, handing the reins to a swampie.

The companions closed ranks with Krysty and Jak in front, the swineherds next, then Doc, J.B., Mildred and Ryan. The one-eyed man stepped to the side so he could watch what was going on at the head of the line. Malosh took only a moment to size up the first person before impatiently waving him to the right, where soldiers waited. The fit-looking young man moved off, presumably to join the fighters.

Zombielike, the line of volunteers advanced. Malosh made quick selections, sending the able-bodied young to the right, the middle-aged but still mobile to the left along with the older children. The elderly and the children under the age of seven he waved back to the doorways of the ramshackle huts. Thus mothers and their breastfeeding babies were separated, the former bound for war, the latter to starve.

This way and that the gloved hand motioned, dividing warriors from cannon fodder, and cannon fodder from those he deemed unfit to even serve as human shields.

As the companions approached Malosh, it became clear that he had yet another pigeonhole. A genetic one. The baron started to wave Krysty to the right, toward the norm warriors, but caught himself. He bent closer and examined the springy coils of her red hair. When he reached out, the prehensile tendrils wriggled away from his touch.

"You hide your rad-tainted blood well," Malosh said. "You almost passed for norm. Of course, almost doesn't count." He hooked a thumb over his shoulder at the swampies clustered behind the well. "Join your fellow muties," he told her.

Krysty didn't argue with the baron. She wasn't ashamed of her heritage. She walked by him with her head held high.

Malosh took one look at Jak's dead-white skin and ruby-red eyes and said, "You, too, mutie."

"Not mutie!" Jak snarled at the man in the leather mask.

"And my mother wasn't a two-bit whore," Malosh said amiably.

"I purebred albino!"

Jak's explosive protest cracked up the sec men of Malosh, both norm and mutie. Even some of the Redbone folk managed to grin.

The baron wasn't interested in a genealogical debate; he was the sole arbiter of genetic purity. He gestured with his thumb again. "That way, mutie boy, or you croak on the spike."

Jak didn't budge a millimeter. In the Deathlands, being branded a "mutie" was the worst insult imaginable.

"Pride goeth before a fall," Doc quoted.

"Misplaced pride in this case," Mildred said cryptically.

"Dark night, what's Jak doing?" J.B. said. "He's not careful, he's gonna get himself chilled."

"Come on, Jak," Krysty urged from beside the well. "Come over here. Don't do this. Don't die for nothing."

"Better listen to your long-legged friend there," Malosh said. "She's trying to save you a big pain in the ass."

It wasn't the first time a dire strategic situation had demanded personal sacrifice from Jak Lauren. As distasteful as this particular sacrifice was, he turned without another word and started walking toward Krysty and the squad of genetic misfits.

The norm fighters didn't let him off that easy. They laughed, catcalled and mimicked the albino in a whining, singsong chant.

"Not mutie!"

"Not mutie!"

"Not mutie!"

Why Malosh was isolating the mutie element was obvious to any resident of the hellscape over the age of three. Norms wouldn't fight alongside muties because they distrusted and feared them. For the same reasons, muties didn't like taking their marching orders from norms. Based on past bloodbaths, both sides were justified in these beliefs.

As it turned out, Young Crad and Bezoar didn't pass Malosh's muster, either. They were too slow of brain and foot, respectively. The baron ordered the pair over with the cannon fodder.

When Doc stepped up next, ebony walking stick in hand, Malosh immediately pointed him in the opposite direction. "Go back to the huts," he said.

"The huts?" Tanner said incredulously. "You have made a grave error, sir."

"No mistake, old man. You belong with the other diaper-wearers, the doddering geezers and the babies."

Dr. Theophilus Algernon Tanner was a courageous man and totally devoted to his friends. No way would he stay behind while they faced death.

"I assure you, sir, I am not ready for a rocking chair," Doc said, unsheathing the rapier blade of his swordstick and with its razor point cutting a wicked *S* in the air an inch from the baron's face.

Before he could retract it, in a blur almost too fast to

follow, Malosh grabbed hold of the blade, trapping it in his fist.

Doc threw his full weight against the baron's grip but couldn't pull the rapier free or make its edge slice through the man's hand.

"Kevlar glove," Mildred said to Ryan over her shoulder.

When Malosh suddenly let go, Doc fell off balance and landed hard on his bony backside.

"Follow the dimmie and the gimp," the baron said, motioning him toward the ranks of the human shields. "You just signed your own death warrant, old man."

Ryan watched stoically as the baron consigned Mildred and J.B. to the norm fighters, but deep down his guts were churning. With the companions split up among the three separate units, their chances of success looked even more bleak.

As Ryan stepped forward, Malosh looked him straight in the eye, then said, "From the way you stare back at me with that blue peeper of yours, I'd say you're a coldheart, chill-for-pay man. A mercie by trade. If you serve me well, mercie, I guarantee you will prosper. If you betray me, I will hunt you down and chill you triple ugly."

Ryan shrugged.

"I'm wasting my breath," the baron said. "Dying hard doesn't scare a man like you, does it?"

"Fear only moves folks so far," Ryan replied. "And it can push from more than one direction. Once you get this kidnapped crew into battle, you lose your monopoly on death threats. What makes you think you can count on me or any of the others when the lead starts flying?"

"The joy of doing unto others as was done to you," Malosh said. "It's what makes the world go around."

Chapter Four

Under the gruesome banner of its hoisted dead, Red-bone ville was sacked to the bare walls. Malosh's army mainly supervised the work. Under its blasters, the ville folk were forced to loot their own homes. Some sobbed brokenly as they sorted and piled their worldly goods in the square—ammunition, blasters, cookware and trade items—but most moved in a trance of disbelief. The hilltop town's food caches were also plundered, yielding up bags of grain, beans, potatoes; smoked joints of meat and barrels of sweet water. This booty was packed onto carts drawn by liberated horses and mules.

As always, the mutie contingent got the brown end of the stick.

Krysty, Jak, the betumored, the extra-limbed and the swampies were given the task of searching the knot of still-smoldering huts where Redbone fighters had made their last stand and removing anything of value that remained. The swampies attacked the job with great enthusiasm. Like a pack of tailless rats, the swampies rooted through the collapsed structures, pulling aside charred rafters, crawling on hands and knees into small, extremely hot spaces. For them, it was a treasure hunt.

As the tall redhead watched, the crew of stumpy

little bastards, dusted head to toe with wet black ash, uncovered another half-cooked norm body in the rubble. After rolling it onto its back and robbing it of anything that would fit into their pockets, the leader of the swampies stood and shouted at Krysty and Jak, "Over here!"

As the swampies moved on to the next hut, Krysty and Jak carefully climbed through the burned-out ruin to where the body lay. She knelt and started to pull off the man's boots. There were no laces. They came off easily. There were no socks underneath.

Jak pulled up the hem of the rough shirt, exposing a pasty, flabby belly. He whispered urgently to Krysty, "Still alive."

Indeed, before her eyes the pale chest rose and fell ever so slightly.

Then the man opened his eyelids. His eyes bulged from a face blackened by soot, the whites by contrast shockingly brilliant. The burn victim wheezed softly, then broke into fit of coughing and choking. He spewed pink foam and bits of ash through blistered lips. The inside of his mouth and his tongue were bloodred.

"Don't get up," Krysty warned him. "Lie still. For Gaia's sake, play dead."

But breathing with scorched lungs was so difficult that he couldn't oblige her. He convulsed, arching up from the ground. The swampies in the neighboring ruin turned at the commotion.

Jak leaned on the man's shoulders with both hands, trying to pin him down and hold him still.

"Look out!" Krysty cried.

As a short, heavy blade flashed down, the albino reacted, twisting out of the way.

With a meaty thunk the predark hatchet smashed the burned man in the middle of the forehead; the wedge-shaped tool split his skull wide open. Krysty just managed to get a hand up in front of her face to block the flying brains and blood. When she looked down, the man's limbs were quivering violently.

And for the last time.

"He don't have to play at nothing now," said the hatchet-wielding chief swampie, who sported an ash-stained, red-knit stocking cap. He put a boot on the man's lifeless face, and wrenching the short handle back and forth, levered the ax head free from the bone. Gore welled up from the inch-wide fissure, crimson rivulets oozed through the coating of soot on his cheeks and ears.

The boss swampie called himself Meconium. Like other members of his kind, he had masses of tiny wrinkles around his eyes and a broad, flat nose. His coarse hands and feet were huge relative to his height. Even though he was only about four-foot-six, he weighed close to 175 pounds. Meconium looked like he was built from a short stack of cinder blocks.

He grinned at Jak as he hefted the bloody hatchet. "Nearly whacked your doodle, Not Mutie," he said.

Sensing some big fun in the offing, the other swampies stopped raking through the debris and circled around. None of them carried blasters. The baron didn't trust them with anything more lethal than edged weapons, nail-studded wooden clubs, and of course, the hellhounds, which were now chained in the square.

With Jak standing just out of reach of his hatchet, and a rapt audience gathered, Meconium prodded, "You ever take a look in a mirror, Snowball? Only a blind man could think you were norm."

The albino stiffened, but he didn't respond.

"Tell the truth," Meconium urged him. "How did you come to be so white all over with those nasty red eyes? Did some scab-assed mutie plow your ma's honeypot? Or did she come naturally with six teats and a chin beard?"

"Not mutie," Jak repeated firmly.

Acting like he had purer blood than the swampies was a very bad move, in Krysty's opinion. But that was Jak all over. He was hardheaded. And she could understand why he was so damned adamant about his genetics. The mutie brand had ugly consequences. Mutated species were at the bottom of hellscape's pecking order, hunted down and chilled for sport by norms, or turned into slaves by them and routinely worked to death.

As a rule, Deathlands's norms were shit-poor and butt-ignorant. Oppressing the visibly different and vulnerable made them feel in command of something. Since they no longer had a great nation or a historic flag to rally round, the only thing norms had to be proud of was their supposedly untainted DNA. Krysty had always felt that, deep down, norms believed that the muties had earned their malformities. They believed that for its own inscrutable reasons, the nukecaust had selected its victims, and had cast plagues upon their houses for generations to come. Muties were tangible evidence of that catastrophe, of the most hated and

feared thing that had ever happened to the human race.
They were evidence that the disaster wasn't over. That
perhaps it would never be over.

Jak hawked and spit a stringy green gob on the
mutie's lapel.

Meconium immediately flicked away the bouton-
niere of mucus. Advancing with the hatchet raised, he
said, "You're dead meat, Snowball."

Jak braced himself for a fight.

"Step back," Krysty told the swampie, her hand
dropping to the grip of her Smith & Wesson.

From the lane behind them a voice growled,
"Enough squabbling, get back to work."

Unlike the swampies, this normal-size mutie carried
firearms. A long-barreled, center-fire revolver hung in
a pancake holster on his hip and he held a battle-worn
12-gauge pump braced at waist height, the barrel
squarely leveled at Meconium's bristling chin. Below
his sweat-stained Bud Light ball cap was a tumorous
growth the color and size of a ripe eggplant. It stretched
the skin on the right side of his face balloon-tight and
balloon-shiny. The growth completely hid his right ear.
Korb was Malosh's appointed captain of the entire
mutie crew—no one in their right mind would turn that
authority over to a swampie. Unlike the swampies, this
tumor-head captain seemed to take no delight in the job
at hand, and he regarded the stumpy bastards he commanded with grave suspicion.

The swampies followed his orders and sullenly retreated. They resumed rummaging through the ash pit
next door.

"Better steer clear of them ball biters, boy," Korb told

Jak. "They pack fight, like dogs. They'll gang up on you first chance they get."

From previous experience, Krysty and Jak had learned a good deal about the nature of the swampie race. They were sour, vicious, greedy, vindictive. And above all, cunning.

Apparently, Korb didn't hold a grudge against Jak for three times denying a mutie birthright. He pointed at the distorted side of his face and said, "You know I cut this blasted thing off me once with a red-hot knife blade. After it was gone I figured it'd leave a triple-mean scar, but mebbe I could pass for a wounded norm. Well, I almost bled to death from sawing it off, and then the rad bastard grew back twice as big in a month."

If the tumor head was trying to get Jak to fess up and admit he had rad-tainted blood, he quickly realized he was wasting his time. As Korb walked away, Krysty and Jak began stripping the dead man. After making a pile of the recyclable clothes, they carried his naked corpse by hands and feet to the cliff and tossed him over the edge like a sack of garbage.

When they returned to the section of burned-out huts, the swampies started making fun of Jak again, speculating further on his origins and the bizarre sexual preferences of his mother.

"They're just trying to draw you out," Krysty said. "To get you to do something stupe."

"Yeah," Jak replied.

"Don't let them."

"Yeah."

They advanced deeper into the jumble of collapsed structures where the swampies rooted about.

"Over here, Snowball," Meconium called. "We got another prize for you."

As the swampies moved to the adjoining hut, Krysty and Jak climbed over a tumbled-down wall. The dwelling's opposite wall stood more or less intact; it supported a shaky latticework of burned and broken roof beams that jutted overhead. They couldn't miss the still form in the middle of the hut floor. It was surrounded by a doughnut of displaced ash and debris. The pockets of the dead fighter's coat and pants were turned inside out.

Jak walked to the far side of the body. As Krysty followed, with a crack and crash, a long, dark shadow dropped from above. There was no avoiding it, no time for Krysty to even look up. The section of scorched beam caught her full across the shoulders, driving her to the ground. Even as the beam's weight slammed her face-first into the ash, a swampie jumped down on top of it. Her arms pinned under her body, Krysty couldn't reach her blaster. She could barely draw breath with 175 pounds of mutie sitting on the rafter on her back. He held a machete to the side of her throat; its edge bit into her skin. Trapped there, Krysty realized the sneaky swampie bastards had set up the deadfall while she and Jak were disposing of the last corpse. In a matter of seconds, she had been taken out of the fight.

As Jak came to her aid, drawing his .357 Magnum from its holster, Meconium hit him from behind with a charred piece of wood that shattered against the back of his head. If the makeshift club hadn't been burned through, the blow would have killed him stone-dead. But Meconium didn't want him to die quickly; he wanted his crew to get in their licks first. Even though the blunt instrument failed, the force of the blow drove Jak to his knees and sent the Colt Python flying out of his hand and into the mound of wet ash beside the body.

Jak sprang up and faced his attackers

The five swampies, three males and two females, had their clubs and blades out. Even the women outweighed Jak by eighty or ninety pounds; he towered over all of them.

"We're gonna bust you up good," one of the swampie females promised, taking a practice swing with her knobby cudgel.

"Then we're gonna hack you into bite-size pieces," said one of the males, waving a predark, made-in-India Bowie knife.

"Don't yell for help, Snowball," Meconium advised.

"You, neither," Jak said.

Krysty expected leaf-bladed knives to start dropping out of his sleeves and fly through the air. At close range, Jak was a dead chilling shot with blades. But no razor-sharp steel appeared in his palms. The albino had unconditionally accepted the terms of the fight. As much as the swampies wanted to hurt him, Jak wanted to hurt them. Like the swampies, he intended to teach a final, agonizing lesson before he dispatched his enemies to the last train west.

Jak feinted right, then darted left, punctuating a 360-spin move with a blur of a back fist. The full power strike caught the nearest swampie in the middle of the face. He could feel cartilage crunch under his knuckles, but even though blood gushed from the broken nose and the eyelids momentarily fluttered shut, the blocklike head didn't move.

That's how strong her neck was.

As the others closed in for the chill, Jak scampered, as light as a spider, over a jumble of scorched and over-turned wooden furniture, to the back of a fallen beam. The rafter lay at a thirty-degree angle, with one end on the dirt floor, the other resting atop the far wall. Like an Olympic gymnast, Jak balanced effortlessly on the six-inch-wide beam.

Hopping to avoid the sideways slash of a short sword, he snap-kicked the stumpy swordsman under the chin. It had as much effect as kicking a boulder. Jak reached up with both hands, caught the end of a loose overhead beam and hauled on it with his entire weight, making it pivot and swing down. As the swordsman lunged with his point, the crossmember landed with a solid thunk between his eyes, driving him backward onto his ass.

Determined to help her companion, Krysty tried to push up from the floor. As she did, the edge of the machete scraped deeper into her neck. The swampie put his boot sole on top of her head and firmly shoved her face back into the ash. At that moment Krysty could have closed her eyes and summoned her Gaia power, the mutie connection with the Earth spirit that gave her superhuman strength for brief periods of time. She could have used the Gaia energy to throw off both the beam and the swampie, but the aftermath of that psychic connection would have left her too drained to be of any use in a fight.

When she looked up again, Jak was running full-tilt along the top of the tumbledown wall. This while the swampies threw themselves at him, lunging with their weapons, trying to cut his legs out from under him. The higher Jak climbed along the wall, the less effective the swampies were. They couldn't jump for beans.

Jak could have easily gotten away by dashing across the tops of the exposed rafters, but escape wasn't on his agenda. Instead, he leaped from the wall, over the swampies' heads, landing behind them. A development that astonished them. Before they could recover, Jak lashed out with a sidekick. It caught the swampie in front of him below the left ear, bouncing his forehead off the mud wall. Then the others attacked all at once.

While Jak danced and dervished, a white whirlwind in their midst, the swampies seemed to be moving in slow motion. He ducked and dodged their rain of blows, they absorbed his like stumpy punching bags. With fists and feet Jak pulped their faces, splitting their brows, closing their eyes, breaking out their yellow teeth. His knuckles and boots were smeared with blood and ash, but they kept on coming.

"Help us get the bastard!" Meconium shouted at the seated swampie.

The crushing weight on Krysty's back suddenly eased as the mutie jumped up and threw himself and his machete into the melee.

Krysty crawled out from under the beam with difficulty, but without using her Gaia power. As she drew her blaster, the battle spilled out of the hut and rolled down the alley in the direction of the square.

When the skirmish burst into view, Mildred was helping J.B. and Ryan strap water barrels onto a wooden wheeled mule cart. Five swampies chased Jak out of the alley, screaming and waving their blades and clubs. The sec men raised their autorifles, aiming not at the new-comers but at the edges of the crowd, this to keep a wider battle from breaking out. With an AK pointed at her chest Mildred couldn't draw and fire her ZKR 551. Likewise, Ryan and J.B. were forced to stand and watch.

Not that Jak needed any help.

He turned and attacked the swampies, splitting the pack in two. His feet and fists found their targets over and over again, smashing into already bruised and bloodied faces. Mildred had never seen him fight with such savage frenzy. She doubted that Jak even heard the crowd cheering him on.

The systematic beating and the victims' inability to return any punishment took its toll. The sword and club strikes began to miss Jak not by inches but by feet; that's how slowly they came. As the muties weakened, Jak isolated one of their number for special treatment. Pivoting as the swampie swung his hatchet, Jak slipped behind the bastard and clapped a forearm across his throat, seizing hold of his left shoulder. He yanked off the swampie's red stocking cap, snatched a handful of coarse brown hair and, straining hard, bent back his head until his scraggly chin beard pointed skyward.

"No, Jak!" Ryan shouted from Mildred's side. "You'll never break that neck!"

But that wasn't what Jak had in mind.

He shook a leaf-bladed knife from the sleeve of the arm that pinned the mutie's chest, then jabbed one of the razor-sharp edges against the base of the hairy throat.

The swampie growled and curled back his lips,

showing bloody fractured teeth as he struggled in vain to free himself.

"Time to die," Jak said.

Over the cries of approval someone bellowed, "Korb!"

A tumor-head mutie in a bill cap stepped behind Jak and shouldered a pump shotgun, taking aim at the back of his skull.

The crowd parted on the far side of the square and Baron Malosh stormed over to Jak. "If you chill that swampie," he said, "Korb will blow your head off. This is my army. You follow my orders. You fight who I tell you to and when I tell you to. Until then you stand down, mutie!"

"Not mutie!"

The edge of the knife drew a fine red line across the exposed throat. It was a shallow wound and only a couple of inches long, but it made blood spill over the swampie's madly bobbing Adam's apple. Jak pressed the blade below the hinge of the swampie's jaw, poised to cut much, much deeper and from ear to ear.

"Nukin' hell!" J.B. groaned.

At that moment the expression on the swampie's face changed from incoherent fury to abject terror. He was certain he was going to die in the next few seconds. Then terror suddenly turned to horror as something fell out of his baggy pant leg and draped across his boot.

He had dropped a turd on his own left foot.

"Let go of the swampie," the masked baron said.

When Jak didn't immediately comply, Malosh moved out of the line of fire and the arc of splatter. "I'm going to count to three," he said. "One…two…"

With a snarl of contempt, Jak shoved the befouled swampie away from him.

"Thank God," Mildred said, allowing herself to breathe again.

"That was close," J.B. added.

"Too damned close," Ryan said.

The baron whirled on the tumor head holding the shotgun. "If you let trouble like this break out again, Korb," he said, "you're the one who's gonna suffer."

Mildred, J.B. and Ryan watched Krysty step from the crowd and hand Jak his Colt Python. Then the two companions were ushered back down the alley at blasterpoint. Jak walked with his back straight and his head high, having defended the purity of his genetics.

It was unclear from Mildred's conversations with Jak whether he had ever actually seen another albino, but she knew it was highly unlikely that he had. Before Armageddon, the U.S. had a population of only about eighteen thousand albinos. Back in the glory days of civilization, their life expectancy was normal. In a cruel and brutal new world, however, the physical deficits that accompanied their condition greatly lessened the chances of survival.

If Jak Lauren had no idea how much he differed from a prenukecaust albino, a late twentieth-century medical doctor and whitecoat like Mildred Wyeth knew exactly. The research of her peers had shown that albinism in humans was the result of defective genes on one or more of the six chromosomes that controlled production of the pigment melanin, which was key to normal development of eyes, skin and eye-brain nerve pathways. Aside from pale skin and hair, the genetic condition caused very poor eyesight and extreme skin sensitivity to sun. Human albino eyes were either blue-gray or light brown in color. Any reddish or pinkish cast was temporary, caused by light striking the iris at a certain angle, like the "red eye" effect in a flash photograph.

Mildred had never seen Jak wear corrective lenses; his vision was perfect near and far. He had never worn a hat or special clothing to protect his white skin from sunburn, which he never seemed to get. His eyes were ruby-red all the time, like a lab rat.

Jak could proclaim himself "Not mutie!" until the hellscape froze over, but he didn't know anything about genetics, or metabolic pathways, or conventional albinism. In point of fact, Mildred was confident that no creature like him had existed before nukeday.

In a world where albinos were virtually unknown, where any sort of physical oddity was ascribed to the curse of mutated genes, it wasn't surprising that Jak was saddled with the mutie label at almost every turn.

She had never told him—or any of the others—how well the label fit. Passing on that information served no good purpose in her view. Besides, Mildred found the whole concept of "pure norm genes" ridiculous. Science and reason told her that post-apocalypse, everyone and everything was a little bit mutie, thanks to cumulative exposure to the increased background radiation. Her own DNA had undoubtedly suffered permanent damage during the companions' imprisonment at ground zero on the Slake City nukeglass massif. That didn't worry her much, either. A century ago, when she was still a medical student, she'd read the statistics on the survivors of Hiroshima and Nagasaki. A-bomb victims with far higher radiation doses than hers lived for many decades before fatal cancers finally appeared. Based on the level of violence and hardship in the hell-scape, the chances were good that she wasn't going to live long enough to die of cancer, anyway.

After all the wags were loaded, Malosh had his troops line up the Redbone conscripts. The masked baron then walked down the row and quickly selected three healthy young men and three healthy young women, apparently at random.

"You six will stay behind," he informed them. "I have left you and the others enough food and water to survive. As you rebuild your ville, remember my mercy."

While the lucky half dozen hurried to join the very old and very young at the doorways of the empty huts, the baron mounted his horse and led the mass exit from Redbone.

Only Malosh's officers rode, either on horseback or in the carts. Everyone else walked down the zigzag path to the fields below. The column of nearly three hundred was a large force by Deathlands standards, and it was segregated by genetics and military function.

"Where the rad blazes are we headed?" J.B. asked the gaunt fighter walking beside him.

"Sunspot ville," the man said. "It's a long march due south. At least two, mebbe three days."

"What happens when we get there?" Mildred asked, hoping against hope for some good news.

There was none.

"We take the ville," the soldier said, "or die trying."

Chapter Five

As Baron Kendrick Haldane crossed the fields en route to his riverside compound, his subjects, old and young, tipped their hats and smiled up at him. They knew nothing of the deal about to be struck. Though Haldane had been made baron by popular acclaim, his fiefdom wasn't a democracy. The good people of Nuevaville didn't want participatory government; they wanted a leader, a father figure, someone in charge who was stronger and more intelligent than they were. Success or failure, survival or extinction was the baron-for-life's sole responsibility.

Parked in the lane in front of the side-by-side, double-wide trailers that housed his residence and administrative offices was a convoy of armored predark wags. Hummers. Winnebago Braves. Military six-by-sixes. One of the vehicles, a veritable landship with a skin of gunmetal-gray steel plate, dwarfed all the others. The metal windshield had two wide rows of louvred view slits for the driver and navigator. There were also view slits above each of the firing ports that ringed its perimeter at four-foot intervals. Bulletproof skirts protected the three sets of wheels; amidships and rear, the wheels were doubled. A full-length steel skidplate protected the undercarriage from improvised road mines and satchel charges. On the roof, fore and aft, heavy, swivel-mounted machine guns controlled 360 degrees of terrain.

The wags' crews and sec men lounged around cable spool tables set out under a pair of oak trees.

Small children peeked at the convoy and its personnel from behind the outcrops that bordered the lane. From their delighted expressions, they thought the carny had come to town. When Haldane angrily waved them off, they scattered, out of harm's way.

The baron had positioned his ville defense force in the surrounding buildings, ditches and fields. From these hiding places, they aimed two old RPGs that had been acquired by the old baron at the parked vehicles and the seated men, ensuring that any attempt at a double cross would end as quickly as it started, a grenade attack turning wags into burning hulks—and men into dismembered corpses—in a matter of seconds.

Haldane could hear the big wag's power generators droning as he approached the crew members and sec teams. There was as much Nuevaville rabbit stew on their beards and forearms as there was on their plates. Those not eating were busy drinking green beer from recycled antifreeze jugs and smoking hand-rolled cigarettes and cheroots. Their predark milspec weapons were prominently displayed. The 9 mm Heckler & Koch MP-5 A-3 submachine guns showed no wear, no scratches in their blueing. They looked brand-new, right out of the Cosmoline.

The visitors didn't rise in deference or salute as Haldane passed. Some ignored him, most stared with unconcealed contempt. The baron had come face to face with plenty of road and river trash in his day, but this gang was different. And not just because of the quality and condition of their blasters. They had no fear of him.

Or perhaps they had a far greater fear of their employer.

The sec men and drivers were uniformly large—tall, well fed and muscular. They all sported an excess of the scarifications and brandings that passed for body decoration in the hellscape. Angry red tears perpetually dripped down cheeks. Mouths were widened at the corners and turned up into obscene, permanent grins. Spiral brands formed symbolic third eyes in the middle of foreheads. Inch-wide, half-round welts, snakes of scars, wound around bare arms from wrist to shoulder. Ground-in dirt caked their hands and faces and the sides of their heavy black boots.

Haldane entered the big wag via a porthole door amidships. The light inside the narrow metal corridor was dim and filled with the most horrible smell, a combination of slaughterhouse in July and deathbed, blood and pus and bodily wastes. It took his breath away. To the right, down the access way, a sec man with shoulder-length, blond dreadlocks motioned impatiently for him to approach.

"Did you talk to your god?" the guard asked, holding the muzzle of his H&K pointed at the baron's bowels, his finger resting lightly on the trigger.

"No," Haldane replied, "my god talked to me, through his chosen oracle."

"Ain't but one true god in Deathlands, Baron, and he's waiting for you back there." The sec man hooked a thumb over his shoulder in the direction of the wag's rear salon.

As Haldane started to walk past, the sentry put out his free hand and said, "Gimme that blaster."

The baron let him take the Remington, then started down the hall. On his right were evenly spaced firing ports and view slits. On his left were riveted metal walls and closed metal doors.

He was fifteen feet from the entrance to the rear stateroom when he heard a shrill, whimpering sound over the generators' steady throb. The sound was instantly recognizable. It made his heart thud in his ears and his blood run cold. He sprinted for the door and without knocking, threw it back and burst into the salon.

Inside everything was in disarray. The lamplit workbenches and tables that choked the middle of the room were cluttered with surgical tools, rusting cans and piles of rags. Under the tables were buckets of what looked like dirty transmission fluid. Floor-to-ceiling metal shelves overflowed with electronic and computer parts. In front of a double ceramic sink streaked with blood was a fifty-five-gallon plastic barrel in which floated human body parts. The concentrated reek of abattoir made his eyes water and his gorge rise.

In the gloom on the far side of the jumble of tables, something moved on the broad, rear bench seat. Haldane caught a glimpse of a face, of sorts. In a full moon of festering flesh sat eyes like chromed hens' eggs.

An ancient, unblinking evil.

That wouldn't let itself die.

When Haldane moved closer, he saw the small

blond-haired child sitting ever so still on the creature's lap. It was his son, Thorne. The boy's blue eyes wore an expression he had never seen before. And never wanted to see again. Thorne was paralyzed with terror. A half metal, half human claw rested easily on the back of the boy's slender neck.

"You have a very inquisitive child here, Baron," the Magus said. "He asked me for a guided tour of my war wag. I think I have satisfied his curiosity."

Thorne Haldane looked up at his father, desperate to be away, but afraid to move a muscle.

As adrenaline flooded the baron's veins, a mechanized hand slipped down to cover the center of the child's chest.

"He has such a strong little heart," Magus said.

The clanking laugh than emanated from the spider-like torso jolted Haldane to the core, as did the implied threat.

Magus wasn't a child molester.

He was something infinitely worse.

"Come here, son," Haldane said.

Steel Eyes held the boy fast on his lap, and the baron sensed the creature's insane jealousy, his envy of the budding young life.

Haldane had a nine-inch killing dirk concealed up his sleeve. A weapon designed to open a wound that would never close. But where to stab, which of the rat's nest of plastic tubes and colorful wires to cut? And failing a one-strike, instant chill, those metal fingers would crush his child's head like a piece of ripe fruit.

The dirk remained in its forearm sheath.

"Son, come to me. You have no business here."

Magus didn't try to stop the boy as he cautiously slipped off his lap. Thorne hurried between the tables to hide behind his father's stout legs. The six-year-old clung to the back of his BDU pants.

From the bench seat came a faint, high-pitched whirring sound as the pupils in Magus's metal eyes dilated. Then he opened his mouth and licked his lips with an all too human tongue. When he closed his jaws, the supporting guy wires slid into the grommets set in titanium cheek braces.

It was said, and widely believed, that this monstrous, suppurating creature experimented with the organs of other people in order to find ways to improve his own ability to function. It was said that Magus was so removed from his human origins that he performed operations on himself. He could turn off his pain centers and yank out and replace his own innards, like components of a wag motor.

There would be no experiments on Haldane's only son. Not while the baron still drew breath. Without a word, he picked up the boy and carried him down the hall, past the grinning sec man, to the porthole door.

"They grabbed me and brought me in here, Daddy," Thorne told him. "I didn't wanna see this place."

"I know you didn't. It's okay, now," Haldane said as he put the child down. He opened the door and whispered in his son's ear, "Run, Thorne. Run!"

The boy jumped to the ground and took off down the lane like a shot, through the first spattering of rain. Lightning arced across the northern sky, and a moment later thunder rumbled.

As Haldane turned back for the salon, his hands

began to tremble and shake. His mouth tasted like he'd been sucking on a bullet. This was how Magus took and maintained control of even the strongest, the bravest of men; this was how he corrupted them. He showed them their most terrible fear, and that he had the power to make it come to pass.

Steel Eyes dealt in weapons of mass destruction, the deadliest instruments that civilization had ever produced. No one knew for certain how he got access to the predark technology, whether he stole it from the secret redoubts scattered around the nuked-out world, or whether, as was rumored, he traveled back in time to rob it from the past. Either way, Magus was much more than a trader in rare and dangerous goods. Although he didn't seek to acquire territory or to amass armies, his spies were said to be everywhere. He didn't aspire to baronhood, but he pulled strings behind the scenes like a puppet master, applying pressure here, pressure there, for motives that were unfathomable.

The baron reentered the salon and stepped right up to Magus. Close enough to see the inflamed joins of live flesh and polished metal. Through the rear window's view slits, in down-slanting shafts of light, fat flies buzzed and zigzagged.

"You shouldn't have touched my son," Haldane said.

"I did him no harm," Magus countered. "I am not contagious. It was an educational experience for him. He saw the greatest miracle of whitecoat science at close range."

With Thorne's life out of the mix, an instant chill strike wasn't necessary. The baron could have taken his time with the killing dirk, absorbing whatever punishment the mechanized hands dished out, stabbing and slashing until the creature finally died. He would have done so with relish, but he needed Magus to save his barony.

"Before we proceed," Haldane said, "I want assurances that the loss of life will be confined."

"I never give guarantees," Magus said. "The weapons systems I have brought you are indiscriminate by design. My sources tell me that even as we speak, the Impaler is advancing on Sunspot with a large military force. He will rout your small detachment of fighters, take over the ville and reestablish his staging point for another hit-and-run attack on Nuevaville. Yes or no, Haldane. I need your decision now."

The puppet master understood the trap in which Haldane and his arch enemy were caught. Both controlled minor fiefdoms with small populations and large, mostly uninhabitable territories. Malosh wanted the natural resources of Haldane's barony, Haldane wanted to protect them. Haldane couldn't defeat Malosh's mobile army, Malosh couldn't defeat his hardened defenses. Neither had alliances of mutual defense with baronies on their other borders.

For the past five years Haldane and his western neighbor had battled across an ill-defined boundary, losing blood and treasure in a steady flow, and the key to staging or holding off successful attacks was Sunspot. The remote ville had the misfortune of standing roughly halfway between the barons' respective capitals, on the most direct overland route. For military purposes, it was a strategic lynchpin, a place for an army recover after the long desert trek, a place to store supplies and gather reinforcements. For years, control of Sunspot had swung back and forth between the adversaries, with the ville folk caught in the middle.

Haldane saw the fighting and the loss of life as a waste of precious resources and time. The constant conflict kept him from developing economic relationships with the wealthy eastern baronies, from building new trade routes, from bringing more prosperity to his people. It kept him from giving them a future.

Magus had appeared on his doorstep with a long-term solution to the problem. The only way to end the stalemate was to obliterate Sunspot ville and make it useless to either side.

For some to live, others had to die.

The price of peace was mass murder.

Haldane knew if Magus offered Malosh the same opportunity, he would jump at it. Not to use against Sunspot. To use against the defenses of Nuevaville. Not to end to the conflict at a gentlemen's draw, but to win a one-sided victory.

The storm had closed in. Thunder boomed directly overhead. A hard rain rattled the landship's roof.

"Show me what you've brought," the baron said.

Magus lurched from the bench seat with speed and agility that surprised Haldane. He whipped aside a tarp on the floor, exposing a pair of lidless crates. They were painted olive-drab and bore the mark of the hammer and sickle. Inside one, in neat rows, were point-nosed artillery projectiles. The second crate held cased propellant charges. Like the wag crews' H & Ks, it all looked straight-from-the-armory, brand-spanking-new.

"The chem weapon warheads are fired by the Soviet

Lyagusha D-30 122 mm howitzer," Magus said. "Its maximum range is a little more than nine miles."

"And you have this gun?"

"Of course."

"Where is it?"

"Safely hidden between here and the proposed target."

Haldane examined the munitions with care. "There are two kinds of shells in the crate," he remarked.

"That's right. You have a choice to make, Baron. Would you prefer nerve or blister gas?"

Chapter Six

Doc Tanner marched with his eyes narrowed to slits and a scarf securely wrapped over his mouth and nose. The cannon fodder contingent to which he had been assigned formed the tail of a 350-yard-long column. In front of the human shields were the muties and the leashed dogs, then came the horse- and mule-drawn supply carts, the norm fighters, with the cavalry taking the lead.

Doc couldn't see the other companions for the shifting clouds of dust and all the intervening bodies. Grit crunched between his back teeth, and when he lifted the bottom edge of his scarf to clear his throat, he spit brown. Beside him, the elder swineherd, Bezoar, walked under his own power, limping on a crudely fashioned, willow-fork crutch. Young Crad kept a wary eye on his mentor, ready to come to his aid in case he faltered.

Like Doc, the others were coated head to foot with beige dirt; like him, most had strips of rag tied over their faces. They looked like an army of the disinterred, children between the ages of seven and thirteen, and men and women with healed, horrendous wounds and missing limbs. Some of the fodder resembled the young swineherd—in Deathlands evocative parlance: triple-stupe droolies.

So far, all those who had tried to escape from Malosh's army had failed. The dust and arid terrain offered little or no cover to conscriptees who broke ranks and sprinted off in the opposite direction. When this happened, the swampies leisurely unchained the dogs, who scrambled after the prey, baying. The deserters got off one, mebbe two shots, then came desperate screams for help amid wild snarling. Screams that were quickly silenced. After the same scenario had played out a few times, there were no more deserters.

Even if successful escape had been possible, Doc would never have left his battle mates.

High above the loose, three-abreast formation, buzzards circled, riding the thermals, waiting for hapless souls to weaken and fall behind. No bullwhips, no threats were required to keep the column of conscripts moving onward. To fall behind was to be abandoned in the desert, and that meant a slow, awful death by heat and dehydration, it meant lying helpless while the carrion birds plucked out your eyes and tongue.

Idle chatter among the ranks had dried up hours ago, along with the rain-soaked soil. The rapid pace of the advance was difficult to maintain, first because of soggy earth, and now because of all the dust the boots, the wheels and the animals were raising. Talking parched the throat and the refreshment stops on the march were few and far between.

Even when wind gusts blew aside the swirling beige dust, there was little of interest to look at. The army trudged down the vast river plain, creeping toward low blue blips on the horizon. The troops and wags and dogs at the front of the column scared off any wild animals.

As Doc put one foot in front of the other, his mind began to wander, inexorably turning inward. This was the first army in which he had served. During his months of captivity before nukeday, he had read about the terrible wars of the twentieth century. Except for the smattering of automatic weapons among the ranks, this army could have come straight from the fifteenth century—or even earlier. It had no mass overland transit. No aircraft. No communications systems. No motor-powered wags.

It was a legion of barbarians, of shabbily clad ground pounders who pillaged the hellscape like locusts.

As AFTERNOON EDGED into evening, Malosh's column climbed out of the river valley into the low, rolling desert hills polka-dotted with clumps of brush. Sunset tinged the mountains to the east, turning the up-tilted layers of folded bedrock into alternating bands of pink and orange. In a notch between the hilltops, they made camp for the night, unharnessing the horses and mules, lighting cook fires, setting up the tents for the men in charge. Everyone else ate and slept in the open in groups segregated by function and the relative purity of their genetics.

While waiting in line with the rest of the cannon fodder for his supper, Doc saw Jak and Krysty standing over by the dog pack. He tried to get their attention, but in the failing light they didn't see him.

Ferdinando, the commander of the human shields, supervised the distribution of their evening meal. His right arm ended in a khaki sock-covered stump just above the elbow. His left hand was badly mangled as was the right side of his throat and face. A thick brown beard covered his cheeks, everywhere but that angry, waxy patch of scar.

Dinner consisted of a single, fire-roasted jacket potato and a dipper of water.

"This is what the baron means by 'plenty to eat'?" Doc said, holding up the charred, stunted spud he'd been given.

"Fighters march faster on empty stomachs," Ferdinando said. "Dogs are more eager for the hunt. Don't worry, there will be feasting enough after we retake Sunspot ville."

"You had control of it and lost it?" Doc queried.

"Our forces were driven out by Baron Haldane's troops. The battle cost me my arm."

"A terrible wound, indeed," Doc commiserated.

"Gren went off under a horse I was walking past. Shrap tore me up bad, and then the horse fell on top of me. Lost this wing altogether, and it crushed my left hand so I can't fire a blaster no more. To tell the truth, I can hardly pick up a spoon to feed myself."

"Malosh's army did that to you?"

"No, no. The gren came from Haldane's men."

"But you were a conscript?"

"No, I volunteered."

"Why in God's name would you do something like that?" Doc asked.

"Because I come from the heartland of Malosh's barony," Ferdinando said. "To the west of here there's nothing but desert, unfarmable hardscrabble for hundreds of miles in every direction. It's a place so worthless nobody has ever bothered trying to invade it. Before

Malosh took power in the territory, the people in my ville were always just one day away from starvation. We had to watch our children die of hunger and disease. Malosh freed us from our fate. He realized that even though we could never win total victory over the neighboring barons because of our limited numbers, we could raid their territory on a regular basis and send the food back to our people. He forged us into a quick-strike fighting force. We survive by our wits, our courage and our speed of foot. If we stop moving, we die."

"Surely you could pack up and move somewhere else. To greener, more hospitable pastures."

"And fall under the bootheel of another baron?" Ferdinando said. "Never. The hard land where we were born has made us who we are. And we are proud of it."

"And in the name of that pride you swear allegiance to the Impaler?"

"Call him whatever you like. He's a hero to his people."

"Perhaps so, but what about the poor souls he has forced to fight and die for him, whose villes he has ransacked?"

"Wait until you see the baron in battle. Wait until you see the effect he has on every person in this army. Malosh has no equal in valor or in daring. His example as a warrior raises everyone up."

"I've seen how he raises people up," Doc said. "He has no equal in brutality, either."

"That is a means to an end," Ferdinando said. "Three die and fifty join us."

"You are saying he takes no pleasure from those ghastly public spectacles?"

"I have fought under Malosh for two years. Because

of that mask he wears I've never seen him smile. I don't know what gives him pleasure. I only know I will die for him because of what he has done for his people, for my kin."

"No matter what he has done to everyone else."

Ferdinando smiled. "Mark my words, when the time comes you will die for him, too. And gladly."

"I will die," Doc said, "but not for the likes of him."

Clutching his miserable meal, Doc found Bezoar and Young Crad huddled close to one of the campfires. The elder swineherd comforted the younger, who sobbed bitterly into his palms.

"She's in a much better place," Bezoar assured his friend. After a minute he limped over to Doc.

"Poor boy's brokenhearted," Bezoar said.

"If you ask me, his attachment to that dead beast seems inordinate," Doc remarked.

"The feeling was mutual," Bezoar said. "That black-and-white hog followed him everywhere he went. They ate cheek to cheek, nose to nose at the same trough. She sat at his feet. She slept beside him in the straw. This is their first night apart since the day she was weaned."

A phrase from Victorian times popped into Tanner's mind. "The love that dare not speak its name."

A florid euphemism that originally referred to another sort of socially—and Biblically—condemned behavior. Perhaps he was overreacting.

Bezoar slammed the door on that happy possibility.

Shaking his grizzled head, the crippled swineherd shared the boy's sad secret. "When it come to getting some of the biscuit," he said, "Young Crad was shit out of luck. None of the norm women in Redbone ville would take him between their legs. And he never earned enough jack to rent out a gaudy slut. Even the ville's female triple-stupe droolies turned up their noses at him. His piggie dear wasn't nearly so picky."

Doc Tanner shuddered as deeply suppressed, horrific memories swept over him. Shortly after he'd first arrived in the hellscape, he'd been captured by Baron Jordan Teague and tortured by Cort Strasser, the baron's head sec man. Strasser, of the skull-like face and skin like tightly stretched parchment, had driven Doc into the baron's pig sties, and at blasterpoint, before an audience of hooting sec men, forced him to have sexual congress with the sows. The ordeal severely tested Doc's staying power; Strasser wouldn't let him leave the pens until he had serviced every single pig. And whenever the mood struck him, Strasser sent Doc back for more.

In the process, the Oxford-educated doctor of philosophy and science, a man of elevated sensibilities, of moral values, had been brought lower than low. A hundred times he had considered suicide. He had already survived kidnap and torture by the whitecoats, the loss of his family; his brain had been scrambled by consecutive temporal leaps. Despite all he'd suffered, his will to live was indomitable. He was only thankful that his beloved Emily and his dear children couldn't witness his utter degradation.

Even years later, the sight of a curly tail made his skin crawl.

The idea that Young Crad might have willingly engaged in similar activity made Doc's head reel. Dropping his dinner to the dirt, he turned away from the fire, clapping his hands over his ears to muffle the swine-herd's cries of anguish.

Chapter Seven

Baron Haldane sat in one of the sunken rear seats of one of Magus's Humvees with his Remington sawed-off resting across his lap. It was slow going on what was left of the main predark east-west road, old Interstate 10. Haldane reckoned he would have made better time on horseback. The ancient roadbed was split and heaved up in places, and missing altogether in others, which made it impassable for the larger wags. The nimble Humvees scouted out a safe route for the heavier vehicles, sometimes on the highway, sometimes off. The convoy made wide detours around the soft spots, the deep craters and the boulders. Even so, Magus's vast landship got stuck. Time and again, it had to be towed out of hole of its own making.

Despite all the stoppages and delays, Steel Eyes hadn't showed his face once.

The baron's three companions in the Humvee were the lowest form of Deathlands road trash. They stank of rancid body oils, spilled beer and diesel fuel. The driver wore a pair of yellow-tinted goggles, the other two wore cracked, wraparound dark sunglasses. All three sported greasy do-rags. The driver's brown hair was braided into a long ponytail.

To break the monotony of the snail's pace journey

and to satisfy his own curiosity about the mysteries of Magus, Haldane asked them how they had been recruited into his service.

The front-seat passenger turned to glare at the baron. "None of your fucking business," he sibilated through the two-inch gap of his absent, top front teeth.

The man in the seat beside Haldane wasn't so touchy about his privacy. His teeth were intact, but mossy-green; the skin of his face was peppered with hundreds of deep pockmarks packed with grime. "I passed out dead drunk in a Siana gaudy," he said, "and I woke up the next day in the back of a six-by-six with some other hungover coldhearts. Truck crew never said nothing about Magus. They fed us good and we did what we was told to the people we was told to do it to. Had nice new blasters to use on them, too. I didn't know it all belonged to Magus until a week later when he showed up. By that time, I didn't care."

"Old Steel Eyes saved my skin," the driver said over his shoulder. "I was all set to be hanged from a lamp post. That's how they do the deed over in Kanscity. See, I got caught chillin' this dirt farmer and his family. I didn't plan no blood bath, I was just tryin' to get my leg over on the little daughter. Dumb farmer heard her yellin' for help after I got in the groove, then it all went to shit in a hurry. Him shooting at me, me shooting back at him. The other kin came a runnin'. By the time it was over, I'd done all five of them. I didn't get far before the neighbors ran me down. Ville folk sold my life to Magus for ten gallons of prime joy juice."

"Do you get a good wage?" Haldane asked.

"Let's say he don't pay in cash, as such," the driver said.

"What does he pay you in, as such?"

"Why are you talking to him?" the front seat guy said. "He don't need to know any of this shit."

The driver waved off the protest. "It depends," he answered. "We get a share of whatever's on the table. Sometimes it's ammo, sometimes it's jolt, sometimes it's something tender and warm."

"Apple pie," said the road trash next to Haldane.

From the salacious look that twisted his filthy mug he wasn't referring to a home-baked dessert.

"Only pie on this job is gonna be miles away and stone dead by the time we're done," the front passenger grumbled.

"A waste of recreational opportunities," the driver said.

"The women of Sunspot don't know what they're missing," the toothless scum whistled.

Actually, they did know.

When Baron Haldane had control of the ville he kept the raping of the population by his troops to a bare minimum. He punished offenders severely, with public lashings. But when Malosh ruled Sunspot, it was another story. And it wasn't only the women who got reamed.

"How many fighters has Magus got?" he asked.

"Who knows?" the driver said "He's got some here, some there, from what I hear. All doing different things for different reasons."

"Where's his seat of power?"

"More like, does he even have one," the pockmarked man said.

"If you're looking for a stationary target," the driver

said, "in case things go sour on this deal, you're shit out of luck. Magus is mighty tight-lipped about such things."

"Jaws like a steel trap," the toothless man said.

A remark that made the road scum laugh out loud.

"Only thing the Magus ever let us grunts in on is his retirement plan," the driver said.

"Yeah," the front passenger chimed in. "Early retirement for coldhearts who talk too much."

"Or ask too many fucking questions," the man next to Haldane said.

Threat taken, the baron looked out the dusty side window. He hadn't come on the road trip unescorted. He had brought ten members of the Nuevaville defense force with him. Fully armed, they rode in the back of one of the six-by-sixes. They weren't along just for his personal protection. Before he initiated an all-out chemical attack on Sunspot, he planned to send some of them ahead to warn the garrison stationed there. His troops had to pull back from the ville and be miles away from ground zero before the gas assault commenced. Baron Haldane was determined to do everything he could to prevent the chilling of his own people.

The baron-for-life was at a disadvantage in the deal with Magus. He didn't know how to load, aim or fire the Soviet-made artillery piece. No one else in his barony did, either. In point of fact, no one had ever even seen a cannon that powerful. According to Magus, it took eight trained men to operate the gun.

So, in exchange for payment, Steel Eyes was to provide the weapon, the chemical warheads and the expertise to lay the rounds on target.

Nuevaville had an ample treasury of precious metals, predark relics, stored food, joy juice, weapons, ammunition and wag parts. All collected as tolls or in trade for other goods and services.

The price Magus had demanded of him was steep. The precious metal gold was a common currency in many parts of Deathlands. He wanted half the gold and a quarter of everything else. But Haldane knew it was worth the cost to end the stalemate. He didn't ask his people to approve spending of their treasure. He didn't have to.

No fool, Haldane had refused to part with so much as a grain of wheat until he was satisfied that Magus could do exactly what he claimed. Which meant test firing the blaster on a practice range and seeing the crew in action. Because the plan was to proceed directly to Sunspot from the test site, it also meant that the dark deed would be done, the ville obliterated, before payment actually changed hands. Haldane wasn't surprised that Steel Eyes agreed to those terms. After all, the good baron had a reputation for honesty and fair dealing, even among the bottom-feeding scabs of the hellscape.

The long ride gave Haldane plenty of time to consider the unfathomability of Magus's true motives. The mechanized creature could have had all of the treasure if he'd used the chem shells on Nuevaville. Perhaps he couldn't enter a poisoned ville because his troops didn't have chem weapons suits? Perhaps he had no way to decontaminate the spoils? Or mebbe the real payoff for him was the monstrous act of mass murder itself? Or its anticipated, long-term consequences? A more prosperous barony for Haldane meant better pickings for

Magus in the future. Steel Eyes always sided with those who had the best chance of turning a profit.

Because of the bad road and heavy vehicles, it took the better part of a day to reach the site of the predark ville of Akela, the rendezvous point with the blaster team. There wasn't much left of the ville—a five-acre patch of pocked-and-cratered asphalt that had been a box-store parking lot, concrete foundation pads sprouting rebar and PVC stubble. A rusted-out water tower toppled over on its side, the holding tank split and emptied. A few telephone and power poles still stood, canted over, draping sagging, rotten wires.

Waiting in the middle of the ruined parking lot was another olive-drab six-by-six. Hitched to its rear bumper was a long, two-wheeled, tarp-wrapped trailer. When the convoy pulled up and stopped, men jumped out of the cab and rear of the truck.

Haldane bailed from the Humvee and walked down the row of wags to join his troops. As they stared at the additional potential adversaries, they looked nervous. Nervous men and automatic weapons were a bad combination.

"Easy, now," he told them in a low, confidential tone. "Keep your safeties on and your fingers off the triggers. We've got nothing to worry about, yet. Just watch me and stay alert."

Then the door to the hulking landship opened. Magus descended to the tarmac and started walking toward the covered trailer. It was horror in motion. The creature lurched forward, swinging its arms, its still-human muscles wedded imperfectly to stainless-steel bones. Despite the convulsive gait, it glided on buttery-smooth, Teflon-coated ball and socket joints.

At a wave of his half-metal hand, the blaster crew began unstrapping and uncovering the steely gray, D-30 Lyagushka. Cannon revealed, they disconnected the lunette under its muzzle brake from the six-by-six's rear bumper hitch. Lowering the blaster's central emplacement jack, they raised the wheels high enough to clear the three trail legs. Then they spread the two outer trails at 120-degree angles on either side.

"Where is the practice target?" Haldane asked as the crew rotated the mount, turning the barrel to the north.

"You can't see it from here with the naked eye," Magus said. He signaled one of the blaster crew. "Give him a scope."

The man handed the baron a spotting scope and faced him in the right direction, pointing out the target over his shoulder.

It was a skeleton of a shack. More of a utility shed, really, squatting on the desert plain. Once it had been connected to the electric grid, but the power poles leading up to it were all blown down. The heat waves rising off the sand made it difficult to see, even with predark optics.

"How far away is it?" Haldane asked.

"Eight point three miles," the crewman said.

Haldane lowered the scope. "You're going to practice with real chem warheads?"

"No, of course not," Magus told him. "To lock in the range and the direction and amount of wind drift on the battlefield, the gunners fire a series of smoke rounds.

They should be sufficient to convince you that I can do what I say."

At his command, the eight-man crew loaded a projectile and adjusted the aim. Then they clapped their hands over their ears.

Anticipating the blast, Haldane did the same.

Magus, on the other hand, simply reached up and turned his off.

Steel Eyes signaled and the gunner jerked the lanyard. With a rocking boom, the Lyagushka jumped on its trails, belching flame and smoke. The 122 mm round squealed as it sailed away.

Haldane raised the spotting scope to his eye and reacquired the target. Seconds later a puff of white smoke erupted downrange, followed by a rolling thunderclap. The impact was about two hundred yards short of the shack and one hundred yards to the left.

Through the lens, Haldane saw a family of mutie jackrabbits hightailing it across the scrub. They had seen enough.

The crew readjusted for distance and windage, reloaded the gun and fired off another round. This time the smoke puff was one hundred yards too long but directly in line with the shack.

Their third shot landed within thirty feet of the ruined shed, pelting it with rock and wreathing it in dense cottony smoke.

The elapsed time from first to last shot was about four minutes.

"You can do that to Sunspot?" Haldane said.

"Sunspot is much bigger, so it will be even easier to hit," Magus said.

"Piece of cake," the gunner confirmed, grinning up at his half man–half machine master. "And nobody's going to be shooting back at us from eight miles away."

"Did you notice how my crew used the wind drift to make the smoke sweep over the target?" Magus asked. "They'll do the same thing with the nerve gas."

"How many rounds will it take?" the baron said.

"To saturate a ville of that size with CW agent, it'll take a dozen of the binary munitions, give or take a few depending on the wind's speed and direction."

"And once that's done?"

"Every red-blooded living thing inside the Sunspot berm will be dead," Magus said.

Haldane couldn't help but ask the awful question. "How badly will they suffer?"

"Charming of you to be so considerate of your intended victims, Baron," Magus said.

The observation wasn't meant as a compliment.

"If we used the liquid lewisite instead of sarin," Magus continued, "their agony would be much prolonged. The blister agent causes immediate burning pain in the chest and eyes, temporary blindness, and after a latency period of a few hours causes severe inflammation of the lungs leading to death. On the other hand, high doses of sarin gas chill relatively quickly, if not painlessly. The nerve agent disrupts the normal functioning of the body's muscles. They go into spasm or cease to operate altogether. Unlike lewisite, its victims once poisoned don't move very far. They collapse, go into convulsions, then total paralysis sets in, which causes suffocation. Salting the earth and water around Sunspot with liquid sarin will make it uninhabitable for many years to come. Anyone who comes within a mile of the ruins and takes a deep breath or touches the ground will get a fatal dose. A permanent solution to your quandary is what you wanted. That's what you've got."

"Yes, so it would appear."

"And you're ready to pay the price?"

"I'll pay what we agreed on, after the job is done."

Magus stared at him in silence for a long moment. It was difficult for Haldane to say whether what passed over that godawful mouth of his was a smile. What lips remained to him turned up at the corners as guy wires slipped through Teflon grommets, coiling somewhere under steel skin onto tiny hidden spools. "Just to make sure you don't change your mind after Sunspot falls, I've brought along an inducement."

"I won't change my mind."

"Nonetheless…." Magus gestured at the landship, steel fingers beckoning impatiently.

The side door opened again and the blond-dreadlocked henchman stepped out, carrying a beige fiberglass box in both arms. The box was a cube two-and-a-half-feet wide, deep and high. At one end was a steel-barred door. The baron had no experience with predark pet carriers, but he could see there was something good-size moving around inside.

As the henchman approached, he saw the small pale fingers clutching at the bars, and behind the locked door, a small, familiar face.

Haldane swung his scattergun up in two-handed grip, bracing himself for sustained rapid fire.

His soldiers shouldered their assault rifles.

Magus's men reacted, raising their weapons, as well.

It was a standoff, unwinnable by Haldane, and winnable only at great cost to Steel Eyes.

"I think we can agree that the boy is in good health," Magus said. "If you want to keep him that way, you and your men should lower your blasters. No way can you chill all of us before we chill him. You need to calm down, Baron. You need to think it through. The child is just a good faith guarantee, a deposit on the full amount. You pay me and you get your deposit back. You withhold payment and I will take him apart just to see what makes him tick."

Chapter Eight

For Krysty, the third straight day of march was by far the most difficult. There was an unfamiliar leadenness in her legs, and the inside of her head felt like it had been scoured with coarse sand. It wasn't just the starvation rations, or the hard terrain, or breathing through a filthy handkerchief, or the distance they had covered. For two nights running, she and Jak had sat back-to-back with weapons drawn, unable to sleep a wink because of the threat the swampie bastards presented. Even now, every time they glanced over their shoulders at her, their faces bruised and battered, she could see it in their eyes.

They wanted a chance to even the score.

And more.

Jak gently nudged her with an elbow, breaking her train of thought. He pointed to the left, to a hilltop to the east. A pair of dark riders had crested the rounded beige summit and were racing down the slope toward the front of the column.

The albino pulled his bandanna off his face. "Scouts back," he announced, showing muddy teeth.

Somewhere out of sight up ahead, Malosh the Impaler called a halt to the advance.

The long line of marchers stood in silence while the

dust settled and the midday sun beat down on them relentlessly. Though they were stopped, no water barrels were opened, no dippers were passed around. The baron was hell-bent on conserving as much of the accumulated resources as possible. If he didn't need to drink, nobody drank.

The cannon fodder unit was standing behind them. Doc slouched about thirty feet away. Krysty watched him peel the long scarf from over his nose and mouth. He didn't shake it out; he wadded it up in his hand while he gasped for air. Under the coating of dust, Doc didn't look at all well. In his too long life the reluctant time traveler had suffered much, both emotionally and physically. The whitecoats' cruel meddling had permanently damaged his brain, creating an intermittent short circuit, a debilitation triggered by stress, by a sound, a sight, a smell, or by Gaia knew what else. From long experience, Krysty knew how to read the signs in his gaunt face and in his body language. If Doc was indeed starting to withdraw into the morass of jumbled memories, of insensate anger, of incalculable loss, there was nothing she or anyone else could do to stop it.

She couldn't see past the carts and the backs of the horses to locate Ryan, J.B. or Mildred.

The six companions were in a unique predicament. Though separated, they had all their weapons and ammo. They weren't bound or hobbled. They were free to move within certain limits, even to regroup if they could manage it quickly enough. But if they regrouped and opened fire with their weapons, they would have been blown apart by a hundred blasters.

It was very hard to do nothing.

To just wait.

Above everything else, the companions valued their freedom. They controlled their own destinies, lived by their own code. They wouldn't be enslaved by anyone or anything. Because Krysty shared that inner core of iron, she would never give up hope while her heart still beat. She was confident that their moment would come. Perhaps in the chaos of a pitched battle or during a lull in a long siege. They had to be ready for it.

She turned her attention to the ranks of dogs and dog handlers waiting in front of her. The hounds were nearly three feet tall at the shoulder, and they looked even taller in comparison to the sawed-off swampies. Their smooth, short coats were brindle-colored. White blazes marked their huge heads and thick necks. She guessed the animals weighed somewhere between 150 and 200 pounds. They were lean and well-muscled. Their pointed ears were bent and notched from blows and teeth. There were dark, crescent bite scars on their muzzles and on the sides and tops of their heads; some were missing their skinny tails.

From what she'd witnessed over the past two days, the relationship between swampies and hounds was not love-hate. It was pure hate. The dogs had either been captured from wild packs or bred and trained to bring out their savage instincts. She had seen hounds suddenly wheel and turn on their handlers, knocking them to the ground and, with a born chiller's hard focus, going straight for the throat.

Most of the swampies showed evidence of these attacks. They had lost chunks of their faces, earlobes, fingers. When a dog pulled down its handler, the other swampies worked together to quickly bring the animal under control. They pounded on its head with their clubs and worked the ends of the cudgels between the grinding jaws to pry them apart.

Krysty caught movement up the line. The scouts were riding down the edge of the formation, in her direction. Both were tall, skeletally thin black men. One wore a leather earflap hat lined with sheep fleece. The other had a shaved head and crude metal wristlets strapped to his massive forearms. Their scruffy brown ponies looked too short to carry them. They stopped their mounts in front of Korb.

"We spotted a Haldane long-range foot patrol," the man with the earflap hat told Korb. "They're a half mile and a couple of ridges over to the west. Baron says we got to take them out before they see our dust. We're only about ten miles from Sunspot now, so he wants as little shooting as we can get away with. He says we got to use the swampies and the dogs on them. Pick a half dozen of your other muties as backup."

Without hesitation Korb chose Krysty and Jak. "I'm taking you two along because you showed me you're not afraid to fight," he told Krysty. "But I don't want any extra trouble. You better keep Not Mutie on a short leash. Otherwise neither one of you will be coming back."

Jak turned his ruby eyes on Korb. Whatever the albino was thinking, whatever he was planning, it was hidden deep beneath those bloodred pools.

"You don't have to worry about us," Krysty said. "We know how to follow orders."

"This way," Earflaps said, waving the muties after

him as he turned his horse. At a gallop he and his partner retraced their route up the hill.

The eager hounds dragged their swampie handlers by their neck chains. Krysty, Jak and the other four muties ran after them, winding around and through the patches of low scrub.

Krysty glanced over her shoulder and saw the column hadn't moved. Malosh didn't want to raise any more dust and perhaps give away his position and numbers.

When they crested the first hill, the riders were already down the other side and climbing the next rise. It was up and down on a dead run for the next fifteen minutes. The horsemen lost them after the third hill, but the chewed-up earth of their tracks was impossible to miss. Krysty was amazed that the dogs didn't bark or howl as they followed the trail. It was as if they somehow understood that the tactical situation required stealth, speed and silence.

Topping yet another hill, they saw the riders waiting for them in a ravine below. There has to be water down there, Krysty thought. Deep water. The notch of land between the summits was crowded with stunted green trees and brush. A perfect ambush site. As the dogs and muties ran down to them, the scouts dismounted.

"They'll be coming along the top of that hill," Earflap said, pointing to the crest on the other side of the tangle. "Take cover in the brush and wait until they pass by."

The scouts opened a gap in the vegetation with machetes, then they led their horses down into the canopied gully, tying them to bushes.

Everyone else followed.

It was very dark beneath the dense undergrowth. And very hot. Along with the others, Krysty and Jak crawled on hands and knees to the far side of the gulch. Muties and dogs lay on their bellies, softly panting.

"Are you going to capture the patrol and make them fight for Malosh?" Krysty asked Korb.

"No, we can't trust 'em to chill their own," Korb told her. "They gotta die. Die real quietlike."

Minutes passed. Krysty lay there, drenched in sweat. The dust trapped under the canopy tickled her nose and made her want to sneeze. Then a soft murmuring sound caught her attention. It was Meconium whispering intently into his hound's torn ear, and as he did so, he was staring daggers at Jak and her. The beast seemed to be taking it all in, its eyes narrowed to slits, its nose, jowls, tongue and fangs dripping.

"Shh," Earflap hissed.

Through the screen of foliage, Krysty saw eight armed men working their way single file along the ridgetop. Every one of them looked warily down into the ravine. None saw the concealed enemy.

The hounds could surely smell their quarry's scent, but they made no noise. Not even a whimper. They had stopped breathing.

The scouts waited until the patrol had vanished over the crest of the hill, then they waved the entire force forward, through the curtain of brush and up the slope. They climbed in a ragged skirmish line, as silent as the dead. Only after they had topped the hill, coming upon the hapless eight from behind, did the swampies turn loose the dogs of war.

At the snarling, growling sound, Haldane's men whirled. Their jaws dropped at the sight of the madly charging beasts. They froze. Before they could bring their blasters to bear, the hounds were in their midst, lunging with bared fangs. They fired their pistols at extreme close range, but jostled by the animals and one another, they missed their targets.

. Two members of the patrol broke and ran down the hill. The man in the lead half turned and frantically, blindly, fired his revolver to the rear, hoping to hit something. Hit something, he did. He shot the man running behind him in the groin, sending him crashing to his knees, then his face. In a second, hounds were tearing into them both.

The six others weighed in with steel-shod rifle butts, and fighting back-to-back, held off the canine onslaught for a minute or two. Then the dogs caught one of them by the leg and dragged him down, and the defensive formation fell apart. The hounds leaped on the backs of the others and sank in their teeth, savagely shaking their heads, pulling the men to the ground by their shoulders, their arms, their necks.

The swampies leaned on their clubs and the scouts held their machetes at port arms while the pack of beasts did the dirty work.

There were many more hounds than victims. Dogs took hold of flailing arms and legs and digging in their paws, pulled against one another. The men caught in the awful the tug of war tried to poke out the eyes of their attackers and clawed at the scarred muzzles. In vain. Spread-eagled on the ground, their bellies were fully exposed. While they screamed, hounds tore into their midsections. And once the animals had opened horrible, gaping wounds, they began yarding out living guts.

Muzzles dripping with blood, the dogs fought one another for the hot goodies. It was competitive eating at its most grotesque. The hounds wolfed so quickly they couldn't keep their meals down. Gagging, they puked up the gray coils, only to gobble them again, even faster.

"Pull off the dogs, for nuke sake!" Korb yelled at the idle swampies. "They're gonna choke themselves to death."

The stumpy bastards laid into the hounds with their clubs, pounding them into submission. After they had rechained the dogs, they hauled them back from the carnage and tethered them to stakes.

Only one member of the Haldane patrol was still alive. And unhappily so. Eyes bugging out in terror and excruciating pain, he thrashed on the ground, trying to shove his ruined guts back into his stomach cavity with blood-slick hands. He stuffed dirt and rocks into himself, as well. Realizing the futility of his effort, he looked up at the muties, desperate for someone to put an end to his suffering.

"You got it, friend," Krysty said, drawing her Smith & Wesson from its holster.

Before she could fire the coup de grâce, Korb's hand deflected the barrel upward.

"No more blastershots," he said.

Beside her, the little albino's hand moved in a blur. Something sizzled through the air. Like magic, a dark star of razor-sharp steel appeared at the side of the wounded man's throat. As blood poured from his neatly severed jugular, he closed his eyes, grimaced once and died.

"Dangerous little fucker, aren't you?" Korb said to Jak.

The albino didn't deny it.

Meanwhile the swampies gleefully fell upon the corpses, stripping them of their weapons and valuables. Then they confiscated and scarfed down their enemies' field rations. They left the torn bodies sprawled on the barren hillside for the buzzards.

After they recrossed the tangled ravine, the scouts climbed on their horses and rode east. With Korb leading the way, the muties headed back for the main column at a leisurely pace and in no particular order of march. Chained dogs walked in front of and behind Krysty and Jak. The animals' appetite for violence was apparently sated. They were no longer dragging their handlers forward. The companions still eyed them warily. And as it turned out, for good reason.

"Hey," a familiar voice called from behind.

Krysty and Jak both turned to see Meconium grinning at them. The hound at the end of the chain leash he held had its ears pricked up. The dense muscles on its shoulders were bunched into knots, and the short hair along its spine stood up in a bristling ruff.

"Oops," the swampie said as he let go of the chain.

The huge brindled dog bounded forward, snarling.

Instead of going for Jak, who was most likely the intended target, for reasons of its own the animal zeroed in on Krysty. She dodged the massive jaws as they snapped shut, then twisted away, pulling her .38 pistol from its holster. Jak drew his revolver, too, and tried to sight on the beast, but it and Krysty were moving too fast, circling, feinting, retreating. He couldn't fire for fear of hitting her, either straight on or with a .357 Magnum round through and through.

"Call it off!" Krysty cried as she sidestepped another headlong lunge.

"My dog's friendly," Meconium protested. "It won't bite."

The swampies found that assertion most humorous.

"Collect that rad-blasted thing before someone gets hurt," Korb ordered Meconium.

The head swampie moved in slow motion to obey.

As Krysty dodged, the dog snatched hold of the edge of her coat sleeve, and with a savage twist of its head, drove her to her knees. Jak darted in and instead of shooting the animal in the head, brought the butt of his Python crashing down on top of its skull. The locked jaws opened and Krysty broke free. Jak took aim, but before he could shoot the redhead was back in the line of fire. As the animal shook off the blow, she drop-kicked it on the point of the chin, snapping its nose straight up. The hound's eyelids closed and it flopped onto its chest, teetering from side to side. For a second it looked like it was going to topple over. Then it recovered and sprang up, madder than ever.

"Call it off!"

"But it likes you."

Krysty cocked her .38 and pointed it at the crouching beast.

"It just wants to be friends."

"Call it off, you stumpy bastard."

"Call it off yourself, Snake Hair," Meconium said.

"You got it," Krysty replied.

As the dog once again launched itself at her, she rammed the muzzle of the Smith & Wesson into its gaping mouth and pulled the trigger. The resounding crack of the report was muffled by flesh and bone. Krysty pivoted to let the thing fly past her.

It landed hard, its legs buckling under it. The back of its skull was a smoking red ruin. As its muscles jerked, its bowels loosed explosively.

The other hounds went berserk, barking, howling, their legs driving, dragging their handlers along as they attempted to get at her and tear her apart. She backed away, blaster in hand.

"You shouldn't have done that," Korb said.

Chapter Nine

Ryan watched Krysty and Jak leave with the dog pack and vanish over the rise.

"Can't trust swampies," Mildred said ruefully.

"Stab their mothers in the back for a line of jolt," J.B. agreed.

"If their mothers don't stab them first," Ryan said. "Krysty and Jak still have their weapons. They'll be all right. They'll lay low and do what they need to do to survive."

"We can't do anything to help them under these circumstances, anyway," Mildred said, looking around at all the blasters that would come to bear if they tried to make a fuss.

Ryan figured they'd be cut down by autofire before the good doctor could empty her revolver's 6-shot cylinder.

At the head of the line of troops, Malosh and his captains had dismounted. The officers hunkered down around their baron, looking over his shoulder while he drew diagrams in the dirt with a pointy stick.

"I'm going to do a little recce," Ryan said.

"Want some backup?" J.B. asked.

"No. This is a solo. Wait here."

The one-eyed man slipped through the milling ranks

of the fighters, over to where the horses were tethered. While he patted a horse on the rump, he strained to make out what the baron and his men were so intently discussing.

Baron Malosh looked up from the dirt and caught him staring. Malosh knew at once that he was trying to listen in on their conversation. "Come over here, mercie," he said, waving him forward with a gloved hand. "Don't be shy. Join the parlay."

Clandestine recce no longer an option, Ryan walked over and stared at the diagram scratched in the dirt.

"Sunspot?" he said.

"That's right," the baron replied.

"Our position?"

"We're about here," Malosh told him, jabbing the dirt outside the diagram with his stick. "There's a thousand-foot elevation gain between us and the ville. It sits in a shallow man-made gorge, blasted out of the bedrock to make way for the road."

In close proximity, in bright sunlight, Ryan could have counted every yellow-headed pimple on his high forehead. But he didn't. He wondered what was hidden under the leather mask that covered nose, mouth, cheeks, chin. Some hideous deformity of birth? Some gross disfigurement of battle? Or of ravening disease?

The baron's four captains stared with rapt attention at their commander. Their respect for his generalship was obvious, and absolute. And it wasn't based on fear. More like hero worship. Though the officers didn't appear to be sadistic lackeys, reveling in their master's excesses, they had taken the Redbone impalings in stride. And presumably all the others that had come before. The skewerings sickened Ryan to the core, but he could see that like the costume the baron wore, they were meant to create particular effects. To mystify, to horrify, to awe.

Malosh was as much a showman as he was a fighter.

The two previous nights, Ryan had kept careful watch on the baron's tent, looking for any signs of weakness the companions might exploit. There had been no female fighters lined up outside, dragged in one by one, and offered up for his scxual pleasure. There had been no drunken revels. No jolt parties.

Counter to Malosh's campfire legend, he was neither a serial rapist nor a debaucher.

Or mebbe he was just saving himself for Sunspot?

That was a distinct possibility.

"My forces have waged three wars against Sunspot ville in as many years," Malosh told him.

"I take it you lost?"

"On the contrary, we won every battle, and we held the ville for extended periods, only to be eventually driven out by a counterattack from Baron Haldane. His men are in command there now."

"If the ville has been overrun six times, there couldn't be much left in the way of spoils to interest you."

Malosh arched a sore-laden eyebrow.

"So Sunspot must have a different kind of value," Ryan said. "Something that can't be taken away or destroyed by either side. It's a staging point for your attacks deep into Haldane's territory, isn't it?"

The baron's black eyes glittered. "Good guess, mercie."

"With so much experience, you must know how to retake the place from Haldane."

"Even though the terrain is unchanged," Malosh said, "what worked once may not work again. There are just three possible courses of action. A full-frontal assault, right up the gut. Or an encircling maneuver, followed by infiltration and a coordinated surprise attack. Or failing surprise, a prolonged siege. Siege is the least desirable choice because it would reduce Sunspot's stockpile of supplies, which would be useful in our campaign. And a siege would also give Haldane time to send reinforcements. The key elements are the size of the force Haldane has stationed in the ville and new defenses, if any, since our last visit. That's what will determine the final battle plan."

One of the captains spoke up. "Shall we send a few of the fighters into the ville to gather intel on Haldane's garrison?"

"Fighters would never get back alive," Malosh said. "Haldane's men would suspect them at once because of their appearance. No, our spies must be nonthreatening. At first or second glance, they must seem nothing but harmless fools." The baron tossed aside the stick, stood and clapped the dirt from his gloves. "Bring the cannon fodder forward," he said. "Let's have a look at them."

After a minute or two the fighters parted ranks to let the human shields pass.

Doc walked within ten feet of Ryan. Urged forward by a man in a baseball cap carrying a battered 12-gauge pump, he smiled a quiet, ready-for-anything smile.

Malosh assembled the human sponges then began sizing up each in turn.

He stopped in front of Young Crad, taking in the odd baby face and stout adult body. "Do you have a name?" he asked.

Crad nodded.

"Well?"

"Well, what?" Crad said.

"Do you have a name?"

Crad nodded again. From his desperate expression, he didn't understand where the conversation was going. Or why. He did understand that his life depended upon his reply.

"Well?" Malosh snarled, leaning closer.

The swineherd drew his head as far back as he could without moving his feet. He swallowed hard a couple of times, then helplessly repeated himself, "Well what?"

"He's just flustered, Baron," Bezoar interjected. "He gets flustered easy. He's called Young Crad."

"A droolie by any other name," was Malosh's comment. "He'll do for this mission."

The baron looked Bezoar up and down for a second in silence, then moved on to the next man in the row.

"Ah, the pants-wetting geezer," Malosh said to Doc Tanner.

"Up in years, I certainly am, Baron," Tanner said. "But I assure you I have thus far avoided the humiliation of senile incontinence."

Malosh laughed. "A well-spoken, pants-wetting geezer. You'll counterbalance the tongue-tied young numbskull perfectly."

"In what regard may I ask, sir?"

"Every idiot must have a loving caretaker. You and the foul-smelling one are going to enter Sunspot ville on foot by the main gate. You're going to count the opposition force garrisoned there, and return to me with the number. It's a very simple assignment. And looking and acting as you do, you shouldn't have any trouble getting past the gate. Or back out again."

Young Crad gave Doc a delighted grin.

"Go south until you hit old Highway 10," Malosh told Doc. "Then turn east and start up the grade. You can't miss it." The baron turned to his chief of cannon fodder. "Ferdinando, give them a few cold potatoes to take along. And a little jack in case they have to bribe anyone."

As the man hurried off to do his bidding, Malosh gave the newly appointed spies a warning. "If you're thinking this is your big chance to just walk away from my army, or that you can give our position to the enemy in return for safety or profit, remember you still have friends on this side. Friends I can hurt in interesting ways. You have until tomorrow at this time to return with the information."

Chapter Ten

Doc heard a distant flurry of blasterfire as he and Young Crad topped the first hill due south. The shooting stopped as quickly as it began. If the hellhounds made any noise as they tore into the Haldane patrol, he couldn't make it out.

With Doc slightly in the lead, they crested and descended a series of low, rolling hills, putting the army of Malosh behind them. The monotonous desert landscape stretched on for as far as he could see. The baking sun was almost directly overhead. Doc kept track of what little shadow he cast to make sure they were headed in the right direction.

After a long silence, he heard another distant gunshot.

A single coup de grâce, Doc reckoned. The dogs hadn't left much for the muties to mercy chill.

A half a pace behind him and three yards to the right, Young Crad moved without speaking. The swineherd whistled, tunelessly, mournfully and very irritatingly through his front teeth. He seemed completely unaware of or unconcerned about the danger they faced. Doc walked well upwind and maintained a constant distance from his droolie charge.

It took the better part of an hour to reach the old interstate. Before them a low four-lane bridge that had once spanned the wash they were following had fallen to blocks of rubble. The jewel of predark commerce stood sadly ruined, vast stretches reduced to their component grains of sand. Having never seen it in its heyday, Doc could only imagine the volume of freight, the motorized traffic flowing back and forth from sea to shining sea.

Gone.

And in all likelihood, forever.

They paralleled the route of the highway, turning east as the baron had instructed. Tiny yellow and white daisies sprouted along the shaded cracks in the ancient roadbed. Here and there on the shoulders of the interstate were signs of previous travelers and long-finished battles: abandoned campfire pits and wags, the latter burned out, bullet-hole-riddled hulks. There were graves, too. Many graves. Though the mounds of beige earth had been protected with heavy stones and chunks of concrete, something had pulled the obstacles aside and then dug down.

Doc looked inside a few of the shallow, oblong holes. He found no bones in the bottom, just strips of dirty rags. He didn't bother looking in any of the others.

Ahead, a dropped vehicle overpass blocked their path. On the ground in front of the massive pile of cracked concrete and bent rebar were huge, green-painted steel signs. The chem rain and sandblasted grit had nearly erased the words. After a few moments of study, Doc decided it read, "Welcome Center 3 miles Sunspot Exit."

When they rounded the far side of the overpass, he could see the gradual rise of the land in front of them, and in the distance the old highway ascended and disappeared through a hilltop gorge. They climbed for a while, then Doc said, "Let's stop for a rest."

The time traveler and the droolie sat on the shoulder of the highway with their backs to the sun. To establish some rapport, and put a temporary end to the soft but shrill whistling, Doc initiated a conversation.

"Have you ever been to Sunspot?" he said.

Young Crad shook his head. "Never been nowhere."

"This is your first adventure away from home?"

"My first adventure," Crad repeated. The small eyes in his baby face twinkled, rather too brightly under the circumstances.

"You realize you mustn't say a word about Baron Malosh or his army once we're inside the ville gates? If you do, we'll both be chilled by Haldane's troops."

Young Crad gave him a blank look.

"And if we die in Sunspot," Doc continued earnestly, "Malosh will chill your friend Bezoar and my friends, too. He will make them suffer first."

The swineherd scratched his smooth chin, his eyes as devoid of understanding as two shiny marbles.

Although Young Crad was an integral part of Doc's cover, it was clear he couldn't count on him for anything else.

"Let me do all the talking, then. Don't say anything."

"I talk good, but people don't hear me right."

"That's why I want you to stay quiet the whole time."

"People back in Redbone always made fun of me," Crad went on. "Just because I get along with pigs."

If "getting along" meant horn-dogging them every chance you got, Doc thought but did not say.

"Pigs are my friends."

Doc couldn't help himself. He said, "More than just friends, from what I've gathered."

"Piggie dear loved me. I loved her. Why is that bad?"

"People consider such a 'love' unspeakable."

"So?"

"I can assure you the vast majority of human beings shares that opinion. A vast majority can make your life miserable."

"I live in a pigpen," Crad said. "I sleep in a pigpen. I eat in a pigpen, out of the pig trough. Only Bezoar ever had a nice word for me. My life could be worse?"

He had a point, Doc decided. "What did Bezoar say about your facility with swine?"

Young Crad chuckled at the memory. "Sometimes he liked to watch."

In the Victorian era, from whence Doc Tanner had been ripped, such behavior wasn't just fodder for shame, but for hard criminal punishment. He knew from his Oxford studies that in medieval times, both the unfortunate animal and its abuser would have been hanged by the neck until dead. Thus bred-in-the-bone depravity was wrung from the gene pool.

If only temporarily.

Because of his lack of interest in females of his own species, and their presumed unanimous revulsion at the sight of him, the chances were astronomically remote that Young Crad would ever sire another human being. That, and the fact that the mission required him to remain alive was all that kept Doc from putting a .44-caliber ball through his forehead.

As they resumed the steady, gentle climb, the

earmarks of battle were everywhere. A maze of neck-deep fighting trenches had been dug in the sandy soil, scorched here and there by overlapping gren blasts, surrounded by uncoiled rolls of barbed and razor wire. The long-established, attack-and-retreat route was deserted.

Near the entrance to the gorge, perched on its rim, Doc saw a crude berm of dirt and eroded concrete. On the highest point of land, overlooking and controlling the floor of the gorge was Sunspot ville.

Just beyond the predark turnoff to the Welcome Center, the interstate was gapped and impassable to wags. A hundred-yard section of the roadway looked as if it had been blown out of the ground with high explosives. The resulting pits and chasms were filled with standing water. The piles of above-ground debris—earth, rock, concrete, rebar—formed an obstacle course that had to be run under the gunsights of the ville. Doc picked out what looked like three cannon or machine-gun emplacements spaced along this side of the berm.

Travel through the highway gorge by foot or wag required a detour through Sunspot and out the other side. Wayfarers who wished to proceed had to mount the rutted dirt road leading from the interstate exit to the berm gates above, walking in the crossed fire paths of a pair of hard-sited M-60 machine guns.

This Doc and Young Crad did at a measured pace.

As they neared the fifteen-foot-high berm walls, Doc saw that one of the gates was moveable. It consisted of a sideways parked tractor trailer that could be hauled aside by a mule team or by human beings. This was the gate for wags and livestock. The gate for foot traffic stood next to it. It was made of an old yellow school bus parked perpendicular to the berm, half buried under rubble, with its front end sticking out. The hood, fenders and grille of the bus were peppered with bullet holes. The engine block protected the sentries who manned it from blasterfire.

"Hold it right there!" someone inside the vehicle shouted.

A pair of AK-47 sights poked out over the dashboard and through the glassless windshield.

"Remember, let me do the talking," Doc whispered to Crad. "Raise your hands in the air. Keep them up in the air until we get to the gate."

"What do you want?" the sentry cried.

"We are just simple travelers," Doc said. "Do not shoot. We are coming closer so we don't have to yell."

As Doc and Crad approached the front door of the bus, two Haldane sec men stood. The men were in their midtwenties, both darkly tanned. One was shirtless and had a narrow, hairless chest. The other was more muscular and wore a sleeveless, coyote skin vest, fur side in.

"Where did you come from?" No Shirt demanded.

"Rado territory," Doc replied.

"Long ways off."

"Plenty of hard walking," Doc agreed. "Not a particularly popular route, either. We haven't seen another living soul for better than two weeks."

"Any sign of Baron Malosh?" Coyote Skin asked.

"No sign of anybody, as I said."

"You and your friend come by yourselves?"

"Yes, it's just him and me."

"You two don't look related," No Shirt said.

"We're not. He's young and I'm old. I'm smart and he isn't. We make up for each other's failings."

"Show us your blasters," Coyote Skin ordered, tightening his grip on his AK and bracing his legs.

"Young Crad doesn't have a weapon," Doc told them. "I can't trust him with one. He's a triple stupe, I'm sorry to say. Given a blaster, he might shoot off his own head."

Doc unholstered his massive Civil War relic and handed it, butt first, to the guards.

"It's got two barrels," No Shirt remarked as he examined the weapon.

"What do you call that thing?" Coyote Skin asked Doc.

"It's a LeMat," Doc replied. "Named after its inventor, Jean Alexandre François LeMat. As you can see, it's a combination pistol and shotgun. The revolver cylinder rotates around the shotgun barrel."

"Was this LeMat a plumber by trade?" No Shirt said, hefting the blaster on his palm. "Was he on jolt? It isn't even centerfire, is it?"

"No, it's a percussion weapon."

No Shirt handed the blaster to his colleague. "What rad-blasted ash dump did you dig this piece of junk out of?" Coyote Skin asked. "Nuking hell, old man, why don't you get yourself a real blaster?"

"I assure you, that one does the job adequately."

"How fast can you reload it?" No Shirt asked. "And how many times can you reload it before you have to tear it down and soak all the parts? You should try something that shoots smokeless powder and cased centerfire cartridges."

"Mebbe he's as dim as his pal?" Coyote Skin suggested as he handed Doc back his pistol.

"Mebbe he uses the butt end to pound nails?" No Shirt suggested.

"With your kind permission we would like to enter the ville," Doc said, holstering his weapon.

"Why should we let you in?" No Shirt asked.

"We saw evidence of a large scavenger at work below here," Doc told him. "There were a number of freshly opened and emptied graves along the highway. We would prefer not to spend the night outside the berm."

"Even critters need to eat."

"Better you than us, old man."

Doc turned his back on the bus and out of sight of the guards, dug into the small leather pouch Malosh had given him. He removed two small, crude bits of gold, each probably cut from a melted gob of wedding rings and wristwatches scrounged from some nearby ground zero. He handed over the nuggets.

The men tested the yellow metal with their teeth and found it to their liking.

"You're good to go," No Shirt said.

"Enjoy your visit," Coyote Skin added, moving aside to let them step up into the aisle of the bus.

Doc led the way. All the seats had been stripped. The intact side windows were blacked out, their outer surfaces blocked by heaped dirt and rock, but the rear, emergency exit of the bus was wide open.

Doc hopped down off the back bumper, into a flat field lined with semitrailers and SeaLand cargo containers. A pall of greasy woodsmoke hung in the air. Tractor wags without doors or wheels, and rusting, immobile Winnebagos and Trailways buses surrounded the only permanent structure, which was the predark Welcome Center. As with the bus gate in the berm, bullet holes in profusion decorated the sides of every dwelling.

Because he had seen similar buildings along other interstates, Doc knew what the Welcome Center was all about. When the world was still intact, it was a place for tourists to pick up brochures and educate themselves on the state's various attractions and points of interest. In this case, the state was New Mexico. The plate-glass windows of the Welcome Center were gone, replaced with sheets of metal and pieces of scavenged plywood. The curved sidewalk and the double-doored entrance, which had once invited legions of curious travelers, were guarded by two men with assault rifles. The Haldane garrison was housed within, Doc assumed. A gibbet made of a predark, portable basketball stanchion, complete with empty noose, stood ominously out front.

Looking at the surround of hammered earth, and the riddled, decaying structures, Doc wondered how many times the place had traded occupying armies. Each time it had lost a little more of its humanity, until it was simply a hilltop junkyard under an unforgiving blue sky.

Young Crad hopped down from the bumper. He kept his mouth shut, as ordered.

As they advanced, Doc noticed the cultivated fields behind the Welcome Center. On closer inspection, he saw they were just truck gardens. The crops were far too small to support the number of people milling about in the enclosure.

Doc could easily pick the sec men from the rest of Sunspot's inhabitants. They were armed; the ville folk weren't. To come up with a force-strength figure for Malosh, he was going to have to count blasters.

He was up to eleven when a group of unarmed people confronted him. The women outnumbered the men by three to one.

"What's your business here, mister?" demanded a tall, blond-haired woman.

"I have no business, as such," Doc said, struck by the unusual color of her eyes, which were pale violet. "I'm just traveling with my friend, here. We're looking for a safe place to spend the night."

"Your friend could use a wash," the woman said, crinkling up her nose. She had tiny wrinkles at the corners of her eyes, and there were a few strands of white mixed in with her yellow hair.

"He could use several," Doc said.

"You still have your blaster," she said. "Are you a Haldane man?"

Doc admired the resolve in her face, her wide mouth and firm chin. She was truly a handsome woman. "I'm nobody's man," he told her. "The guards at the gate found my sidearm less than terrifying. That's why they didn't take it from me, I imagine."

"It does look like it might blow up in your hand."

"Looks can be deceiving."

"So they can. Are you harmless?"

Doc smiled, displaying his remarkably excellent teeth. "When called upon to be."

"Are you a spy for Malosh the Impaler?"

"I am no one's spy," Doc lied. "Why do you persist in questioning my allegiance?"

"Because," the woman said, "you are either with us or you're against us. Either aligned with one or the other baron, or with the people of this ville. We have learned there's no difference between our occupiers. One is just as bad as the other."

"But surely Malosh has a reputation…"

"Deserved, no doubt," she said. "But he doesn't torture or abuse us. He doesn't dare. When he has control of Sunspot, he depends on our labor, our food and our water. Whether it's Malosh or Haldane in charge, it doesn't matter to us. Both barons rob us, and the sec men of both chill us every time they attack."

"Why do you stay here, then?" Doc said.

"It's our home. We don't have anywhere else to go. But even if we wanted to leave, we couldn't. Malosh and Haldane would never let us. They need us here to farm, to maintain the ville. If we were gone, they'd have to move their own people into the chill zone and risk their lives. Neither baron is willing to do that because their populations are too small to be stretched that far. If we were gone, the armies would have to carry enough supplies to last them through their campaigns. And without long convoys of wags and overstocked storehouses, that just isn't possible."

"You are caught in a terrible dilemma," Doc said.

"Our community is slowly dying under the weight of it," she said. "When our members get chilled, they can't be replaced. As you can see, most of our menfolk are gone."

It occurred to Doc that no one else had spoken a

word. The others had all deferred to this lovely woman.
She was in fact the leader of the tragic little hamlet.

"I have jack," Doc told her. "May I purchase some
food and drink, and acquire lodgings for the night?"

"Jack's no good here anymore," she said. "We've got
nothing left to sell. Water's free. The only thing nukeday
ever did for us was to open up the sweet springs over
behind the Welcome Center. You can't buy food here,
but you can come along with us and catch your own
dinner if you like."

"Much obliged, madam."

"Call me Isabel."

"I am Theophilus Tanner. Please call me Doc for
short. And this is Young Crad."

Isabel sized up the hulking, odoriferous man. Her
evaluation only took a few seconds, but evidently included an IQ test. "If the dimmie's hungry, bring him
along, too," she said.

Chapter Eleven

Baron Haldane's kidneys ached, his butt ached, his neck ached. For the better part of two-and-a-half days, he had been a pebble trapped inside the constantly shaken tin can that was Magus's Humvee. The military SUV lurched and bucked, breaking its own trail across the hardpan, throwing its occupants this way and that, slamming them against the doors, the full length, central console, the head liner, compressing their spines as the seat springs bottomed out over and over again.

With the artillery piece in tow, Magus's convoy had virtually crept along. The first day they covered fewer than forty miles. This from ten hours of running time and eight hours of breakdowns, backtracking and retrieving stuck wags from potholes. Once they crossed the predark interstate and headed due south, the going got even slower.

In Haldane's opinion, traveling on horseback or even on foot would have been preferable; they could have dragged the gun carriage behind a mule team and made more speed. But the baron had no say in the matter.

To avoid being spotted by Malosh's army, the convoy had made a wide detour to the south of Sunspot. Their snail's pace kept the dust clouds to a minimum. There was no way to keep out of sight of the ville because it stood on a prominent high point, the gorge rim, and had a panoramic view.

Haldane was on the wrong side of the Humvee to check on their progress. With all the jolting he couldn't have focused on the horizon even if he could have seen it. Except for the front windshield, the windows were coated with fine, beige dust.

One thing was certain—when the convoy could see the gorge rim ville, the gorge rim ville could see them. There was no cover for the big wags among the low hills and broad stretches of flatland. The baron knew his hilltop garrison would do nothing but watch them creep by. A group of wags as large and well-armed as this one could defend itself against anything but an all-out attack. Because of the distance involved, engaging the convoy would mean leaving Sunspot unprotected for an extended period of time. His men would follow orders, stand their ground and wait.

There was another reason for the detour, as Magus's chief gunner had explained. The prevailing winds swept through the narrow gorge from the west. To prevent the deadly gas from blowing back on the artillery position, a healthy tail or crosswind was absolutely necessary. Something a southerly approach provided.

By nightfall, if all went well, the weapon would be in firing position, seven or eight miles from the target. The sarin gas barrage would commence the next day, after Haldane's garrison had been withdrawn and Malosh's army had reoccupied the ville. Shelling Sunspot with gas while the masked baron and his raiders were caught inside its berm would end the threat from the west for the foreseeable future.

But at what price?

Haldane had entered into the deal with deep moral misgivings. To protect his people and their offspring, he had sold his soul to the devil.

And in the process placed his own beloved child in the devil's half-steel hands.

Could he trust Magus to let his son go once the murderous deed was done and the jack was duly paid?

It was a question he couldn't answer without help. And help was forthcoming.

The ponytailed driver caught his eye and noted his dour expression in the rearview mirror. "Did you really think you could do business with Magus and not come out holding the shit bag?" he said. "Baron, you are a major disappointment."

"What would Magus want with my son?" Haldane said. "He doesn't need a guarantee of payment other than my given word. Everyone knows I've never robbed a living soul."

"Mebbe that's Steel Eyes' game," said the shotgun seat passenger. "You being such a straight-shooting, noble fucking bastard, mebbe he wants to knock you down a peg or two."

"You think you're so much better than us," the driver said, "but you're not. You're paying Magus to poison gas an entire ville. Haldane, you're a mass-chilling, coldheart son of a bitch."

"To me, the kid looked too old and too young to interest Magus," the man sitting next to the baron said, showing off his verdant teeth.

"What do you mean?" Haldane demanded.

"Magus likes his young 'uns fresh from their mamas'

bellies, or big enough so he can use their organs for transplant. Like I said, your boy's too old and too young."

"What does he do with the newborns?"

"Makes milkshakes out of them," Mossy Teeth said.

Haldane's hands clenched into white-knuckled fists. "Nukin' hell, you say!" he snarled.

"Hey, easy, now," the driver said. "Don't blow a gasket. He's just messin' with your head a little, Baron."

"Yeah, actually Magus makes spaghetti sauce."

The Humvee crew guffawed over the vile joke while Haldane seethed in impotent silence.

"I'm sure he's showing your kid all sorts of interesting things right now," the road trash in the shotgun seat went on, shrilling every "s" like a steam whistle. "Good old Uncle Steel Eyes and his Rolling Shop of Horrors. Poor kid'll never be right in the noodle again."

"He'll be pooping in his drawers for the rest of his life," the man with the mossy teeth stated.

"If he hurts Thorne," Haldane said, "he knows I'll chill him. I'll chill him dead."

"Don't think that ain't been tried, Baron," the driver told him. "Magus's been shot, stabbed, some big-time heavy shit's been dropped square on top of him, and he's still ticking, still kicking. One time he even got himself blown up. Lost a little meat from the blast, but the metal parts held everything together and he pulled himself right out of the crater. Still got a bit of a tranny leak from that one."

"Magus ain't afraid of anyone or anything," said the whistler. "He does what he wants to whoever he wants."

"I once saw him crush a gun barrel with his bare

hand," Mossy Teeth said. "A 7.62 mm AK. Mashed the sucker flat. Some folks say he started out life flesh and blood like you and me, but now he's made himself all nuke-powered and bionic. If you ask me, Steel Eyes never was human. He started out as a machine, not the other way around. Whitecoats put him together before the nukecaust. They all got fried on the big day, but he survived. Over a whole lot of years, he added human bits and pieces to himself because they were easier to come by as spare parts. He's always tinkering with his innards, trying to make them work better. He tinkers with the world the same way, ripping stuff out, jamming new stuff in to see what happens. I swear the clanker thinks he's God. And who knows, mebbe he is."

"Ugliest god you ever saw," the driver added.

"Meanest, too," the shotgun passenger whistled.

"See," Mossy Teeth went on, "it's just like I said. He wasn't born with a regular heart. He don't feel things the way regular people do. He was assembled with a rad-blasted pneumatic pump in his chest. Sounds like a bag of cheap alarm clocks. Deep in his soul, he's a machine, but a real curious one. Baron, you shouldn't have let Magus take your kid."

"I didn't 'let' him do anything," Haldane reminded the man, barely able to control his anger. He shifted the sawed-off Remington on his lap, pointing its muzzle across the console, at Mossy Teeth's rib cage. Slipping his finger inside the trigger guard, he took a firm hold of the pistol grip, clamping the forestock against the top of his thigh. The weapon was already cocked. A high brass buckshot round was in the chamber.

"Get your mind around this little fact, Baron," the

driver said, a big grin plastered across his mug. "Now he's got your boy, he's never going to give him back."

The baron realized that it was possible the road trash were just jerking his chain again, trying to get a rise out of him, seeing if they could make him fall to pieces, but the stupe louts had opened a gigantic can of worms. Essentially, they were telling him if he played it straight, as he had intended, he was going to get double-crossed.

In that case there was no point in playing it straight.

A dangerous conclusion to come to.

Chapter Twelve

At the edge of Sunspot's truck gardens was a banked wood fire, on top of which the ville folk set water-filled caldrons made from fifty-five-gallon drums. Wreathed in the pungent smoke, women and children stooped between the garden's rows and began carefully harvesting very small piles of new potatoes, greens, carrots and onions.

"Given the quantity of liquid," Doc said, "those are the makings of a rather thin and unsatisfying stew."

"We're going to do something about that," Isabel said.

She led Doc, Young Crad and a dozen others to the back bumper of the school bus. The eight ville women were armed with pitchforks or long wooden clubs. The two pairs of men carried empty, lidded, sheet steel garbage cans by their handles.

As they passed through the stripped school bus and out the front door, the no-shirt sentry said, "Good hunting."

Stepping down from the bus, Doc remarked, "I take it that the occupiers don't help with the foraging?"

"The troopers can't leave their posts," Isabel said. "Baron Haldane's orders. It's down to us to feed everybody inside the berm."

"How come you got no pigs in the ville?" Young Crad asked her.

Doc knew the droolie was thinking about something less wholesome than garlic-smothered pork chops. He gave the swineherd a swift, hard jab with his elbow to shut him up.

"They're all gone," Isabel admitted. "The last of the hogs went three weeks ago."

"The invaders appropriated them, I presume?" Doc said.

"No," the head woman said. "And unfortunately we didn't get to eat them, either."

"What happened, then?"

"You look like a man of imagination, Doc. A man who enjoys unraveling a mystery…"

"Yes, I will admit to that."

"Well, here's a little mystery for you to play with. Trust me, the answer will be apparent soon enough. In the meantime, feel free to puzzle it out, yourself."

When she walked ahead of him down the path to the interstate, Doc found his gaze immediately dropping to take in her backside. It was the instinctive, hardwired reaction of a human heterosexual male, an automatic response that even a quarter millennium span of existence couldn't extinguish. To Doc's credit, he refrained from openly leering at her charms. He only glanced long enough to appreciate the shapeliness of her bottom outlined against the well-worn seat of her BDU pants. Tight, muscular but unmistakably and heartrendingly feminine.

Ever the chivalrous gentleman, Doc Tanner turned his head, forcing himself to stare at the bleak horizon. The woman stirred him in a most pleasant and unusual way; that was undeniable. Not just her mature physical beauty, which was a rare enough thing in a land where tragedy, hardship and the elements sent men and women reeling into premature old age. It also turned them into burned-out emotional wrecks long before they reached thirty. Isabel still had her serenity, and a vital spark. A bright, wonderful spark.

Lost in the warmth of its afterglow, for a few remarkable seconds Doc was able to forget everything.

His past.

His mission.

In a single file, the ragtag food gatherers descended from the mouth of the gorge onto the shoulder of the ruined highway. After traveling a short distance down the grade, they crossed the interstate and started to trek south, over the arid hills and the barren plain.

Doc surveyed the terrain that stretched in front of them. He saw nothing remotely green. It was a moonscape of beige on beige. Of sand and sandstone. For many years Doc and his companions had been on what amounted to a permanent scavenger hunt, themselves. Experience was a cruel teacher. In this sort of sun-blasted geography the best that could be hoped for was to stumble onto a nest of mutie rattlesnakes sleeping in a deep, cool, rock cairn. Or if there was an oasis hidden somewhere ahead, it might be possible to set up an ambush, waiting for birds or antelope to come to drink—although how pitchforks and clubs could help bring down either was beyond him. Perhaps the ville folk already had nets stashed away at the site?

Doc voiced his growing doubts to the lovely Isabel. "There appears to be nothing alive here," he said. "No plants. No animals. No source of water in this direction."

"As you said before, looks can be deceiving," she told him.

"Frankly, my dear, all I see is desolation."

"Ah, that's where you're wrong, Doc. You're only looking at what's on the surface. You've got to look harder, deeper, to see what's really here."

"Deeper? I am sorry…"

"Until a month ago my people were starving to death. We had been bled dry by successive waves of invaders. Most of us were convinced that the next winter would be the ville's last. Then it came, like manna from heaven. Like the sweet spring gushing forth from the rock. And we were saved."

"Madam?"

"A wonderful plan is unfolding before our very eyes, Theo Tanner. You will see it, too, I am convinced of that."

He started to ask another question, but Isabel reached up and placed her finger gently on his lips, stopping him from speaking. "Wait. It won't be long. It isn't far now."

The food gatherers walked without hesitation, on a route that was well known to them. Whatever their destination was, they were heading straight for it.

With Isabel in the lead, they descended into an arroyo and began following its meandering course. Dried stalks of grass the color of gunpowder sparsely fringed the gully's rims. The dry streambed was filled with soft, fine sand. There were no signs or sounds of life. Not even the buzz of an insect.

Despite his attraction to her, Doc found himself starting to question the head woman's sanity; looking on the darkest of dark sides had become a habit, a survival instinct. Then he had a sudden uncomfortable twinge. It occurred to him that perhaps she and the others were cannies. It occurred to him that he and the swineherd had been taken out of earshot to be slaughtered, then lugged back in quarters that would give body and substance to the evening's pot of stew. Young Crad would certainly be no help, even in a fight to the death.

And there was plenty of him to eat.

Except of course brains.

"Look," Isabel said.

Across the arroyo, a strip of white rag tied to a stick marked a hole about a yard across in the waist-high bluff.

"It appears to be a burrow of some sort," Doc said. "Something quite large, based on the diameter. What's in there?"

"Dinner on the hoof," Isabel told him.

Doc noticed other, similar holes spaced at irregular intervals along the length of the low bank.

While the ville menfolk set down the garbage cans and the women leaned on their pitchforks and clubs, Isabel waved for Doc to follow her. "Be very quiet, now, and don't get too close to the hole," she said.

They hunkered down on either side of the opening. Isabel cocked her head, listening at the burrow entrance. Doc listened, too, but he could hear nothing but the pounding of his own pulse in his temples. An odd odor emanated from the hole. Both fecund and fecal with a hint of ammonia.

Then in a scrambling rush that sent Doc rocking back on his boot heels, a huge, shiny black creature lunged partway out of the hole. Its horizontal, pincer jaws snapped shut, making a sound like punch press. Blue-black jaws that could cut a man—or a hog—in two in a single bite. Doc glimpsed a broad, domed, eyeless head, segmented, armored backplates, and thousands of short, bristling yellow legs beneath.

As Doc and Isabel jumped out of the way, the creature darted in a blur back inside its hole.

"By the Three Kennedys!" Doc exclaimed. "What was that?" As he spoke, Doc pointed his cocked LeMat shotgun barrel at the burrow, prepared to unleash a chamber packed with "blue whistlers."

"A mama scagworm protecting her nest."

"That was a scagworm? Good Lord, the ones I have seen were much smaller than that. Perhaps two feet long, and four inches across. And even at that size they were triple-mean chillers, virtually impossible to dispatch with blade or blaster."

"Those were just the babies," Isabel informed him. "The breeders are like that one, mebbe three or four hundred pounds."

"A bit testy, was she not?"

"She's still carrying her young in her belly. We don't want to mess with her. We're looking for a worm that's just given birth. We've learned the hard way that timing is everything."

The entire crew advanced along the bank as quietly as possible. Isabel and Doc moved from burrow to burrow, listening from a safe distance.

At the fourth hole, they heard strange noises. Quite loud noises. They sounded like grunting, wet sloppy, sloshy, slurpy grunting, and high-pitched squealing.

"We have to wait until the babies finish," Isabel said.

"Finish what?" Doc asked her.

"The ultimate gift of a mother worm to her offspring," Isabel said. "Their very first meal is her living flesh. And in turn the baby worms give their flesh to us."

"I had no idea they were edible."

"The mamas aren't. Their meat tastes like old snow tires."

"How do you remove the little ones from the burrow?"

"We smoke 'em out," she said.

On her signal, some of the ville folk wrapped oily rags around the ends of sticks, lit them on fire and tossed them into the den. In seconds, dense gray smoke was billowing from the hole.

"We lost some mighty good folks figuring out how to harvest these muties," Isabel said. "The trick is to catch them at just the right moment, when they pop out of their mama's minky."

Doc couldn't help but recall his initial experience with scagworms. They were like shadows flying low over the island battlefield, shadows weaving erratic trails through the heaps of the dead to reach the living. He aimed his LeMat at the center of the gushing smoke, once again cocking back the shotgun barrel's hammer.

"You won't need that," Isabel assured him.

The creatures that spilled from the burrow were identical to those he had seen before—slick armored shells, blue-black bullet heads, rippling rows of crisp insect feet—but they moved much more slowly.

Half suffocated by the dense smoke, packed to the gills with their own mother's meat, they slithered sluggishly across the sand.

The womenfolk set upon the newborn worms with pitchforks and clubs. Leaning all their weight on the fork handles, they pinned the snapping, squirming muties to the ground with the tines. The club-wielding women brought their weapons down on top of the eyeless heads, again and again. These weren't love taps. The thick carapaces withstood multiple, full-force blows without denting or cracking, but the peabrains inside took a shellacking. After a moment the worms stopped squirming.

Scooping up the stunned creatures on their forks, the women tossed them into the waiting open garbage cans. With the lids slammed closed, the worms regained consciousness, banging and scrabbling around inside. They couldn't bite their way to freedom because their jaws couldn't get a purchase on the curved surface.

While this was going on, the burrow's last worm burst through the veil of smoke. It made a hard right turn and ran along the foot of the bank. It seemed much livelier than the others.

"Get it!" Isabel cried. "Don't let it get away!"

The woman nearest to the worm lunged with her pitchfork. She tried to lead the fleeing creature, but as if sensing the strike, it stopped dead in its tracks. The fork speared deep into the bank, missing the bullet head by inches. Before she could jerk back her weapon, the worm jumped onto the handle and scampered up it. Its jaws snapping like bolt cutters, the two-foot-long mutie attacked. It bit through her trousers and flesh in an instant, then twisted its head into the flesh of her upper thigh, trying to bore up into the warmth of her body cavity.

"Yee! Yeeee!" she shrieked, staggering backward, grabbing the armored shell in both hands. With a supreme effort, she corkscrewed it out of her flesh and flung it away. Bright blood sprayed between her fingers as she desperately clutched the inside of her thigh. She couldn't stop the bleeding. Nothing could stop it. Her femoral artery had been severed.

The gory scagworm landed at Doc's feet, jaws snapping. Instinctively he stomped on its head with one boot, then both boots. It was all he could do to keep the thing pinned to the ground. Then help came in the form of a well-aimed pitchfork. The women clubbed the trapped creature senseless, then flipped it into one of the garbage cans.

By that time, the unfortunate victim had bled out in the sand. The ville folk stood around her still form, staring down ashen-faced and stunned. Some wept into their hands.

"Margie knew the risks," Isabel told them. Her face showed strain and sadness, but she didn't give herself permission to cry. Because she was the leader she had to be a rock the others could lean on. "It could have been any one of us. We're not going to carry her body all the way back to the ville. She wouldn't have wanted us to. We'll bury her here."

Using the pitchforks and their bare hands, they dug a shallow grave in the arroyo, then unceremoniously rolled in the limp, still warm corpse. No one said any words over the dead woman before they filled in the hole with sand. Maybe they were all out of goodbyes. The men moved two slabs of heavy rock on top of the earth.

Doc thought about mentioning the evidence of a grave-digging critter, but it didn't seem in good taste, or politic.

Solemnly, and much more warily, they moved down the low bank, repeating the procedure at each likely burrow. Before they had gone forty yards, the men were straining under the weight of half-full garbage cans. And the food gathering was complete.

Doc was amazed at the density of the scagworm population. "Good grief, how many of those things are there?" he said.

"There weren't any until about a month ago," Isabel said. "Now there doesn't seem to be an end to them. More and more are moving up from the south every day. And they're damn good eating. Like I said, it's manna from heaven. We don't have to feed them, either. When they can't get pigs or prairie dogs, they happily eat each other."

"Doesn't that happen when they're piled up inside the containers?"

"No, they go right to sleep in the dark."

"Remarkable," Doc said.

"The only rub is, they aren't housebroken."

AN HOUR LATER, when they were back at Sunspot, Doc realized the extent of their unhousebrokenness. The men tipped a garbage can against the rim of one of the caldrons, then carefully opened the lid, sliding the scagworms into the boiling water. The muties were no longer black. They were streaked end to end with vile-smelling, ochre-colored excrement.

The scagworms squealed and writhed, trying frantically, vainly, to swim before succumbing to the intense heat. The few that managed to reach and cling to the barrel rim were immediately knocked back with clubs.

An ochre froth billowed upon the water's roiling surface, spilled over the rim and oozed down the sides of the barrel.

Doc moved upwind to escape the ghastly aroma.

"We scald them awhile to chill them good and dead, and to clean off all the runny shit," Isabel told him.

After a fifteen-minute boil, the ville folk sieved the dead worms out of the barrel with pitchforks. The drum full of nasty, clot-choked water was unceremoniously dumped on the ground. When the worms were cool enough to handle, the men shoved sharpened iron rods under their belly plates from tail to throat. They fitted four worms to a rod, then started roasting them over the coal bed. Clear juices dripped down into the fire, spitting clouds of steam. Post-boiling, the aroma was much improved.

"They smell like shellfish when they're broiling," Doc said. "Like lobster or crab."

As the cooks rotated their skewers, the black shells gradually turned gray, then glowed red. When the shells finally split along the backs, the worms were removed from the heat. After they had again cooled and were unskewered, the women used claw hammers to shatter the fire-weakened, armored heads, exposing the end of a tube of meat that was easily pulled free of the carapace. An inner liner like a sausage skin protected the lump of muscle.

After they had stripped the meat from the liner, the women used carving knives to hack it into bite-size chunks. They dropped the flesh into the second fifty-five-gallon drum of boiling water along with the collected vegetables and a few bunches of herbs. The vat of stew cooked at a slow simmer until after sundown, when portions were finally ladled out.

As Doc had hoped, all of Haldane's sec men lined up for chow. It was a no-fuss, no-muss way to accomplish the mission Malosh had given him. His head turned slowly as he took them in.

Isabel noticed the focus of his attention. Perhaps his lips were moving. "Are you counting the sec men?" she asked.

The question startled him, but he covered himself. "It's a habit," he said. "An old road warrior likes to know what he's up against. It appears the opposition numbers sixty. Is that all of them?" The question came out naturally, effortlessly. And was answered in the same fashion.

"All but the eight stationed on the wag and foot gates. And there's another eight still out on patrol. Sometimes they spend the night outside the berm, depending on how far they've gone on their sweeps."

"A sizeable force by any measure. Shall we take our suppers over to the fire?"

They carried their pint cans of stew to a fireside log and sat hip to hip, a foot apart.

"What do you think?" Isabel said after he had taken a bite of double-cooked scagworm.

"It's chewy, but in a pleasant way. It doesn't taste of the sea, like I thought it might. It's rather more like possum, only less greasy."

"This," Isabel said, hoisting her stew can to the heavens, "is the answer to our prayers."

"Indeed."

"The Almighty has chosen to save the people of Sunspot from a horrible death. To lift our impossible burden. It has to be for some reason. For some great purpose. Can't you see the hand of God in this, Theo?"

Somehow Doc managed to swallow the food in his mouth. He said, "I do."

But it was a heartless God whose hand he saw.

And he was that God's lying instrument.

With his assistance, Sunspot was about to change occupiers again, with the accompanying loss of life. It was possible that the woman beside him would be killed in the process. That wasn't a concern he had anticipated a few hours ago. Though he wanted to warn her, he couldn't for fear the word might reach Haldane's men, which would put his companions who were part of Malosh's assault at greater risk. If Isabel survived the coming battle, she would certainly take his action for the cowardly betrayal that it was.

He had his friends' lives to consider.

And yet Isabel was sending unmistakable signals with those violet eyes of hers. He could see that she found him attractive. His strange Victorian manners, speech and bearing, and his innate sadness, had cast a romantic spell. Even as he resolved not to press this advantage, he found himself leaning over and kissing her. Her mouth was soft and warm and pliant beneath his. And a surprising sensation passed between them. It was electric.

When Doc broke off the kiss, he saw the rosy color rising in her cheeks. The experience though brief seemed to have sucked the very breath from his lungs.

He knew he had to stop before things went any further. He could not in good conscience court this lovely, brave woman. That would be heaping betrayal upon betrayal.

"What's wrong?" Isabel said.

"I cannot," he told her, rising to his feet. "I am sorry."

She called out to him as he walked away, but he didn't look back.

"Not our ville." The companions' standard disavowal of responsibility had never rung so hollow.

Chapter Thirteen

As a salmon-pink sunset faded to black on the horizon, Magus's convoy circled and stopped on a flat stretch of desert hardpan. Just enough daylight remained to make camp and batten everything down for the night. Thus far, the chem weapon caravan hadn't attempted to travel after dark. Even with every headlight blazing, it would have been far too dangerous. The potential road hazards and risk of rollovers would have forced an even greater reduction in speed. Now that they were within spitting distance of Malosh's army, creeping along in a parade of halogen lights was a very bad idea.

When the road trash piled out of the Humvee, Baron Haldane followed suit; only then did he realize they had reached their destination. To the north, some eight miles away, along the summit at the mouth of the gorge, were the pinpoint firelights of Sunspot ville.

After tomorrow, lights would never again dance on that black ridge of rock. Haldane stifled a shiver. There was a decided chill in the air now that the sun had gone. The first stars of evening were coming out.

"In an hour it's gonna be colder than a bull doomie's tits," Mossy Teeth quipped.

"Only there won't be no fires for the likes of us tonight," the driver said. "Don't want to draw attention to the camp in case the Impaler has long-range patrols out."

In the purpling light, Baron Haldane left the Humvee and headed for the side of one of the six-by-sixes, where his sec men waited. He looked from face to shadowy face and saw uniformly grim expressions. And with good reason. First of all, they were outnumbered if not outgunned by Magus's coldhearts. Now, as they looked on, the gun crew unhitched and unwrapped the Lyagushka at the edge of the ring of wags. Very soon their Nuevaville kin would be under the sights of the Soviet artillery piece, inside the kill zone of the predark WMDs, and the hand on the trigger cord had steel fingers.

Haldane took his men aside, out of earshot of Magus's crew. He hunkered down while they huddled around him.

"I want my son back," the baron said, "alive and in one piece."

"We need to know where Magus has got him stashed," said Bollinger, Haldane's head sec man. He was tall, squint-eyed, lantern-jawed and harder than predark steel. Unscratchable. A man after the baron's own heart. "Before we make a plan."

"He's in the landship with Steel Eyes," Haldane said.

"That wag is gonna be a tough nut to crack," Bollinger told him. "We can't see inside. They've got all the bulletproof shades pulled down. What's the floor plan?"

"There's a long, skinny corridor running the full length of the thing," Haldane said. "And just one armed guard that I saw. He could have more, now. There are steel doors spaced along one side of the hall. The salon at the back end is where Magus does his experiments. Thorne could be in any of the cabins. Or with Magus."

"Seems like Magus would keep him close by, for safekeeping," the head sec man said.

"We've got problems unless we can force Magus to show his hand. Sweeping that wag room by room is going to get my son chilled."

"Are we going to try and rescue him before the gas attack?" Bollinger said. "Tonight mebbe? I wouldn't mind chilling a few dozen of these road scum in the bargain."

"If we do that, Magus might not fire his chem weapons at Sunspot. He might turn them on Nuevaville, out of pure spite."

Haldane paused for a second then added, "Nothing can be decided until we evacuate our garrison from the ville. Once they've joined us, we have a chance against Magus. We'll outnumber his blackhearts by almost two to one."

"When you send men to Sunspot to collect the others," Bollinger said, "you reduce your force down here by that number. If there's a hang-up, if something goes wrong, you won't have enough guns left to free your son."

"That's why I'm only sending three runners to the ville tonight," Haldane said. "Bollinger, pick a pair of men to go with you. Steer clear of Malosh and bring our soldiers back."

The head sec man chose his team, and they battened down and rattle-proofed each other's gear. Magus knew the baron was going to pull back his troops before the barrage, so there was no need to conceal the operation. The runners had eight miles to cross at night, with only stars to light their path. Haldane knew the trip could take three hours or more. Each way.

As Bollinger and the others shouldered their blasters and walked off into the gathering gloom, one of the baron's men looked over his shoulder and said, "Uh-oh, we got company…"

The huddle of troopers gave way, letting the dread-locked sec man from the landship approach Haldane.

"Magus wants you to eat dinner with him in his wag," the man said. "He told me to tell you that it was to 'celebrate the eve of your great victory over Baron Malosh.'"

It wasn't an invitation the baron could refuse.

"Grub's on now," the sec man told him. "Magus doesn't like to be kept waiting."

As Haldane followed the man down the circle of wags, he heard the throb of the landship's generators. When they reached the wag, Dreadlocks again relieved Haldane of his Remington 12-gauge, then pulled the side door ajar. The baron was bathed in bright electric light.

"Go on," his escort said, waving him inside.

The sec man pointed him to the third doorway along the corridor instead of the rear salon. Haldane was glad to see that supper hadn't been laid out in the butcher's grisly playpen.

The baron opened the door and looked into a tiny, windowless olive-drab–painted cell. A single, bare, 100-watt bulb hung from the riveted metal ceiling. The table was also made of painted metal. There were two steel benches built into the walls on either side. On the right-hand bench sat Magus.

"Where is my son?" were the first words out of Haldane's mouth.

"Safely tucked away."

"I want to see him, now. To make sure he is safe."

"Please close the door behind you."

After the baron complied, Magus said, "Your boy is perfectly fine. You can see him after dawn tomorrow, when our transaction is completed. Sit down. Our meal is growing cold."

Various uncovered serving dishes were set out on the table. Roasted sliced meats, some in their own juices, some in thick gravy. Stewed vegetables. Piles of long, thin noodles. A gallon jug of foaming ale. If not for the company and the circumstances, Haldane would have found the platters appetizing.

The baron didn't press the issue of seeing Thorne. He hadn't expected Magus to give him access to his son. The most he could hope for was a clue where he was being held in the wag. Haldane took his place on the opposite bench, across narrow table from Steel Eyes. He was practically knee-to-knee with the creature. The smell of transmission fluid and fleshly decay competed with the delicious aroma of the food. Baron chose not to show his disgust, for fear it would be seen as a sign of weakness.

"Please, begin," Magus said. "Help yourself."

Haldane filled his plate and his glass, then waited for Steel Eyes to do the same.

"It's very good," the baron said, swallowing the first heaping forkful of yam.

Magus nodded as he chewed, guy wires spooling, unspooling into his cheekpieces, motorized jaws grinding away. After a moment he picked a plastic squirt bottle from the table, opened his still full mouth and sprayed what looked like water between his lips. Then he resumed chewing.

It occurred to Haldane that perhaps Steel Eyes either lacked or had inadequate saliva glands, which meant he had to lubricate every mouthful with water to fully pulverize it.

Though the baron watched and waited for Magus to swallow the bolus, he never did. Instead he spit a golf-ball-size wad of finely masticated food onto his steel fingers and slapped it onto the side of his plate.

"Eating for the purpose of sustenance is a dim memory for me, I'm afraid," Magus said, "but there is still the pleasure of the taste."

To illustrate, the creature stuck out his human tongue.

"Why don't you try some of the spaghetti sauce," Magus urged him. "It's my own recipe."

THORNE HALDANE WAS ALIVE, but not "perfectly fine."

The boy was still crammed in the tiny, predark pet carrier. The only position he could assume was fetal. The carrier sat on an unmade bunk in a pitch-dark cabin. Before the lights went out, he had gotten a good look at his surroundings. The room was packed with junk—moldy papers and electronic parts in disintegrating cardboard boxes. Because the air vent was open, he could hear every word of the conversation between his father and Magus in the cabin next door.

Likewise they could hear him.

Thorne would have shouted or kicked the cage to let his father know he was close, but Magus had booby-trapped the cage, placing a shaped explosive charge on the carrier door. The creature had shown him the remote detonator, a whitecoat gizmo the size of a deck of playing cards. Magus had threatened that if he made so much as a sound, a split second after chilling him he would chill the baron.

"There is only a tiny bit of plastic explosive on the door," Steel Eyes had told him. "Just enough to mebbe rattle the wag's walls. A little bitty boom to pop a little bitty head from a little bitty neck."

Like all Deathlands children, Thorne was used to hearing tales about the monsters that roamed the hell-scape. Wild animals. Muties. Maniacs. Awful creatures that ate raw human flesh and sucked the marrow from the bones. Or kept children captive to satisfy their sick urges. Tales devised, and often repeated, to instill fear and caution in the vulnerable. But all those horror stories had done nothing to prepare him for the suffo-cating terror he'd felt as he'd sat on Magus's lap in that room full of death.

Steel Eyes's hands were incredibly strong. When he made a fist, it sounded like it was motorized. Thorne's wrists still ached from the rough handling he'd received.

Just as alarming to the boy, Magus didn't seem to ever wear clothes. If he had any private parts, they were covered by a stainless steel cup arrangement that was bolted over his crotch. It had no hinge, no lock. To get it off took a box wrench. Thorne Haldane had guessed that urination, a prime curiosity of someone his age, was accomplished through one of the clamped plastic tubes that dangled between his legs. Sitting on that horrible lap, he could feel ice-cold, metal long bones under his butt. The bare flesh that was attached to them was feverishly warm. Some of the greenish gunk that oozed from the places where muscles met metal had gotten on his pant leg. It smelled real bad. Like fish guts left in the sun.

Thorne blamed himself for what had happened. He kept replaying his last moments in Nuevaville, trying to undo them in his head. The convoy road scum had snatched him up in an old gunny sack as he tried to beat the rain back to his front door. If he had only been able to run faster, or dodge better, mebbe he could have gotten away.

By letting himself get caught by Magus, he had put his father at a terrible disadvantage. And he had put him in terrible danger. He knew his dad would never give up until he was free.

Chapter Fourteen

"Why do we have to leave here?" Young Crad asked Doc. "I like this ville." He tipped up his stew container and tapped on the bottom to get the last dribble of scagworm juice. "I got my own can of food. And people don't spit on me all the time."

Sound reasons for staying.

"Remember your friend Bezoar?" Doc said.

Young Crad's too small eyes lit up at once.

"If we don't depart Sunspot ville tonight," Doc told him, "by this time tomorrow your friend is going to be fifteen feet in the air with a maypole wedged up his backside."

After a moment of strain, the swineherd made the mental connection. And was aghast. "Like in Redbone?" he muttered.

"The self-same. We have got to go."

"Can we come back?"

"Yes, of course," Doc assured him, "and we'll be returning very soon." He didn't bother to add, "So we can absorb the first salvo of lead from sixty-odd blasters."

After a pause, a sly grin twisted Young Crad's mouth. "You like the one with the pretty eyes, don't you?" he said.

"I beg your pardon?"

"You kissed her. I saw you."

As might be imagined, a hulking, swineherd pervert's attempt at coyness was nothing short of horrifying.

Nonetheless Doc replied in the affirmative, if briefly. "Yes, I kissed her. But we must put that aside and leave this ville. Bezoar's life depends on it."

Doc pulled the droolie into the shadows beyond the reach of the firelight. There they waited for the dinner party to break up. Eventually the Sunspot folk began to slip away in ones and twos to their pallets in the cargo containers and rusted-out Winnebagos. Haldane's sec men retreated to their barracks in the Welcome Center. As the last of them crawled off to bed, the unattended campfires burned low and the flames winked out, leaving beds of glowing red coals.

"We're going to climb the berm," Doc informed Young Crad.

The droolie looked up at the shadowy, fifteen-foot-high pile of loose rubble and dirt, but asked no questions.

Doc had decided that they couldn't leave Sunspot via the foot gate. If they'd tried, they would have had to explain to the sentries why they were heading out into the hellscape in the middle of the night. Something that would have looked very suspicious. And they couldn't risk waiting until daybreak to make their exit. There was a chance they wouldn't be allowed to leave, even then. Moreover, they needed all the time available in case they got lost en route, or if Malosh had moved the column from its last position.

Given the dark, moonless night and their distance

from the Welcome Center and ramshackle shelters, as long as they moved quietly they would attract no attention.

"Make no noise," Doc warned the swineherd as they slowly started up the forty-five-degree incline. Because the berm wall was made of loose piled debris, and there was only starlight to see by, it was difficult to locate solid hand- and footholds. Young Crad's weight caused a minor collapse in the structure. Small chunks of concrete rattled to the ground below. They froze near the top of the berm, but no one burst out of the semitrailers to challenge them. Given the building materials, such mini-avalanches no doubt were common occurrences.

After descending the other side of the perimeter wall, Doc and Young Crad turned left and skirted the edge of the heaped riprap. Outside the front gates, bonfires were burning, presumably to deter predators. The light they cast only penetrated thirty or forty yards into the darkness. Doc made a wide detour around the pyres before rejoining the path to the interstate on the slope below.

As they walked down to the predark highway, the only sound came from Doc's bootsoles softly crunching on the starlit track. The old man could feel his back muscles bunching up into knots. Night was the worst time to be out and about in the hellscape. Unless you were trying to commit mutie-assisted suicide.

As dim-witted as he was, even the droolie was aware of the extreme danger.

"So dark," Young Crad whispered.

Below them was the eerie, vaguely outlined, colorless landscape of ruined four-lane and towering, canted light stanchions.

"We're fine," Doc said. "We'll just follow the interstate and retrace our route back to Malosh."

As they moved along the highway shoulder, Doc felt the hairs on the back of his neck stand erect. He had a powerful sense of being watched.

"Wait a second," he said, drawing the LeMat.

When he held his breath and listened, he could hear something moving stealthily in the dark, just beyond the range of his vision.

"Stinks here," was Young Crad's choked comment.

The stench of a freshly excavated grave was unmistakable.

That the swineherd could smell it over his own pungent aroma was a true measure of its intensity.

Thirty feet ahead was a pile of heaped earth and overturned stone slabs. Approaching cautiously, Doc reached down and grabbed a handful of soil. It was still damp. On the other side of the mound was the source of the terrible odor: severed body parts. Strewed long bones. A headless torso. The rotting corpse had been devoured belly first.

Had they scared off whatever it was?

Did it only feed on the decaying dead? Or did it also take its food warm and kicking?

Was there more than one?

Questions without immediate answers.

Doc doubted that he was looking at the handiwork of a scagworm. A worm wouldn't have bothered pulling the body out of the ground to feed upon it. It would have just burrowed in and done its dining out of sight, on the buried pocket of protein. The creature that had disturbed the grave had to overturn the heavy capstones and pull its meal out of the earth. Which meant it was bigger, stronger than the mama worms, and to grapple with the stones, at least two-armed if not two-legged.

As he scanned the darkness at the edge of the shoulder, Doc considered the possibilities.

A five-hundred-pound scalie?

Scalies were lazy, low-moving bastards, and they liked weak or injured prey, or prey they could ambush at close range or trap in some way. The grave robbing could also have been the work of a band of roaming cannies. He couldn't recall seeing any bootprints around the opened graves the previous afternoon. And it was too dark to make out any now. For cannies to dig up graves, they had to be triple desperate. Congealed human blood and decaying tissue being preferable to no blood and tissue at all. Their alternative to starvation was to eat one another, which they usually only did when a member of the band became too sick to live.

As Doc turned his attention west, something crossed the four lanes left to right in front of them, about forty yards away.

Though the light was dim, he could see that it was neither scalie nor cannie. It was the size and height of a full-grown bull or an ox. And it had more than two legs. He squinted, hard.

It had more than four legs.

For its size, it was amazingly quick and light on its feet. In a crouching run, it disappeared soundlessly into the pitch-dark desert.

Doc swept the highway shoulder with the sights of the LeMat. There was nothing to shoot at.

"Damnation," he said.

Young Crad had glimpsed it, too. "Whuh-whuh-whuh-whuh?" he stammered.

Doc got the swineherd's drift. "Your guess is as good as mine," he said. "I think it is running back along the road to the east, trying cut us off from the ville."

They looked behind them, at the distant fires perched on the silhouette of ridge.

"We go back now?"

"That isn't an option. It's already probably lying in wait for us."

"We go on, then."

"If we do that, it will run us down from behind."

There was only one choice, Doc realized. Most unpleasant. Because he could shoot, he had a chance in hell of holding off the creature long enough for Young Crad to get away.

"Can you find your way back to Bezoar?" he asked the droolie.

Young Crad nodded. "Broken bridge. Broken bridge."

"That's right. Turn at the broken bridge. If I tell you a number can you remember it?"

"What?"

"This is very important," Doc told him. "To save Bezoar and my friends, can you remember a number?"

"What?"

There was no time for droolie games.

Doc set down the LeMat and unsheathed his sword-stick. He said, "Give me your palm."

When Crad extended his hand, Doc seized it by the wrist. "Hold still," he said. "This will only hurt for a moment." Holding the sword near its razor-sharp point, he dragged the edge across the droolie' skin, making quick, shallow slashes.

"Ow!" the swineherd yelped, jerking his hand back.

"Find Malosh and show him that mark on your palm. Can you do that?"

Young Crad looked down dumbfounded at the scratches in his flesh, which oozed a thin trickle of blood.

"Can you do that?" Doc demanded.

The swineherd nodded.

"Then, go! Now! Run!"

Young Crad took off without further prompting, clutching his injured hand to his chest, lumbering barefoot into the darkness below.

Doc resheathed his sword, picked up the LeMat, and started back up the grade. There was no way of knowing whether the droolie would find the column in time. He could only hope.

Grimly, Doc advanced with the heavy pistol raised. Every broad puddle of shadow, every low hummock along the road's edge could have concealed his enemy. He was determined to confront the monster head-on and to at least cripple it. He had his LeMat to accomplish the task. After that, he only had his swordstick to rely upon.

As he neared the highway exit for the Welcome Center, between the turnoff and the one hundred-yard-wide blown-up section of road, the creature reappeared from the shadows. It squatted in what was left of the slow traffic lane, all eight of its legs bending at the first joint. With its belly about three feet from the ground, it made a distinct hissing sound. The body was a vague, flattened oblong. As the beast turned back into the darkness, the silhouette didn't change, which told him the body was roughly circular in shape.

Doc knew he had to lure it closer, to within sure-chilling range of the black powder pistol. He advanced to the spot where it had just stood, his eyes were skinned for the slightest movement, ears pricked up to catch the faintest sound.

Before him was a wide pool of semiliquid excreta. The creature had marked its turf.

As Doc rounded the wet spot, the thing suddenly raised up from a depression in the roadway ahead.

Doc reacted, opening fire with the LeMat, sending a .44-caliber ball into the center of its body. The rocking blast echoed in the gorge above. The resulting plume of gunsmoke momentarily obscured the creature. Undaunted, Doc walked through the twinkling haze, straight for his target. Because of the combination of the weak light and unfamiliar animal, he wasn't sure precisely what to aim at, but he gamely continued to fire a fresh round at each forward step.

His bullets thwacked into and presumably through its torso as they whined off the boulders of concrete farther up the road.

The beast seemed impervious to lead balls and content to wait for its dinner to come to it. As Doc advanced through the smoke, he got an impression of shaggy hairiness. And of savage cunning if not intelligence.

Doc emptied all his .44-caliber rounds into the dark shape. With those gunshots still echoing, he cocked the hammer on the blue whistler barrel. Then he heard shrill shouts from the ville gate above. When he stole a glance in that direction, he saw a line of torches bouncing down the path toward him. Haldane's fighters were coming.

Instead of leaping upon him straightaway, the creature scuttled to the right and took cover behind a rubble pile. The .44-caliber balls might have stung it a little, after all.

Doc knew he couldn't stop to reload the revolver. He had to press his advantage, if indeed he had one, relying on the LeMat's single-shot, scattergun barrel. Perhaps a load of grapeshot at close range could create a wound grievous enough to kill or hobble it.

Perhaps.

Doc stepped unblinking into the jaws of death, with raised pistol in his hand.

The many-legged thing surprised him by springing away in a tremendous bound. He instinctively led it with the LeMat's sights and as he did so he touched off the shotgun barrel. The pistol boomed and bucked in his fist, spitting a yard of blue flame and choking pall of smoke.

Unable to see anything through the plume of burning black powder, his ears momentarily ringing, he holstered the empty weapon and drew his blade, preparing to pursue his quarry into the darkness.

Before he heard the crash of footfalls behind, someone shouted at him, "Stop there! Don't move or we'll fire!"

Doc turned to face torches and assault rifle muzzles.

"Put that stabber away," one of the men said.

Doc scabbarded the rapier without protest.

"What the hell are you doing out here?"

The old man knew that "taking the night air" wouldn't suffice. Nor would "feeding the animals." There was no good explanation for leaving the berm's protection before dawn.

"He didn't go through any of the gates," one of the sentries said. "He must have jumped over the wall."

"Why did you sneak out of Sunspot?"

Again, Doc had no credible answer, so he kept quiet.

"He showed up this afternoon with a droolie," another trooper chimed in.

"Where's your droolie pal?"

"The creature took him," Doc replied in an even tone. "I tried to help him, but bullets didn't stop it."

A reasonable enough story, but the men didn't buy it.

"Rad bastard's got to be a spy for Malosh."

"We hang spies around here."

Chapter Fifteen

Bollinger didn't make a headlong rush for Sunspot. He had six hours to get there and return before the gas barrage started. There was time for caution, though forcing himself to take it slow made his stomach jittery. Safety was far more important to his mission than speed. He knew if he didn't make it to the ville and warn the garrison to pull out, all of Haldane's soldiers would die. Either by the hand of Malosh, or the hand of Magus. These were troopers Bollinger had personally helped train and had commanded in battle. Moreover, he had grown up with all of them. He knew their families.

The sec boss sensed his two subordinates were jumpy, too. It wasn't just because they were traveling at night. They had an awesome responsibility. Many lives depended on their success.

With starlight dimly reflecting off the sand, Bollinger led them along the clearest route, keeping to open ground as much as possible, keeping away from pitch-dark patches of brush, boulders and deep, narrow gullies. That way, if they were ambushed by men or muties, they had a chance to return fire and beat off the attack.

Bollinger could see their goal ahead, rising above the shadowy hills. Firelights twinkled against a black backdrop. He didn't let his gaze linger; the danger was much closer and all around.

The sec boss knew everything there was to know about Sunspot. He had helped Baron Haldane take the ville from Malosh twice, and had been stationed there himself for months. During that time, he had learned to hate the rank shit pile and its people. He had lost many dear friends during the campaigns' advances and retreats. He had come to view the ville folk as sneaking, lying, cheating bastards. And murderers. While he had been in command of the Sunspot garrison, they had assassinated four of his soldiers in one night. Bollinger had caught the guilty parties and hanged them in front of the whole ville. He had strung up the ville leader for good measure. He still wished he could have hanged them all, men, women and children.

Though the prospect of their impending annihilation with gas pleased him, he was less enthusiastic about Malosh's receiving the same fate. Given the man's history of atrocities, it seemed far too easy a way out. If offered a choice, the sec boss would have preferred to drag the still-living baron by his heels behind a wag for twenty or thirty miles, until there was nothing left but leg bones and feet.

Bollinger was sweating hard as they hopped down into a wide arroyo. His mouth was bone-dry. Not from the exertion of the trek or the lingering heat. The tension was starting to get to him. A man could only stay hard-focused, listening for the slightest sound, looking for the tiniest movement, for so long without losing his edge.

"Let's stop a minute," he said.

It was okay to move across open ground, it was definitely not okay to take a rest break there. His assault rifle braced against his hip, finger resting on the trigger, Bollinger headed toward a low, grass-fringed bank on their right. The crumbling, undercut bluff was draped in deep shadow. He approached it carefully, making sure that nothing hid in the darkness.

When he had completed the recce to his satisfaction, he told his men to sit in the shadows. With their backs against the bluff, they broke out canteens and sipped water. They kept their weapons ready and their senses alert. They spoke in near whispers.

"How far to go?" one of the soldiers asked.

"Mebbe five more miles," Bollinger answered.

"I'm thinking the ville folk are gonna know something's up when we pull out all our troops at once," the other soldier said. "We've never done that before."

"Yeah, but they won't know what the something is," the sec boss said. "Until it's too late…" Even though they were sitting quite close to each other, it was so dark Bollinger couldn't make out their faces.

"All those dead people are really gonna stink up the place."

"That'll bring on the buzzards, big time. Do you think the poison will chill them, too?"

"Yeah, stone dead," Bollinger said. "Them and anything else that wanders by. That sarin gas is triple nasty. Breathe it, you die. Taste it, you die. Touch it, you die."

Dirt exploded with tremendous force and a grinding roar from the bank at their backs. The man sitting next to Bollinger let out a yelp that lasted about one-tenth of a second, cut off along with his head, which toppled forward into his lap and bounced out of the shadows, landing face-up and bug-eyed in the starlight. Bollinger and the other soldier sat frozen as the still-thrashing body beside them was suddenly jerked backward, out of sight into a hole that hadn't been there moments before.

Bollinger jumped to his feet, but the other soldier never made it that far. Before he could rise he was seized around the waist from behind and shaken so violently and so rapidly that his body actually blurred before Bollinger's astonished eyes. Caught in that monstrous, crushing grip, the trooper couldn't break free, he couldn't breathe or scream. The only sound came from avalanching rocks and rib bones cracking. All the poor bastard could do was kick his legs and flail his arms. The extended limbs acted as brakes when he was slammed backward into the mouth of another fresh hole. Dirt rained down from the collapsing bluff. Again he was slammed backward, again he just managed to stay out of the burrow. The third time he hit the hole, he doubled over like a ragdoll at the waist and vanished.

Bollinger vaulted away from the bank, crow-hopping over the severed, drop-jawed head.

He hadn't clearly seen what had just taken his men. He was left with a vague impression of smooth, domed heads, like the noses of five-hundred-pound bombs. And heavy, powerful jaws. Jaws that could cleanly sever a human neck in a single bite. Whatever the hell they were, they were very large, very quick and very deadly.

When he glanced down the arroyo behind him, his heart sank. In starlight, the dry river channel was alive with movement. Glistening, sinuous movement as the earth vomited forth dozens upon dozens of black segmented creatures. They poured out of the ground and slithered toward him, moving like streaking shadows above the sand. Even if he could have hit them, there were way too many for him to shoot.

"Oh, shit, oh, shit," Bollinger groaned as he turned and broke into an all-out sprint. He felt good, felt strong, light and fast on his feet. Thanks to a jet-assist of adrenaline rush, he could make it. He was sure he could make it. He had to make it. There was no time to dump his gear and lighten his load. The effort would have slowed him a few fractions of a second, and he would have lost precious ground to the pursuit. He had to concentrate on running.

Running like all holy hell.

He pushed past his own limits, trying to put as much distance between the muties and himself as he could. Distance was the great dissuader. If he could make them give up hope of catching him, he had a chance. That was the only way he was going to reach the ville alive. He no longer had the luxury of picking an easy, meandering path through the clearings; he raced overland, busting brush, beelining it for the ruined interstate.

He didn't think about how far he'd run, or how far he had to go until his legs started burning and growing heavier and heavier. He could hear his own breath rasping in his ears and he couldn't seem to suck down enough air. Even as his pace faltered, as he began to stumble, from behind he heard scratching sounds, growing in volume like an onrushing storm, crisp feet scurrying, tens of thousands of them.

He knew then that he wasn't going to make it. That his mission was lost. In that last moment of despair, he begged his doomed friends in Sunspot for forgiveness, and cursed the god that had abandoned them all.

Something heavy latched on to his right ankle and wouldn't let go. As he dragged it along with him, the creature writhed and shook its head, the savage movement caused its serrated jaws to sever tendons and ligaments and score deeply into the bone. Hot blood squished inside his right boot. His foot went dead. He screamed as he ran a step or two more, unable to kick it free.

In the distance he could see the firelights of Sunspot.

Help was far away.

Too far away.

Pain lanced into his other leg and he tripped, crashing facedown in the sand. The creatures swept over him in a chitinous wave. Rolling over onto his back, he instinctively raised his hands to cover his face, which opened his torso to attack. Once the two-foot-long black worms sank their jaws in his belly, there was no getting them out. While he pulled and pounded on the powerful armored bodies and the rippling rows of scratchy bug feet, the worms shook, snapped and burrowed in a frenzy. Over his shrill screams, he could hear his ribs breaking like dry sticks and then they were squirming inside his torso, fighting over the choicer bits.

Only when one of them made a meal of Bollinger's beating heart did his agony end.

Chapter Sixteen

Young Crad hightailed it downhill, his injured hand raised and clenched in a tight fist, blood trickling steadily down his arm. He ran parallel to the ravaged highway. The loose flesh of his face bounced and jiggled with each impact of bare feet slapping sand, as did the heavy muscles of his chest and stomach. Snot in twin clear streams trailed down his cheeks and swayed from his chin. The swineherd was a strong man, in the prime of his life, and if he knew how to do one thing, and one thing only, it was how to flee.

He had been fleeing pretty much his entire life. Usually to avoid kicks, sticks, spit, hurled stones and howled insults. Young Crad understood human cruelty, having received it for as long as he could remember, yet he had never once asked himself, "Why me?"

Because he knew why.

He had been marked at birth, abandoned by a mother who either sensed his mental deficit or shared it. Like most Deathlanders, the barrel-chested swineherd knew nothing about the predark myths that described orphaned babies being wet-nursed by wild animals. Supposedly, Romulus and Remus, the founders of the ancient city of Rome, had been raised by a she-wolf. Young Crad, the discarded droolie, had been suckled by pigs. Domesticated pigs. It was likely that his mother had deposited him inside the pen to be eaten by the hulking, omnivorous beasts.

Waste not, want not.

Instead, miraculously, he had been adopted into a sprawling litter of piglets. His earliest memories were of grubbing about in the sty with his oinking littermates. Young Crad had lived his life in constant, close proximity to the porcine species. Now that he was torn from the familiar, he felt terribly alone, and once again abandoned.

Being born a droolie in the hellscape wasn't unusual. There were a number of ways fetal brains could be damaged between conception and birth, and little in the way of prophylaxis. After the fact, there was no remedy at all, save death. Accordingly, every ville had among its number a few button-eyed Young Crads; some had more, some less.

In Redbone, all the other dimmie girls and boys had had futures, of sorts. When they became old enough to control their respective sphincters and gag reflexes, they found gainful, lifelong employment in the ville's lone gaudy. The gaudy master and his customers had no use for the pig boy. Not only was he scorned by every other human being—except for Bezoar, who was also an outcast and fellow swineherd—the ville folk actively sought to do him bodily harm, just like his birth mother had. It seemed he was always ducking, dodging, barely escaping their wrath.

Young Crad was a morally degenerate triple stupe, but he was smart enough to be scared shitless. The memory of the creature he'd just seen put wings on his heels. A dim memory. He hadn't seen it all that clearly. But what stuck in his mind the most was all those legs, and the sheer size of it. Not only did it have twice as many legs as normal, eight instead of four, each leg had too many knees. Four or five, it seemed. All capable of bending. When it straightened its legs and stood to its full height, he could have walked under its belly without crouching. Crad was a bona fide droolie, but he instinctively sensed the creature was a stone chiller, not just a grave robber. And that it was looking for its next meal.

Then he heard the sound of blasterfire from up the grade behind him. Boom after rocking boom rolled against his back. The old geezer was blasting away like there was no tomorrow—if he was missing his target, there probably wasn't any, either. The awful silence after the shooting stopped made him run even faster.

Other than Bezoar, Young Crad had never had a human friend. And he'd certainly never had a friend who would sacrifice his life for him. That's what Doc Tanner had just done. The act of selfless heroism amazed him. That it had been done on his behalf made him feel wonderful and horrible at the same time, and he didn't understand why. His new friend Doc had hurt him, cut on him, but he was accustomed to being hurt. Sometimes Bezoar beat him with a stick to drive home a point he was trying to make. It was useless of course, but it seemed to make the elder swineherd feel better.

Young Crad was crushed that he had lost a friend like Doc so soon after finding him. He blubbered a bit over a man he'd hardly known. Pathetic and limited and grotesque as it was, his world was collapsing around him.

For the life of him he couldn't quite recall why he

was returning to the baron's army. Young Crad was a three-dimensional person with a two-dimensional mind. A cardboard cutout who walked and talked and ate and crapped. He knew he was in mortal danger, though, and that he would be safe when he reached the camp.

Broken bridge, he muttered as he ran.

Broken bridge.

Broken bridge.

A two-word prayer to ward off the thing with too many knees.

He was still muttering to himself when the shattered blocks of the collapsed four-lane span came into view below him. He scrambled over the uptilted plates of roadbed and dropped down into the dry riverbed. Without pausing to look behind him, he ran north, up the wide channel. After traveling a quarter mile, he climbed out of the riverbed and into the low hills.

He didn't have to think about where he was headed, and he didn't look to the stars to find his direction. Which was a good thing because if he had he would have become lost in a hurry. Below the conscious level, some ingrained homing sense told him which way to go.

He ran up and down the slopes of the low hills for what seemed like a very long time before he crested a rounded summit and looked down on a wide hollow where Malosh's fighters had made camp for the night. Though there were no fires and no lights, he could make out horses, mules, dogs, carts, tents and, scattered everywhere, the dark forms of men sleeping curled up on the ground under the stars.

Young Crad was so relieved and so excited to see them that he didn't think to yell or to wave his arms to announce his return. It didn't even occur to him that there would be sentries on duty and that they would be armed. He raced full-speed down the hill toward the camp.

No one challenged him.

They just opened fire.

From behind rock outcrops on either side of him came starburst muzzle-flashes and the raucous clatter of automatic weapons, and he was caught in a withering cross fire of lead. Bullets whined all around him, kicking up dirt, zinging off into the night.

Young Crad didn't know what to do, so he shut his eyes and kept on running.

Chapter Seventeen

Ryan Cawdor couldn't sleep. He sat crosslegged on the ground beside Mildred and J.B. Though they were curled up side by side, they weren't asleep, either. In the starlight he could see that their eyes were open. He figured they were thinking about the same thing he was, and feeling the same extreme sense of urgency.

The whole camp was dark. The baron had ordered no fires. Even though they were settled in a hollow, the combined glow would have lit up the surrounding hilltops and given away the position to Haldane's force in Sunspot. Darkness presented a perfect opportunity for the companions to slip away. All that kept Ryan from organizing an escape was Doc Tanner, who hadn't returned from his involuntary spy mission, yet. As soon as he showed up, they could sneak past the perimeter guards, moving in ones and twos so as not to attract attention, and join up somewhere to the west well after dawn.

There was of course a possibility that Doc wouldn't return from Sunspot at all, not by choice, but due to circumstances beyond his control. If that happened, Ryan vowed before he'd let the others get spiked he'd take out the baron personally. Shoot the horse out from under him and empty the rest of the SIG's mag into the side of his head. Before he was shot down in turn, he'd rip off that black leather mask just to see what was crawling underneath.

The mask, the man of mystery, the black gear, the big horse, the legendary cruelty and ruthlessness was the kind of stagey, cornball shit that worked on dirt-farmer audiences in a carny show.

But in real life there was a downside to theatrics.

The sudden death of the seemingly invincible commander would leave a power void that would send his army into chaos. Fighters would turn on one another to avenge old scores. Norms versus muties. Norms versus norms. Sec men without axes to grind would hightail it for their homes. Without Malosh's presence the officers couldn't maintain control. Ryan figured his companions could even get away in the resulting confusion.

The sound of rapid footfalls from the summit above broke Ryan's train of thought. Whatever it was, it was coming downhill full-tilt. As he looked up, the sentries opened fire.

By the light of flickering muzzle-flashes, he saw a lone, shadowy figure running with arms raised through a withering hellstorm of slugs.

The figure only managed a few steps before crumpling and falling, then driven by gravity and its own momentum, it rolled head over heels down the slope.

"Hold your fire!" Ryan shouted.

Although they were unsure who had given the order in the dark, the guards did the safe thing and stopped shooting.

"We got him!" one of them said.

"Nailed that sneak-ass piece of shit," said another.

Ryan was already dashing over to the still form. When he got close, he was relieved to see that the man lying on the ground was the Redbone swineherd and not Doc. He rolled the man over onto his back, expecting him to be shot full of holes and stone dead. He was surprised to see the barrel chest heaving and the button eyes blinking.

The stammered sounds "whuh-whuh-whuh-whuh" came out of the swineherd's mouth.

Ryan turned to shout for Mildred, but she and J.B. were already beside him.

Mildred quickly, expertly, checked his body for bullet wounds and, finding no evidence of serious injury, made him sit up. "It doesn't look like he's hit except for his hand," she said.

"Luck of the dimmie," was J.B.'s wry comment.

"Come on, let me see your hand," Mildred coaxed Young Crad. She carefully opened his balled fist, and held it that way while she poured a little water from her canteen on the wound to soften the congealed blood and dirt. Then she started to gently clean it with scrap of rag.

Behind them, the whole camp was on its feet, blasters out, adrenaline pumping. Malosh the Impaler had burst from his tent and was calling for his officers.

"Where's Doc?" Ryan growled through clenched teeth. "Where's the man who went to Sunspot with you?"

When Young Crad didn't answer, Ryan took hold of his baby-smooth chin, squeezed until the first two joints of his fingertips disappeared into the fleshy cheeks, and repeated the question. "Where's Doc?"

"A thing chased us…"

"What kind of thing?"

"Big. It was hunting on the old road. He told me to run and he went back to chill it."

"Did you see him chill it?"

"No."

"Did you see it chill him?" Mildred asked.

"No. He shot and shot and shot, then it got quiet. I was running hard as I could."

"You didn't go back?" Ryan said.

Young Crad shook his head. "He said to come here."

"Ryan, we don't know that he's dead," Mildred said.

"That's true, but if he was okay, he would have caught up with the droolie. He'd be here by now."

"Mebbe he's hurt?" J.B. said. "Mebbe he's down?"

Ryan swore in frustration.

"This isn't a bullet wound," Mildred told them as she poured more water over the swineherd's open palm.

At that moment Malosh stepped up behind them, accompanied by his cadre of staff officers. The baron held a burning torch that cast a ring of weak, flickering light on the ground around the companions and gave off a steady hiss. He leaned down in all his black-masked, black-caped glory. "What did you find out?" he demanded of the seated swineherd.

Crad looked up at the baron. He swallowed hard, he opened his mouth, but no sound came out. There was blind panic in his eyes.

"You'd better have found out what I asked you to. Or it's gonna be heinie-stretching time."

Crad responded by making desperate little squeak. He didn't have a clue what the baron wanted of him. But it was clear he remembered the heinie stretching.

Some things were unforgettable.

"Look!" Mildred exclaimed, raising the swineherd's palm up to the torchlight for them to see. "Look, it's the number 76! Doc must've done this. He knew Young Crad wouldn't remember it. He cut it into his hand so he couldn't lose it. So we'd have to see it."

"Smart geezer," the baron said.

"Triple smart," Ryan said.

"If there's only seventy-six soldiers in Haldane's garrison," one of the officers said, "we can overwhelm them with main force."

"Where's that scout?" Malosh said. "Get him over here."

When the scout approached, Malosh held the burning end of the torch close to the sand. "Draw the defenses for me again," he ordered.

The scout knelt and started making a sketch in the dirt with the point of his knife. Ryan had to squint his good eye to see it. First, the man drew the circular oblong of Sunspot's berm. On the south side, he put in the gorge with the interstate running through it. He crosshatched a section of highway directly below the ville, indicating a major break in the road. On the north side of the berm, and parallel to it, he sketched some narrowly spaced contour lines, which were meant to describe the steep back of the hill on which Sunspot sat. He added a path on the gorge side running from the interstate up to the ville and out the other side, bypassing the disrupted section of highway.

When the scout put in the heavy machine gun positions, Malosh said, "They've moved the emplacements since we were there last."

Together, the gun positions provided overlapping fields of fire, nearly 360 degrees of kill zone. On the south or gorge side of the berm, two widely spaced emplacements controlled the western, uphill approach from the interstate and the westernmost path leading to the ville. The path leading from the ville to the east was controlled by two more emplacements. A fifth machine gun was positioned on the north side of the berm, defending the steep hillside approach.

Malosh stuck a gloved finger in the sand, pointing out the weakest point on north side, the widest stretch of undefended berm wall.

It was the very spot Ryan would have picked.

"The main force attacks here at first light," the baron said. "On my signal, the norm fighters will breach the berm and take out the two gun posts on the west, here and here. The muties and dogs will follow them through the breach and contain any resistance inside the ville. Before I call for the main attack, I'll lead troops up the gorge in a feint, to draw the garrison's fire. Once the berm is breached and the defending gunposts are knocked out, I'll take the western path and break through on that side. Any questions?"

There were none.

Apparently it looked like a piece of cake to the officers. Ryan didn't consider five machine guns and seventy assault rifles a dessert course.

"Assemble my army," the baron said.

When the three-hundred-odd fighters stood packed in a solid mass before him in the hollow, Malosh mounted his horse and walked it a short way up the slope, far enough so he could look down on them all.

On his command, the big chestnut reared up on its hind legs, slashing its forelegs in the air. The two of them formed a stunning black silhouette in front of the starry field of sky.

A carny act, Ryan thought.

An opinion that only grew stronger when Malosh began to address his troops.

"They say life is cheap in my barony," Malosh shouted to the crowd. "They say it's thrown away on a madman's whim. They say that I'm a monster without conscience. I say that's all lies. Life is the most precious thing, that's why we fight and chill and die. To preserve it.

"We have the right and the obligation to those we hold dear to take what the rich barons in the east are too weak or too careless or too stupid to protect. The wealth of their baronies is waiting for us, but first we must conquer Sunspot. We must take it and hold it. With Sunspot in our control, we can bleed the bastard rich barons dry, and convoy the food and the loot back to our home villes and our families.

"Some of you here have not come of your own free will. Even now you are thinking about escaping before the fighting starts. I say there is no escape from death for any of us. And the only brief victory that death allows is glory, glory while we still live and breathe. I offer you the chance for that glory, the chance to carve your own bloody mark on this land, to take what is yours from it. Follow me and I will lead you into that place where the bullets whine and men scream. My glory is there, too, in the teeth of that howling gale. If a baron isn't afraid of what's to come, why should you be? You have nothing left to lose. I have everything to lose, but I won't hide from the reaper's blade."

The crowd stirred and shifted on its feet, unsure where Malosh was headed, but mesmerized by his physical presence.

"Show no mercy to any of Haldane's fighters," Malosh said. "With bullet or blade or club, dispatch them straight to hell. But let the Sunspot folk who drop their weapons and surrender live. They can fight alongside us in the battle for Nuevaville.

"The norms and the muties will follow my officers. As for those I have consigned to be cannon fodder, I would never ask another to do something I would not do myself. I will proudly lead the cannon fodder into battle."

The revelation drew an astonished gasp from the crowd.

Even Ryan was taken aback by it.

Leading a suicide squad was the last thing anyone would expect of a Deathlands baron. As a rule, barons delegated the really dangerous work to the highly expendable, easily replaceable and utterly despicable muties under their command. If barons rode into battle at all, they did so only after the conflict was well under control, to exercise their backhands by hacking off a few enemy heads, maybe emptying a few banana clips of 7.62 mm rounds into rows of bound captives.

Around him, Ryan saw awe in the faces of the new Redbone conscripts, the wounded and the young and the old and the lame. The seasoned cannon fodder, those who had marched behind Malosh before and survived, sent up a raucous, jubilant cheer at the news. When the

newcomers realized it wasn't some kind of sick joke
being played on them, they joined in the celebration.

With a single, totally unexpected gesture, the Impaler
had turned the tide of sentiment from dread and fear to
something that approached real enthusiasm for the
coming battle. He held them, not just the fodder, but the
entire three hundred in his gloved fist.

Malosh was no sham of a carny master, Ryan
realized at that moment. He was something infinitely
more dangerous.

The coldheart bastard was a rad-blasted hero.

"Nuking hell!" J.B. exclaimed in disbelief. "Most of
the fodder don't even have sticks to swing. What the
fuck is he up to?"

"He's trying to convince Sunspot that the main attack
is coming from the west, up the interstate," Ryan said.

"No better way to do that than to ride at the head of
the force himself," Mildred added. "He's a little hard to
miss in that outfit."

"And he said I had some balls," Ryan said.

"Don't tell me this rah-rah stunt changes your
opinion of the Impaler," Mildred said.

"A big set of balls doesn't make him a sweetheart."

"Any more than it makes you one?"

"Exactly."

MALOSH'S ARMY DIDN'T break camp as much as they
walked off and abandoned it. They left behind everything that wasn't vital to the battle—the tents, carts,
mules and food supplies.

The troop of cannon fodder limped after the masked
baron and his chestnut steed, heading over the hill in the

direction of the interstate. As the sacrificial ranks filed past, Ryan saw that the two Redbone swineherds, Bezoar and Young Crad, had been reunited. Not that it really mattered to him one way or another. Their fate was, well, their fate. It no longer had anything to do with his.

From horseback the baron's officers organized the procession of norms, muties and dogs. Norms moved to the front of the file, with the muties and their panting beasts bringing up the rear. Once they were in position, they began a deliberate, careful advance to the northwest, keeping to the hollows and saddles between the low hills as much as possible. The only light came from the stars, and it turned the desert into shades of gray spattered with pockets of impenetrable black.

The long row of troops in the main column was easy to get lost in. There were at least 250 souls, not counting dogs. Ryan moved slowly enough so the other norms had to pass him. In this way, without drawing attention to himself, he gradually dropped back to the end of the norm ranks, along with Mildred and J.B.

Figuring Ryan would do just that, Krysty and Jak advanced to the front of the muties until they were walking right behind their companions.

"Doc never turned up," Ryan said over his shoulder to Krysty.

"But the droolie did," J.B. said.

"For Gaia's sake, don't tell me Doc got chilled up there," the tall redhead said.

"Truth is, we don't know," Ryan told her. "He could be dead already. Or he could have been captured by Haldane's men. There's no way of finding out before we attack the ville. Malosh isn't going to let us wander off and search for him."

"We can't desert Malosh's army without making sure Doc is beyond our help," Krysty said. "We just can't."

"From the way the droolie tells it, Doc sacrificed himself to get the word back, so Malosh wouldn't skewer us," Mildred said. "So we'd have a chance to get away."

"That's why we're not going to leave him behind," Krysty said.

"He would never leave us like that," Mildred agreed.

At the sound of a snarling dog, Ryan looked over his shoulder. A swampie in a red stocking cap had moved within ten feet of them. He held the massive animal by a chain around its neck. Swampies were sour-faced by nature, but this one was extra unhappy.

"That swampie looks like his dog just died," Ryan said.

"It did," Krysty said. "I blew its head off earlier. I didn't want to, but he didn't give me any choice. That's Meconium, the boss swampie. I would've shot him, too, but I was outnumbered."

"Isn't he the same bastard who shit his pants back in Redbone?" Ryan said.

"I bust his nose good," Jak said with pride.

Ryan squinted to see. "Yeah, it's kind of flattened and bent over to the left," he said. "Can't breathe a lick through it, I'll bet."

"Doesn't bother him. He's a mouth breather," Krysty said. "And he's got himself a new dog."

And it was some dog.

The beast was nearly as tall as Meconium. It had pointed ears and huge feet. Slobber swayed from its pendulous jowls as it glowered at Ryan, head lowered, chain biting deep into its thick neck.

Ryan slipped between Krysty and Jak and spoke in hushed tones as they walked along.

"We're going to get split up once we reach the ville," he said. "The norm unit is going over the berm first."

"What are we going to do?" Krysty said.

"We don't have any choice. We have to follow Malosh's orders," Ryan told her. "It's the only way to get into Sunspot and locate Doc. If he's there, we've got to find and free him as quickly as we can, while the battle is still under way. If he isn't there, he's got to be on the interstate, mebbe wounded, mebbe dead. Whether we find him nor not, we need to regroup once we're inside the ville. We'll meet close to the western gate. We can use the confusion to slip out and head down the interstate."

"If he's in the belly of some mutie," Mildred said, "we're never going to find him."

"If we don't find Doc on the road," Ryan said, "we've got to face facts. He's on the last train west."

"Get your mutie ass back here where it belongs," growled a voice behind them.

Ryan glanced back at a man in a baseball cap armed with a 12-gauge pump.

"Belongs square on my hairy face," Meconium said, waggling his tongue between bruised and split lips.

Jak faked a move toward him and the swampie not only flinched but jumped backward behind the dog, which snarled in defense of its new master, showing long fangs, top and bottom. The animal started towing Meconium forward in the hope of taking a chunk out of Jak.

Krysty looked at the head swampie, her hand resting on her pistol butt. "Better hold that pooch nice and tight this time. I think you remember what happens if you don't."

"No more of that, rad-blast it!" the keeper of the muties said, swinging the shotgun's muzzle around. "You shoot another dog, and I'm going to blow you clean in half. Move to the rear of the line, you two. Do it, now!"

Krysty gave Ryan a wink, then she and the albino dropped back among the shuffling shadows and disappeared from sight.

IT TOOK THE BETTER PART of three hours of steady walking to circle to the north of the gorge entrance. Looking up at that side of the ridge, Ryan could only see two bonfires burning. From Sunspot's vantage point the column was invisible. Without a moon, there wasn't enough light to pick out the formation's approach.

At the base of the ridge, the officers began dividing the norm fighters into three assault waves. Ryan leaned close to one of the officers and said, "Me and my two friends would like to be in the first bunch that hits the berm, as a matter of personal pride. Is that a problem?"

The officer shook his head and whispered back, "We're gonna tear Haldane's bastards a new one this time."

Ryan waved for J.B. and Mildred to follow him to the head of the line. If they were the first ones over the breach, he figured they had the best chance of locating Doc before someone else shot or clubbed him to death.

At the officer's signal, Ryan, Mildred and J.B., and the rest of the first wave, began to climb single file up a kind of deer or goat trail that was no more than a foot wide. It zigzagged up a slope that varied between forty-five and sixty degrees. Half the time, they had to use both hands and feet to advance. There was no vegetation; it was bare rock. And they couldn't see more than a few yards above them.

The north side of the gorge was both the toughest route to attack and easiest route to defend. If Haldane's soldiers got wind of what they were doing, they were dead meat. They had no cover but the side of the hill. If the enemy started firing down on them from along the edge of the ridge, they didn't have a chance. And it was a long way to fall.

Which was why Malosh was making such a show of coming up the gorge. The feint was designed to draw attention from the real spearhead of the attack until it was too late to do anything about it.

When they neared the ridgetop, at the officer's command they fanned out in a line that paralleled the berm. Lying flat on their stomachs, they slowly crawled closer to the lip of the cliff.

Close enough for Ryan to hear the bonfire crackling and snapping. J.B. and Mildred could hear it, too. They were almost directly across from the gun emplacement.

Ryan raised his head, just to the level of his good right eye, confident that his black hair and the black night would hide him. The weapon they faced was a predark heavy machine gun, .308 caliber, belt-fed. The

M-60 was swivel mounted on the roof of a Chevrolet Suburban in front of a large hole that had been hacked in the sheet metal. Steel plate replaced the windshield and side windows. Its rear end wasn't just backed up against the berm; it was buried by it. From the looks of the vehicle, no tires on the front rims, dozens of rust-ringed bullet holes in the fenders and grille, it hadn't run in more than fifty years. Beside the emplacement a well-stoked fire roared from a fifty-five-gallon drum.

Ryan counted two soldiers behind the gun, although there could have been more inside the SUV. There was seventy feet of open ground to cross before they reached the berm.

When Ryan ducked back down, he gave J.B. and Mildred the info using hand signs. Two enemy. Then he signaled the letter M and Six-Oh. It was all they needed to know.

The sky to the east was already starting to turn from ebony to lavender. False dawn was almost upon them.

Ryan checked the SIG by feel, easing back the slide, reaching in with a fingertip, making sure he had a live round chambered.

J.B. carefully snicked back the bolt of his Uzi, putting a 9 mm round under the firing pin.

Mildred wiped the sweat from her palm on the tail of her T-shirt, then regripped her Czech wheel gun.

On the other side of Mildred, Malosh's officers knelt with a satchel charge and predark frag grens at the ready. Below them in the dark, the rest of the norm force and the muties and dogs crouched on the slope, waiting in considerable discomfort for the signal to charge the summit and break through the berm.

Then the hard clatter of blasterfire erupted from the gorge side of the ville. As the firing continued, Ryan's empty eye socket started to itch.

The fight for Sunspot had begun.

Chapter Eighteen

"For nuke's sake, don't give the droolie that fucking thing!" Bezoar protested.

Ferdinando, the one-armed leader of the cannon fodder, paused as he handed Young Crad a well-worn AK-47, steel shod butt first.

"Don't give him that blaster," Bezoar said, "unless you're looking to get shot in the ass yourself. He doesn't know one end of a blaster from the other."

The young swineherd had never been offered a functional firearm before. For him, it was a coming of age moment. He eagerly grabbed hold of the rear stock and the curved magazine and tried to pull the AK to his bosom with main force.

For a crippie, Ferdinando was triple quick. He snap-kicked Young Crad in the groin. When the stupe's knees buckled in slow mo, he jerked the weapon out of his hands and passed it over to the ten-year-old boy standing next to him.

Though the baron's cannon fodder was meant to absorb lead not dish it out, they had to throw up some blasterfire or the Haldane force would realize their assault was a ruse. As Bezoar looked around, he saw weapons being passed out to some of the old, the young and the ambulatory infirm. Even though it was dark, he could see the rest of the AKs were battered old blasters, too. Not a speck of bluing was left on the barrels or the receivers; in the starlight, they reflected silver as if chrome-plated. Their front and rear stocks were missing or held together with metal plates and screws or with overlapping winds of duct tape. Fire selector levers were busted off in either single-shot or full-auto position.

Scary ass guns.

But then again, there was no reason to give decent weapons to the walking dead.

Baron Malosh spurred his huge horse, and with a wave of his gloved hand, led them out of camp.

The uplifting sense of power and pride the baron had instilled in Bezoar with the eve of battle/get your glory speech faded with every limping step. The elder swineherd knew they were going to die.

And soon.

Unlike the men, women and children marching behind him who were still bright-eyed and eager for the fight, he had a hard time seeing anything positive in drawing his final breath.

"You shouldn't have come back for me," he told the baby-faced swineherd at his side. "You should've run off when you had the chance. Now instead of just me, we're both gonna be dead."

"I was too scared to run," Young Crad admitted. "I had nowhere to go. Are we really gonna die?"

"Where do you think we're going now? To a picnic breakfast? Hell, yes, we're gonna die. We're gonna all get shot to pieces."

The elder swineherd fell into the hypnotizing rhythm

of the march. Step, limp, step, he leaned heavily on his willow fork crutch, thinking about the life he had lived. Bezoar was weighing days already long spent. Young Crad was too dimwitted to comprehend the need to make an accounting. And besides, every day had been pretty much the same for him since he was a baby. All pigs. All the time. Bezoar, comparatively speaking, had lived a rich, full life.

In his thirty-eight years, he had had several common-law wives and had fathered many children. Once he had owned more than a hundred pigs, and he had paid others to take care of them. Then he lost everything, thanks to jolt. Wives. Family. Jack. Pigs. Youth. Mental stability. The only job his jolt-holed brain could handle was herding swine. Sometimes he could still taste the white crystalline powder, hot and bitter in the back of his throat, and he caught himself waiting with every muscle tensed, every nerve poised to receive the unholy, wipeout rush that never came. Bezoar's life in retrospect was a cause for both regret and celebration. But mostly regret. And at the end of his allotment of hours and minutes, his only friend in the world was a triple-stupe droolie who smelled even worse than he did.

He could feel the pain building in his bad leg as he hopped along on his crutch. The original damage to his knee, like every other catastrophe in his life, had been jolt-related. When he had failed to pay the local supplier of the drug, he got his kneecap shattered with a ballpeen hammer. It was meant to serve as a warning. It should have been taken as a warning.

It wasn't.

Beside him, Young Crad tunelessly whistled through his front teeth.

"Shut the fuck up," he told the droolie.

They walked along in silence for a long time, following the horse tracks in the sand.

When the cannon fodder column finally reached the interstate and the dropped bridge, Malosh turned them toward Sunspot, detouring around the dropped overpass. On the far side of the rubble, because of the highway's upward incline, the going got more difficult for Bezoar. It forced him to lean even harder on the crutch. It was too dark to see the mouth of the gorge in the distance, but the silhouette of the ridgetop against the stars and the fire lights on the left-hand rim gave Bezoar a sense of its size. And menace.

To him it seemed like the killing chute of an immense slaughterhouse.

Where was the glory in being led single-file into an abattoir? he asked himself. And unlike slaughtered cows or a hogs, their meat would rot in the desert sun. Fly food.

In front of them, Baron Malosh's big chestnut suddenly reared and sidestepped, detouring around a section of ruined road.

Bezoar caught a powerful reek of ammonia. It got stronger as they advanced farther. Some kind of vile liquid spoor had been sprayed over the ground.

Young Crad recognized the stench. "It's the thing," he said. "It's what dug up all the graves."

"Where?" Bezoar said, swiveling his head to look from one shadowy side of the road to the other.

"Take it easy," Ferdinando told him. "It won't dare attack. There are too many of us."

"How do you know that?"

"It was hanging around the last time I fought here, when the dead horse fell on me and I lost my arm," the head of the cannon fodder said. "Seemed like there was only the one. Like a big cat, I guess it needs a lot of territory to hunt. We never saw it during the day, we just found the tracks in the sand along the side of the road. And the piss or shit, whatever it is it leaves behind. It probably lives in a hole somewhere out in the bush. Only comes out at night. Can't bury the dead deep enough or pile enough rocks on the graves to keep it from digging them up. Free eats for a big-time scavenger."

"What the hell is it?" Bezoar said.

"Nobody knows for sure."

"Legs," Young Crad said. "Lots of legs."

"Yeah, and it moves so fast your eye can't hardly follow it. We never found any part of the dead ones that it took, either. Snatches up its live victims the same way. Zip and they're just gone. Probably carries them back to its hidey-hole."

"Alive?"

"Let's hope not."

After they'd walked a little farther up the grade, Ferdinando asked, "You made your peace, yet, pig man?"

"Working on it," Bezoar said.

"Well, don't work too long. Once we step into the gorge, nukin' hell's gonna break loose. You and your triple-stupe buddy better be ready to meet your maker."

For somebody in exactly the same position they were—about to be shot to shit—Ferdinando was pretty fucking chipper. But not nearly as chipper as Baron

Malosh. The masked man rode tall in the saddle, cantering his horse this way and that, leading the column around the scattering of open, emptied graves.

False dawn was breaking in front of them as they neared the entrance to the gorge. In the faint light, Bezoar could just make out the looming walls of rock that bracketed the interstate. Blazing fire cans on the ridge lit up the sides of the three gun positions that commanded and controlled the stretch of ancient highway. The line of sacrificial lambs was about to enter a well-established kill zone. Bezoar knew the heavy blasters outside Sunspot's berm had to have the range locked in. It was too dark to see clustered bullet holes and rows of spawl marks strafed into the roadbed. And of course, there were no bodies or body parts to stumble over, as the creature had taken care of cleanup.

Malosh's strategy was to move in just before the break of dawn so the ville defenders couldn't see that they were up against a token force of cotton tops, peglegs and eight-year-olds.

Dread hung over Bezoar in a sickening fog as they advanced into the jaws of the gorge. Had they been seen by the enemy already? There was no cover that he could see ahead. It was a four-lane highway, with no divider except for a dirt strip. He couldn't make out the gun barrels on the high slope above but he imagined their gun sights. Tracking. Tracking. Tracking. He lowered his head and trudged onward, though it was even harder for him to walk, what with one knee stiff and the other gone all to rubber.

If the gunners on the ridge saw them, they held their fire, letting the column advance until it was completely within the kill zone.

"Get ready to run," Ferdinando said.

"Where to?"

"There's cover on the far side of the turnoff."

At that moment Malosh turned to his troops and shouted, "Run!" As the cry echoed through the gorge, he spurred his horse, galloping the last hundred feet to the edge of the blown-up section of road.

It was all Bezoar could do to keep from being trampled by the people running for their lives behind him. Young Crad grabbed him under the armpit on the bad knee side and half carried him forward or he would have certainly been swept under and crushed.

On the other side of the predark turnoff to the Welcome Center, Bezoar could see weak light reflecting off small pools and trenches filled with standing water. The ruined stretch of road was littered with mounds of earth and thick, uptilted slabs of concrete reinforced with rebar. Such was the only cover on offer.

As Bezoar and Young Crad three-legged raced to the disrupted zone, Sunspot's gunposts cut loose, raining blasterfire down on them from above. Heavy-caliber slugs sparked off concrete and steel, kicking up dust and sending shards of road metal flying.

Ahead of them, Ferdinando leaped over the first of the water hazards and dived behind a three-foot-high pile of rubble. Young Crad gave Bezoar a hard shove, sending him and his crutch skidding into an open trench. The water was cold and hip-deep, but it was shielded from incoming fire by a canted slab of concrete.

As Crad jumped in the water beside him, other fodderites dashed or limped or crawled past, looking for a place to hide.

Although it was getting lighter by the second, Haldane's gunners couldn't have seen exactly what they were shooting at. They laid overlapping waves of machine-gun fire onto the road, hosing it down with lead.

The effect was like random meat grinder.

The slow and the unfortunate were chopped down in droves. Flicked to earth. Staggered. Not just chilled.

Disintegrated by converging, triangulated blaster-fire.

A man in his forties lurched toward them, his right shoulder blown off, arm hanging by thread of sinew. As he clutched his terrible wound, he was hit in the back by dozens of down-angled rounds. Which opened his torso from throat to crotch and emptied his body cavity in an awful whoosh.

The wash of hot blood and guts sprayed over Bezoar's head. Gagging, he crouched lower, chin under water, unable to breathe for his own fear. He could feel the ground shaking underfoot from the ravening impacts of machine-gun bullets.

The sky was lightening apace.

In dawn's glimmer, Bezoar saw piles of still bodies. He saw quivering bodies. Others crawled, mortally wounded, screaming as bullets stitched up their backs, swallowed up in clouds of dust. The water in the swine-herds' trench had turned red.

Of the hundred or so who marched into the valley of death, eighty survivors had found cover.

Bezoar was astonished to see that Malosh the Impaler was still astride his horse, riding back and forth while bullets sailed all around him, taunting the gun positions.

The other fodder was stunned by his bravery, too. The baron and his horse seemed impervious to alloys of lead. When he spurred his steed behind a wide, uptilted section of roadway and dismounted, the shooting from above abruptly stopped.

"Ready for some payback?" he shouted through a gloved hand to his human sponges.

A ragged cheer went up.

A bit less enthusiastic than before, Bezoar noted. If Malosh's life was in fact charmed, sprawled on the ground all around them was proof that charm wasn't catching.

"Open fire!" the baron cried.

Ferdinando echoed the order to the troops. "Shoot! Shoot! Get the bastards!"

The armed fodder poked their scarred assault rifles around and over chunks of concrete and mounds of dirt. AKs barked single-shot and streamed blasterfire along the destroyed section of highway. The more cautious shooters fired blind and one-handed, upward in the general direction of the ville. Others stuck their heads out from behind cover and actually aimed.

They were the unlucky ones.

Sunspot's gun positions resumed firing, this time with muzzle-flashes to aim at. Whether what happened next was the result of concentrated incoming fire or some of the junk AKs blowing up on their own, blow up they did, like frag grens. What metal and wood the shooters didn't absorb with their bodies and heads flew through the air.

Young Crad shielded Bezoar with his wide chest, and jammed his head under water. When Crad let him up, the elder swineherd sputtered and choked, but he didn't complain. Not ten feet away, a cotton-topped shooter clutched a shattered buttstock driven through the side of his throat. Moaning, he struggled in vain to pull the thing from his neck. A little farther along, a young boy lay with his cheek pressed to the ground. Jutting from between his dead staring eyes was a dark shape. Part of the receiver and gas cylinder had been driven through his forehead.

Those with assault rifles that didn't explode or jam kept on shooting. Ferdinando moved up and down the ragged firing line and passed out extra 30-round mags. The thousands of unaimed rounds being expended weren't a waste, any more than the dead fodder that decorated the battle field. They were the cost of victory. The enemy for its part was unleashing tens of thousands of rounds. And every bullet fired in this direction was a bullet that couldn't be used to turn back the main attack.

When there was lull in the firing from Sunspot, Bezoar could hear Malosh laughing. "Conserve your ammo!" the baron shouted down the line. "Space your shots. Let 'em burn out their gun barrels."

The elder swineherd saw Malosh turn to his horse and open one of the saddle bags. He took out a fat-barreled, orange-colored handblaster. He broke open the barrel to make sure it was loaded, then snapped it shut. Cocking the strange weapon, the baron aimed it over the top of the concrete slab that protected him and his horse.

The pistol made a hollow pop when he fired it. The round trailed a thin coil of smoke as it sailed away. It didn't sail fast. Bezoar could easily follow its path. It flew in a high, looping arc toward Sunspot. High above the berm walls, it exploded.

The bright red flash against the lavender sky signaled the beginning of the end.

Chapter Nineteen

Doc Tanner sat huddled with his back pressed against a wall of hurricane fence, his long legs tucked up under his chin. His hands and feet were unbound, but his LeMat and swordstick had been confiscated by Haldane's men. The holding cell in which he had been placed was actually a cage, with wire on five sides and a six-by-twelve concrete pad for a floor. Completely open to the elements, it stood next to the Welcome Center building. Before the nukecaust it was a locked utility and storage area.

Now it was death row.

Twenty feet away, a fire blazed in a fifty-five-gallon drum. Two armed guards stood beside the barrel. Behind them were the ville's extensive communal gardens.

Doc tried to move as little as possible. Moving hurt. He was sore from his lengthy interrogation by Haldane's sec men, which consisted of short periods of questioning interrupted by long periods of kicking and punching. They had asked him how close Malosh's army was. They had asked him if attack was imminent. How many troops he had? Did he have artillery? They asked him what happened to the triple-stupe droolie.

Doc had chosen to say nothing except "I do not know."

To offer any information to his interrogators meant committing to something that he would have had to keep track of.

After a few hours the soldiers realized they could kill him but they couldn't break him. Killing him would have robbed the garrison of the drama of the hanging ceremony, certainly the high point of the week. And on top of that, they had gotten tired of knocking him around.

During the questioning, Doc flashed back to torture he had previously endured, at the hands of Cort Strasser. Compared to him, Haldane's men were pikers.

The knowledge that Malosh and his army were coming, and soon, helped Doc endure the punishment. He knew that Haldane's men were outnumbered, three to one. If he wasn't going to survive the battle for Sunspot, he was confident that most of his torturers weren't, either. He would dance at the end of a rope, satisfied that he had saved his dear companions' lives and that they in turn would avenge his murder.

The sudden roar of heavy machine guns from outside the berm made the guards at the burn barrel jump. As the clattering blasterfire roared on and on, the Welcome Center garrison doors banged open and armed troops raced to their battle stations. One of the barrel guards took off, as well, disappearing around a corner on a dead run.

The remaining guard, who had enthusiastically participated in the interrogation, looked over at the caged Doc Tanner.

Doc rose to his feet as the short, skinny man stepped up to the wire, a nasty look on his weather-seamed face.

"Think your pal Malosh is gonna save you?" the guard said, dropping his AK's fire selector lever to full-auto and sticking the muzzle through the fence. "Think again."

There was nowhere for Doc to go in the narrow cage, nowhere that bullets couldn't find him, so he stood perfectly still.

Before the guard could pull the assault rifle's trigger, he was hit from behind and slammed face-first into the mesh, grimacing in pain. Steel points protruded through the front of his T-shirt, pitching four little pup tents in the fabric. Black blood drooled from his parted lips, spilling down his chest.

Moving out of the now-fixed line of fire, Doc saw Isabel standing behind the guard, her hands gripping the handle of a pitchfork. She had stuck the soldier in the back with such force that she had driven the eighteen-inch tines through his chest.

With a vicious twist, she freed the fork. And when the guard staggered backward, clutching his chest with both hands, she pivoted from her hips, slamming the end of the fork handle into the side of his head. He dropped to his knees, vomiting blood in a torrent.

She jabbed him with the business end of the fork and he toppled to his side on the ground, twitching helplessly.

Doc had no doubt that either of the blindingly fast blows would have been enough to chill him. They were that savage.

Isabel put down her weapon and searched the dead man's pockets. She quickly found the keys to the cage's lock.

"Madam, I am forever in your debt," he said as she opened the door to his cell.

"No time for thanks, let's go." She pulled the AK from the wire where it hung by its muzzle and front sight.

"I must collect my own armament before we proceed," Doc told her. "I know where it is."

Ignoring her protests, he trotted around the side of the building and pushed through the Welcome Center's front doors. Leaning against the cinder-block wall was a pair of huge, two-inch-thick steel plates designed to reinforce the flimsy entry doors. Torches in stanchions lit a hallway that led to the reception area. It was obvious that men had been sleeping on the tiled floor. There were mattresses of piled cardboard, ratty blankets and dirty clothes scattered around. There was also evidence that at some earlier time, intense fighting had taken place inside the building. Everywhere he looked there were bullet craters.

Doc made a beeline for the information desk, which was pocked and splintered with slug holes. He rounded the counter and bent behind it. Fumbling on the top shelf he found his ebony-handled walking stick. He unsheathed the rapier blade to make sure it hadn't been damaged. Satisfied that the edge was intact, he started looking for his handblaster.

"Hurry up," Isabel urged him.

As she spoke, the door behind the counter banged open and a soldier stepped out. He was as surprised to see Doc as Doc was to see him.

Before the man could swing his assault rifle around on its shoulder strap and bring the muzzle to bear on

Doc, before Isabel could swing her own weapon up to shoot him, the old man snatched up his sword and lunged from his knees, driving with both legs. The rapier's point entered just below the soldier's sternum, and lickety split it slipped into his torso like a well-oiled scabbard, all the way to the hilt. As Doc whipped the blade out, he rolled his wrist and forearm, cutting a precise, overhand figure eight, which severed the heart from its major blood vessels. The soldier was dead before he hit the floor.

Doc wiped the blade on the man's shirttail.

"Get your blaster, let's go!" Isabel said.

Doc found the LeMat and its Mexican rig holster in a cardboard box on the bottom shelf. "After you, my dear," he said as he strapped the hand-tooled belt to his waist.

Outside the Welcome Center, blasterfire from the ville's gun positions raged on, unabated. He could hear intermittent answering fire from attackers at the bottom of the gorge. Ineffective fire, as it was directed at hardened positions and yards-thick berm walls.

Doc followed Isabel past the portable gibbet where he had been scheduled to hang. As he ran under the basketball backboard and its stiff, empty noose, he smiled.

It was a fine day to die, but not that way.

The ville's head woman cut across the compound, moving low and fast. She took him between the rows of wheelless Winnebagos, converted semitrailers and cargo containers where the people of Sunspot made their homes. No one stepped out of the shadows to challenge them. All of Haldane's soldiers had moved to defensive positions on the berm. Accustomed to invasion, the ville folk had taken cover.

Isabel led him to one of the cargo containers and pushed aside the sheet of opaque plastic that was its door. The windowless space was lit by a single torch. Tiers of wooden bunks lined one wall, all empty; an oil drum stove stood in the far corner. Two men were waiting inside. At Isabel's signal the two men shifted the cold stove off its wooden platform, then swung the platform aside, revealing a hole braced with timbers, leading down into blackness.

At that moment Doc realized that the folks of Sunspot weren't the meek victims that they seemed.

Isabel shoulder slung her AK and grabbed the torch from its stanchion. "Stay close, or you'll get lost," she warned him.

Doc followed her into the hole. Four feet down was a dirt floor. Ahead in the hissing torchlight, under timbered bracing, was a narrow, dusty tunnel. The ceiling was so low that Doc had to drop to his hands and knees and crawl.

After thirty feet or so, the tunnel grew taller and the earthen walls, floor and ceiling gave way to bedrock. Doc got to his feet, though he still had to lower his head to keep it from hitting the roof. The passage was triangular-shaped, narrower at the bottom than the top, a natural fissure in the stone.

Because of the tunnel's gradual turns it was difficult for Doc to keep track of their direction. Though the heavy machine-gun fire was muffled by the stone overhead, he could still hear its ominous rumble. They encountered numerous pitch-dark side passages in the bare rock. He had no way of telling whether they were dead ends.

Doc tapped Isabel on the shoulder and said, "Do these passages provide the scagworms access to the ville proper?"

"They do, unfortunately. We've blocked off the tunnels we know they are using, but they keep finding new ways in."

"This is how they decimated your stock of pigs."

"Hogs are no match for the big old scagworm sows. They burrow up under the sty, get hold of the hogs' legs and pull them down into the tunnels. Even though we knew what was coming, when it happened, it happened so fast we couldn't stop it. The poor bastard guarding the last pig jumped into the hole after it. He let out a scream and was never seen again."

"So they're fond of long pig, as well."

"They like their food alive and kicking. And warm-blooded."

After they had traveled for a few minutes more, Isabel hopped down into wide, low-ceilinged stone chamber brightly lit by a ring of torches. Doc paused on the verge. Leaning against the far wall he saw a row of AKs and olive-drab ammo cans. Armed men and women, at least twenty-five of them, stood waiting, grim-faced.

As Doc dropped down into the room, the muzzles of all the assault rifles swung up to cover him.

"Put up your hands," Isabel ordered him.

"As you wish."

"Are you a spy for Baron Malosh?" she demanded.

Doc momentarily considered denying the accusation, but decided it was time for him to start telling the truth. "A most unwilling spy," he told her. "Malosh holds my dearest friends as hostages. Their lives hang in the balance. I had no choice."

"You bastard. You lied to me."

"Would you lie to save your people?"

"I have lied. I have chilled to save them."

"And you are ready to die in that cause?"

"Of course."

"Then what separates us is a distinction without a difference, my dear."

"The difference is you put my people at risk," she said.

"The risk existed, whether I cooperated with Malosh or not. He is intent on retaking this ville."

"Why did you walk away from me last night?"

"I would no more dishonor you, Isabel, than I would myself."

Isabel gave him a searching look. She was handsome, brave, intelligent and utterly capable. There was the promise of great tenderness in her lovely eyes.

"It was not for lack of desire, I assure you," Doc said. "I could not betray you in that way. Thankfully such an abomination was not part of the terms the Impaler dictated to me. Madam, I did only what I had to do in order to save my friends, nothing more. I owe them my life, many times over. If it costs me my life now, so be it. Do what you will."

After a pause, Isabel waved for her people to lower their weapons.

"If you thought I was really Malosh's spy, why did you not just let them execute me?" Doc asked.

"My husband was hanged by Haldane's head sec man, Bollinger," Isabel said. "Have you ever seen a person chilled that way?"

"Regrettably, yes."

"It broke Paul's neck and stretched it until it was two feet long," she told him, her violet eyes flashing in the torchlight. "He was Sunspot's duly elected leader. Paul never personally raised a hand against either one of the barons, or their sec men. He was trying to hold things together, trying to keep as many ville folk alive as he could. Some people here called him an appeaser. But it wasn't true. He wanted freedom for the ville, an end to occupation. He did his best to protect the emerging underground. It was Paul who discovered the honeycomb of tunnels under the ville. The same slippages of rock that produced Sunspot's sweet springs also produced the underground passages, which haven't been completely explored because there are so many of them, and because of the danger of falling into deep chasms or being trapped by cave-ins.

"Though Paul tried, he couldn't control a small group of ville hotheads. They insisted on not just sabotaging, but chilling our oppressors. It started with poisonings in the garrison mess, which were blamed on bad water, bad food, or contagious disease. Bloody revenge murders weren't so easily dismissed. Bollinger caught the guilty ones and hanged Paul, too, because he hadn't turned them in."

"Why didn't you side with Malosh, then?"

"One baron is just as bad as the other. Both of them bleed us dry. Which one was in charge at the time didn't matter. It could have as easily been Malosh who hanged Paul."

"How have you kept this tunnel system a secret?"

"The entrances are concealed inside the cargo containers. For reasons of personal safety, the barons' troopers don't like to enter them. When they do search our homes, it's over quickly. There is another entrance near the latrines in the garden."

"You intend to throw off your shackles by force of arms?"

"We have been planning it ever since Paul's murder. We have armed ourselves with good weapons and ammo, stolen from our enemies."

"Do you really think you can defeat both Malosh and Haldane?"

"We have no choice."

"Indeed, it appears you do not."

Isabel stepped up to him and said, "Will you fight with us?"

"Either my companions are safe or they are not. Either way, there is nothing more I can do for them at present. Under the circumstances I would be most honored to join your cause. My gun and my sword are at your service, madam."

No sooner had he finished speaking than a string of muted explosions burst almost directly overhead.

"Grens," Doc said.

Then came the clatter of machine-gun fire, likewise muted by the layers of intervening rock.

"Malosh's real attack has started," Isabel said.

A moment later the subterranean room was jarred by a rocking blast. The walls and floor shuddered violently, and with an awful grinding roar, a section of the stone ceiling broke free and came down on top of them. As Tanner grabbed Isabel's arm and swung her out of the path of the massive deadfall, clouds of dust whooshed over them and the other survivors, extinguishing most of the torches.

They coughed and gasped in the dim light. More gren explosions came from above; though less powerful, they still shook the chamber. With a groan, another chunk of the weakened roof broke loose and crashed to the floor.

"Gather the weapons and ammo!" Isabel shouted. "We've got to get out of here before the rest of the ceiling comes down."

The ville fighters hurried to obey her.

Doc picked up a dropped torch so he could help. As he stepped forward, he almost kicked a man's head that was sticking out of the rubble on the floor. The face was a strangled black, the eyes popped out of their sockets and dangling upon his blood-suffused cheeks. Hidden from view, his torso had been crushed flat by a huge block of stone. He had bitten off his own tongue by reflex.

It lay on the floor under his nose.

Chapter Twenty

Ryan stretched the cramps out of his legs while blasterfire raged on the gorge side of ville. He figured the Haldane sec men who weren't assigned to defend the north wall would be scrambling up the slope of loose scree on the south side, eager for the chance to rip off a few clips at a pinned down enemy. The machine gun in front of them was his one and only concern.

The steady chatter of blasterfire was loud enough to cover conversation. Ryan waved for J.B. and Mildred to come closer to him.

"The big gun position is going to be tough to crack," he said. "Its kill zone runs through nearly 180 degrees of arc. And there's just bare ground between it and us."

"The officers brought along plenty of grens," Mildred countered. "Fraggers."

"The emplacement's SUV is buttoned up tight with plate steel," Ryan told them. "Windshield and side windows are covered. The wag is sitting on its rims, and the undercarriage is mebbe six inches off the ground. The only decent-size opening is in the roof behind the machine gun, the port for the gunner. It's going to take a hell of a pitch to drop a gren down that hole."

"Nothing but net," Mildred said.

"Nukin' hell!" J.B. exclaimed, looking up as a flare

burst high over the ville. It reflected in his spectacles, casting a sickly red light as it drifted down out of sight behind the wall of dirt and rubble.

If they could see Malosh's attack signal, the trooper behind the Haldane machine gun could, too.

So much for surprise.

"Get ready," Ryan said, tightening his grip on the SIG-Sauer and bracing himself to charge over the top of the cliff.

Farther down the cliff edge, he saw Malosh's officers yank the pins on the grens they each held. Counting out loud, they let the safety levers flip off, then lobbed the bombs in high arcs toward the emplacement.

Pure chuck and duck.

The machine gun opened up at once, strafing the edge of the cliff with 7.62 mm NATO rounds.

Ryan couldn't hear the grens land because of the roar of blasterfire. The hard, cracking explosions were impossible to miss, however.

Whump! Whump! Whump!

As the companions crouched, shrap sizzled and whined through the air scant inches above their heads. The stench of burned Comp B swept over them.

And the machine gun went dead.

Mildred and J.B. started to move forward. Ryan put out both arms, holding them back.

Other norm fighters concealed below the summit weren't as cautious. Following their officers' command, the first twenty vaulted the cliff edge and charged.

The M-60 came to life at once.

Amid the 550-round-per-minute thunder and the howl of flying lead, men and women screamed and fell.

Those who weren't flattened by gutshots or head shots in the first twenty-five feet abruptly reversed course and tried desperately to dive or jump over the cliff edge to cover.

Some of these unlucky ones were lifted in the air by multiple bullet impacts and thrown over the cliff. They toppled soundlessly down the cliff face. Others reached the edge only to be cut down before they could make the headfirst leap. A man whose skull was largely shot away slipped past J.B., who instinctively reached out for his arm and missed. The body slid by, limp as a rag bag, rapidly gathering speed.

The first wave of the attack was over. None of the attackers had survived it.

When the officers reared back and chucked a second round of grens, the emplacement ceased fire. This time the gunner wasn't caught off guard. When he saw the grens arcing toward him, he abandoned the gun and ducked into the protection of the armored wag.

With three distinct thunks the grens hit the hood of the Suburban and bounced or rolled off.

Again, they hadn't managed to hit the hole.

Explosions ripped the air, shrap screamed and smoke billowed.

"Go!" the officers shouted to the norm fighters.

The second wave of attackers surged over the hilltop, shouting at the tops of their lungs. They burst onto the killing ground, now a blood-slick obstacle course of sprawled bodies. The machine gun roared from its hard site, sweeping through the skirmish line like a weed trimmer. The fire was so concentrated that some of the poor bastards were nearly cut in two. All were cut down.

Before the wounded could crawl over the edge to safety, the gunner methodically stitched up their backs with lead.

This was going nowhere.

"Give me a gren!" Ryan bellowed through cupped hands at the officer closest to him.

Without hesitation, the man dug out another fragger from his bag and underhanded it to him.

Ryan caught the bomb in his left hand. "Cover me," he told J.B. and Mildred.

He waited for the officers to pitch the third helping of predark grens. He waited for the rocking triple blast. But he didn't wait for the smoke to clear to gauge the effect.

An instant after the overlapping explosions shook the air, with the shrap still flying, Ryan was up and over the cliff edge. He ran low and quick through the rolling white smoke, his bootheels sliding and crunching over the bodies and body parts.

Blasterfire rattled at him from another gunpost far to his right, the one that defended Sunspot's western gate. The machine-gun bullets slapped and shook the bodies at his heels, but no fire came from the smoke-shrouded emplacement in front of him.

As he raced for the bumper of the SUV, the gren smoke began to thin out. A dark head and shoulders popped up behind the roof-mounted M-60. Ryan saw the gunner shoulder the stock and grip the foregrip. Then he tipped the barrel down to put him in its sights. Ryan threw himself against the Suburban's grille as the machine gun cut loose, blasting ragged rents through the leading edge of the hood, just above his head.

Smoke gone, target acquired, J.B. and Mildred opened fire on the shooter from the edge of the cliff. A combination of 9 mm rounds and .38 caliber slugs rained on the makeshift gun turret, sparking off the steel-plate armor.

The gunner reacted by swinging up his sights, walking a stream of hot lead toward them.

With the machine gun howling overhead, Ryan holstered his SIG and pulled the gren's safety clip and yanked the pin. Holding down the safety lever, he crawled from the front to the left side of the wag. When he was below the front passenger door, as close to the gunner as he could get, he let the lever flip off. He sprang to his feet and stuffed the gren in the gap between the edge of the hole and the very startled man's back.

One thousand one.

The gunner tried to turn the muzzle on him, but Ryan blocked the barrel and gas cylinder's swing with his forearm. Suckers were hot, too. Burned his skin right through his jacket.

One thousand two.

Ryan looked into the man's eyes.

A dead man's eyes.

One thousand three.

The gunner pulled the machine gun's trigger and held it pinned, firing wild, trying to take the one-eyed man to hell with him.

One thousand four.

Ryan dropped to his knees, letting the roaring barrel pivot over his head.

Whump!

The explosion knocked the one-eyed man flat on his butt and made him go both deaf and blind for an awful instant. But the real force of the blast was focused upward, through the aperture in the SUV's roof. It blew the gunner clean out of the makeshift turret. He landed facedown and smoking on the Suburban's hood. Half of him did, anyway, from the waist up. The rest was a goulash of bloody shreds and stripped bones.

Smoke continued to pour out of the turret hole and for a few frantic seconds belted .308 rounds cooked off, hammering in vain against the inside of the armor plating.

When the cook-offs stopped, Ryan waved J.B. and Mildred forward.

The gun emplacement at the gate tried to nail them as they crossed the bloody ground in a sprint. A volley of 7.62 mm rounds plowed the earth and spanked the bodies in their wake. They dived for cover behind the smoking hulk of the Suburban. Protected by the side of the emplacement, J.B. and Mildred knelt next to Ryan, gasping for breath.

The one-eyed man looked back toward the cliff edge and saw one of the officers running toward the berm with a hefty satchel charge.

The smoke from inside the SUV had thinned.

Way too quickly.

Cross ventilation.

J.B. noticed it, too. His eyes widened behind his smeared spectacles.

"The gun position has got an open exit door on the ville side of the berm," Ryan said. "Let's use it."

J.B. climbed into the hulk first, followed by Mildred.

"Oh, man, there were at least three guys in here," she groaned as she dropped down. "They're all turned to spray paint."

Ryan slipped behind the ruined M-60 and lowered himself through the hole in the roof. At once he was slammed by the coppery sweet reek and the intense residual heat. Blood and pulverized bone and pureed intestinal contents dripped from every interior surface. Eyes on the prize. Stuck through the Suburban's open rear doors was a three-foot-wide, corrugated steel culvert pipe that ran through the berm wall. J.B. had already disappeared down it. Mildred was right on his heels.

As Ryan dropped to his knees, something heavy landed on the backs of his calves. He looked over his shoulder to see the canvas satchel of high explosives. About thirty pounds worth, he figured. He didn't try to throw it back out again. If the strap got hung up on the machine gun, or if the officer was still outside, throwing it wouldn't do any good. Throwing it would just eat up precious seconds. He didn't waste them cursing, either.

"Move!" he yelled at Mildred and J.B. "Move!" Then he crawled over the slimy gore like a madman, hurling himself into the narrow culvert. He couldn't fault the officer's strategy, even if he was about to be made a victim of it. It made perfect sense to set a charge in a tunnel under the wall. Get a much bigger hole that way.

Ryan slid out of the open end of the pipe and hit the ground running.

J.B. and Mildred were moving toward the nearest cover, ignorant of what was coming. There was no time to fill in the pertinent details. "Hurry!" Ryan cried. "Faster!"

A split second before the explosion, they ducked behind a rusting cabover camper propped up on concrete blocks.

Too close to the SUV as it turned out.

Way too close.

The boom was tremendous. It made the previous gren blasts seem like firecrackers. The pressure wave alone knocked the camper off its blocks and it tipped over, almost landing on top of them. A heartbeat later came a flash of intense heat, then boiling clouds of dust and smoke. Big rocks and chunks of concrete sailed down through the obscuring smoke, thudding to earth all around them.

The satchel charge had blown the Suburban apart and taken out a pie-shaped wedge of berm. As the smoke lifted, Malosh fighters poured through the gap.

Only to be met by ravening waves of automatic weapons fire from the Haldane defenders.

Bullets slammed into the roof of the overturned camper, slicing ragged holes in the sheet aluminum. Ryan, J.B., and Mildred whirled to face the fresh attack. Some seventy-five yards away, Haldane soldiers crouched next to the culvert opening of the gateside gunpost, firing assault rifles.

Ryan swung the SIG up in a two-handed grip, punching out a tight string of single shots.

KRYSTY AND JAK WERE waiting on the path halfway up the cliffside when the satchel charge detonated with a sudden flash of light and a rolling boom. The concussion shook loose dirt and scads of small rocks, causing minor avalanches all along the slope. Krysty had to put a hand out to steady herself.

Then it started raining.

Boulders and chunks of concrete blown sky-high bounced down the cliff face, as did the gun post's front axle and V-8 engine block. The norms closer to the summit were swept off the path by falling heavy debris. Screaming, cartwheeling bodies flew past. Along the base of the cliff, a rubbish heap of rock, metal and torn flesh accumulated.

Krysty thanked Gaia that she hadn't seen Ryan in free fall. That didn't mean he or the others were okay, though. The explosion was much more powerful than she'd expected, and that worried her.

Someone shouted down from the cliff top. "They've broken through the berm. Let's go! Everyone up!"

Krysty and Jak advanced behind the last of the norm fighters. Behind them came the swampies and their highly excited dogs. The hellhounds could smell the blood and the fear in the air. Krysty could smell it, too. The drooling animals scrambled up the path, half dragging their stumpy handlers.

As Krysty climbed toward Sunspot ville, the small-arms fire above intensified. Haldane defenders were trying to turn back the spear point of the assault.

With Jak at her side, she jumped onto the summit, her Smith & Wesson 640 in her hand. The first thing she saw was the smoking ruin where the SUV gunpost had been. The satchel charge had blown a twelve-foot gap in the berm. Nothing of the wag remained. Ryan, Mildred and J.B. were nowhere in sight. Heavy blasterfire sawed back and forth inside the berm as they ran through the litter of bodies and body parts. The corpses closest to the explosion were burning like guttering candles.

Jak led Krysty into the breach. The norm fighters were jammed up on the far side, pinned by blasterfire from the maze of wags and semitrailers, and from the sides of the Welcome Center and the garden behind.

"Follow me!" Korb shouted to their backs, turning left along the inside of the berm wall.

There was no time to locate their companions. To stand still was suicide. Krysty and the albino melded into the mutie force, sprinting across Sunspot's hammered ground with the swampies and their slathering dogs. The norm fighters put up a wall of covering fire, allowing most of their genetically challenged comrades to safely slip into the northernmost edge of the wag-and-trailer shantytown.

Korb led the forty-five-mutie unit into a narrow, rutted path between rusting vehicular hovels, the tallest of which was about fifteen feet high. The back streets of Sunspot weren't laid out in anything that remotely resembled a gridwork. The tracks between structures wound back and forth, and the bends concealed what lay just beyond them. Empty clotheslines sagged across the lanes. No ville folk were in evidence. They either were hiding under their mattresses or they'd taken cover elsewhere. The norm contingent was drawing the defenders' full attention. For the first time, Krysty heard grens detonating inside the berm. There was no way of telling whose grens they were.

They had only traveled about fifty feet into the maze

when blasterfire barked at them from the rear corner of a semitrailer dead ahead. With bullets whining around their heads, the mutie fighters ducked into the crudely hacked doorways and between the junkyard wags. The shooting abruptly stopped.

"Let the dogs have 'em!" Meconium shouted to his fellow swampies.

Krysty and Jak watched as the hellhounds were unchained and released to do their worst.

The pack took off down the path like greyhounds after jackrabbits. Gleefully baying, they disappeared around the bend.

A fraction of a second later the muties heard snarls, screams and bursts of blasterfire.

"Forward!" Korb cried, waving his 12-gauge pump.

The muties advanced to the bend; clubs, machetes and axes ready for the mopping up.

When Krysty and Jak reached that vantage point, she raised her .38 and he aimed his Colt Python, but neither of them fired.

Four of the swampie hell mutts had a Haldane trooper trapped in front of a shambles of a Winnebago Brave. When he looked away, one of the beasts coiled and sprang at him, stretched out full length. The trooper pivoted and fired his AK from the hip. The close-range, full-auto burst blew through the dog's torso, blowing its ribs out its side in a spray of bloody splinters. The hound twisted in midair and crashed lifeless to the ground behind him. The other dogs celebrated the death of their packmate by seizing the man's arms and shoulder in their jaws and dragging him down. As he fired the AK's last rounds in the air, a combined 450 pounds of dog tore at his flesh.

With sharp fangs and shaking heads they pulled clumps of flesh from his arms. The dogs gulped their prizes and went back for more. One of the animals jumped on his chest, knocking aside the muzzle of the AK, and bit into his face, from cheek to cheek. The hell-hound threw its body from side to side, using the weight and the leverage to tear away the tender flesh.

Without being ordered to, one of the swampies jumped from a doorway and joined the dog-bites-man melee. He had a thin, red-orange beard and large-lobed ears; he wore faded denim bibfronts. Extra-wide, extra-short bibfronts. Facing his swampie pals with a grin on his face, he swung an iron pipe down on the trooper's skull, shattering it like a raw egg. The bastard didn't give a damn about ending the man's suffering; he just wanted to get in some free licks.

Amid the din of the raging battle, an assault rifle barked once. From the loud report, it was very close. The club-wielding swampie jerked forward, waving his short arms to keep his balance. As he opened his mouth and screamed he was struck by another single shot. Again, the mutie jerked like a puppet on a string; this time he fell to a knee. Shot twice in the buttocks with full-metal jacket 7.62 mm rounds, he somehow managed to get to his feet. As he tried to run stiff-legged, clutching his behind in both hands, he was hit a third time. The bullet impact twisted him sideways.

The seat of his bibfronts was gone, his double-wide rear end shot to hamburger.

His fellow swampies yelled for him to take cover.

Before he could do so, a fourth rifle shot caught him in the back of the neck and came out under his chin, parting his wispy red beard. Blood from the horrendous throat wound poured down his chest and gushed from his mouth. He dropped to both knees.

As he toppled in slow mo onto his face, two of the dogs jumped on his back. They worked as a team, dragging his limp body into the shadows under a semi-trailer. It didn't take a doomie to know what was going to happen next.

There was no calling off the dogs. Loosed from their chains, they were independent purveyors of mayhem.

"Forget him," Korb said. "We've got to cut off Haldane's men, take out as many as we can before they hole up in the Welcome Center."

Korb waved his muties forward, his 12-gauge pump braced against his hip, its muzzle sweeping the line of predark wrecks. When he neared the spot where the swampie had been shot, he flattened himself against the side of a cargo container. He thought he was well out of the line of sniper fire.

He was wrong.

The ass-shooter had either moved to get a better angle, or it was somebody else potshotting.

Another rifleshot cracked and Korb's baseball cap whipped off his head. His skull slammed into the steel wall, and he slumped for a second, then he gathered himself and straightened up.

He looked all right.

Like the shot had just ripped off the hat. A near miss.

Then he turned his head.

A high-power military round had caught him square in the eggplant-colored, balloonlike mass that covered the right side of his face. A growth whose blood supply had grown even more tangled and elaborate, thanks to his earlier, unsuccessful attempt to remove it. Gore geysered from the grievous, fist-size wound, pouring over his shoulder from half a dozen severed vessels. He tried to squeeze off the flow, frantically digging the fingers of both hands into the mess of exploded purple tumor.

He couldn't stop the hemorrhaging. He couldn't even slow it.

He bled out before help could reach him. Not that there was anything that anyone could have done.

With their leader's death, with blasterfire and grens blasts on all sides, all illusion of unit cohesion evaporated. It was every mutie bastard for him- or herself. Like the hellhounds, the swampies and the variously malformed immediately beat feet, disappearing through gaps in the rows of wags and trailers.

Krysty had had no bone to pick with Baron Haldane or his troops. No blood grudge to settle. No matter of unpaid debts or stolen property. Neither had Jak. All they wanted was to locate their companions and depart, leaving the fighting to those who gave a shit, or had no choice. Then a rifle round screamed past her head, close enough to feel the breeze. Her prehensile red hair pulled into even tighter coils.

And all bets were off.

Jak grabbed her arm, and they dashed across the narrow path to the side of a derelict truck. By crossing the road in the sniper's direction, they had cut off his narrow shooting angle, which ran between the parked wags and trailers.

Jak and Krysty rounded the rear of the vehicle,

moving into the next lane. As they stepped out from
cover, a figure to their right ducked around the bend in
the otherwise deserted path. The sniper had been trying
to reposition to get off another clean chillshot. Realizing that pursuit was after him, he was beating a hasty
retreat, presumably toward the Welcome Center.

The Welcome Center was the key.

None of the combatants on either side wore uniforms
or insignia. Indeed, Malosh was the only fighter recognizable at a distance. Once the berm wall had been
breached, after preliminary defenses were overrun, attackers scattered by counterattack, it was almost impossible to tell friend from foe. In the narrow, shadowy
lanes, and across the stretches of open ground, whoever
shot at you was the enemy.

Haldane's men did have a strategic advantage,
though. They could keep from accidentally chilling one
another by withdrawing to the Welcome Center. It was
a fort within a fort. They could hold out behind its
concrete block walls for a long time, perhaps until reinforcements arrived from Nuevaville.

Jak dashed after the escaping sniper. Krysty had
longer legs than he did, but she couldn't match his ac-
celeration. By the time she reached the bend in the lane,
he already had his Colt Python up and aimed. The
blaster barked and bucked in his outstretched fist.

Forty feet away, the .357 Magnum slug found its
running target. The sniper stumbled forward, struck
beneath his right shoulder blade. Caught in midstride,
the bullet impact bowled him over. He landed spread-
eagled on his back in the middle of the path. His Kalashnikov flew from his grasp, sliding beneath the

undercarriage of an ancient motor home. The sniper flopped around in the dirt, unable to draw breath. From the size and position of the exit wound in the front of his chest, the 158-grain hunk of lead had taken out most of his right lung. Shock trauma had probably collapsed the other one.

As the shooter was no longer a threat, Krysty and Jak hurried past him without a backward look. Neither was willing expend a live round to send him west. They left him to die at his own pace.

Krysty and Jak leapfrogged each other from bend to bend, running between the scabrous huts and wrecked wags. They glanced into the crudely sawn doorways and windows, but there was no sign of the ville folk. When the end of the lane came into view ahead, they could see fighters moving across the mouth, from left to right, in the direction of the Welcome Center. They couldn't tell whether the fighters belonged to Malosh or Haldane.

In the pauses between volleys of blasterfire and the whumps of grens, Krysty could hear dogs baying and barking from the other side of the ville. The noise seemed concentrated in that area. It sounded like the hellhounds had formed into a hunting pack, which was bad news for anyone they happened to come across.

When Krysty and Jak reached the end of the path, which was framed by a refrigerator semitrailer and a Trailways bus, they stole a cautious look around the corner. They had a clear view of the ville's gardens and the Welcome Center beyond. The rows of crops— staked tomato plants, waist-high corn, pole beans and peppers—ran east and west, perpendicular to their point

of view. Haldane's men were holding off attackers from
the behind the building's pillars and concrete planters,
allowing their comrades to withdraw to the center's
front doors. A fighting retreat.

There were only a few Haldane troopers left on the
berm's southern ridge. The roar of machine-gun fire had
fallen off markedly. It sounded like just two of the heavy
guns were firing into the gorge.

The ville folk appeared to have vanished.

It occurred to Krysty that they'd all been herded into
the Welcome Center so they could be used as hostages.

Protected from blasterfire by the garden's row of
concrete block compost bins, hellhounds fought over
something in a snarling, snapping mass. Swampies
hiding inside the bins shouted encouragement to their
pets' bristling backs.

"Look!" Jak exclaimed, pointing to the left with his
Python.

Krysty had already seen it. Behind a row of four-
foot-tall tomato plants a head bobbed along at high
speed. It was wearing a red stocking cap.

Meconium.

His hand swung up and silver flashed.

The hatchet.

Ahead of him, something else was moving at high
speed, something even more vertically challenged. At
first Krysty thought it was just more swampies, perhaps
a pair of females. On closer inspection, the runners
were way too short to be swampies.

Two towheaded boys dashed out of the tomatoes
into the stands of corn. They ran as if their lives
depended on it. And from the looks of things, they did.

With the hatchet-waving swampie gaining on them, the children abruptly turned left, bursting through the cornstalks side by side, heading straight for Krysty and Jak.

As the children exited the garden, the smaller of the two tripped on the top of a row and landed hard on his stomach.

Before he could get up, Meconium was astride him with his stout legs, raising the hatchet high overhead. There was blood smeared on the razor-sharp blade. And the blood and gobs of brain matter in the swampie's beard weren't his own.

Jak snap-fired the Python as Meconium reared back to strike the boy. The movement shifted his blockhead just far enough to save his life. The Magnum bullet missed his skull, but only by a hairbreadth. It whizzed between hatchet and head. Meconium let out a yelp and clutched his ear with the hatchet hand.

The other blond boy skidded to a stop, taking cover behind Krysty's long legs.

"You wanna lower that chopper," she told Meconium, taking two-handed aim at his forehead with her revolver.

Meconium obeyed, dropping his hatchet arm, thick blood leaking from his ear hole.

While Krysty held the rad bastard covered, Jak grabbed the kid by the shirt collar and dragged him out from between the swampie's legs.

Meconium's eyes glittered with malice. He turned his head toward the compost bins, sucked down a deep breath, stuck two grimy fingers between his lips and whistled. The single, shrill note stretched on for about twenty seconds. It was so piercing they could hear it between bursts of blasterfire.

When the swampie faced them again, he smiled. "You're in for it now, Not Mutie," he promised.

Over his shoulder, the tops of the plants whipped back and forth, stirred not by wind, but by dogs as they bounded across the rows.

Not all of the hounds had responded to Meconium's summons.

Just the ones still hungry for blood.

Krysty and Jak grabbed the boys and raced back into the lane. Sweeping aside a sheet of tattered opaque plastic, they ducked into the first doorway, dragging the children up the steps of the ancient Trailways bus. It was dim and dank inside, and it reeked of sour woodsmoke and mildew. The driver's seat had been torn out, but the steering wheel and pedals were still there. No passenger windows survived; the openings were blocked by plywood or sheet-metal scrap. What light there was came through the doorway's plastic and through rows of small glass rectangles that decorated the seam between walls and roof.

As Jak backed away from the lone doorway, dogs scrambled up the steps, fighting one another to be the first to get inside. The albino aimed his Python at the top step, ready to fire.

Krysty shoved the boys in front of her. All the passenger seats had been pulled out. Except for a narrow path down the middle, the floor was covered with straw-stuffed pallets and plastic bags full of wadded-up clothes. A table had been built-in along one wall. Made from a scavenged interior door, it held a junk-store collection of mismatched plates, cups and steel silverware. Beyond the end of the table was a woodstove fashioned from an oil drum. Its stovepipe angled outside the bus through a hole hacked in a piece of plywood. The back of the bus was the most defensible position. Krysty pushed the boys in the direction of the narrow stainless-steel cubicle that had once housed the Trailways' walk-in toilet. The toilet door stood ajar.

When the first dog leaped into the bus, Jak's Magnum blaster unleashed a deafening roar and its big, bony head exploded, sending hot, wet flesh splattering around the steel room. Jak rode the muzzle climb, bringing the blaster back on target for a second shot. He held his fire.

Instead of scrambling over their dead packmate, the dogs in the stairwell busied themselves by licking up the cranial splatter that had showered them. Typically, they fought tooth and nail over the last of the juicy bits.

"Once they get a taste of blood, they won't never quit," Meconium shouted up from the lane.

Something clicked outside the bus. It sounded like a metal latch opening. Then a rusted hinge squeaked.

A second later, directly beneath them, they heard heavy thuds and the sounds of claws scrabbling on steel.

Krysty was making tracks for the back of the bus, herding the kids in front of her, when a dog jumped out of the open toilet cubicle. Head lowered, fangs bared, ears back, it slinked toward her.

"Jak! They're coming in back here!" Krysty cried. Without taking her eyes off the stalking beast, she guided the boys around her and pushed them toward the unlit oil barrel stove. They scurried into the skinny hiding space behind it.

Krysty sensed the dog was about to spring and

nipped the attack in the bud. She fired her .38 once, hitting the hound between the eyes. In the confined space, the blaster's report made her wince. The animal's bony skull held together, but it was instant death. The dog collapsed in a heap and didn't move again.

She stepped over the corpse and looked into the toilet cubicle over the sights of her Model 640. There was a big hole in the floor where the toilet fixture had once stood, which created a connecting passage to the luggage compartment underneath. The compartment that Meconium had opened.

Even as she glanced in, another hound's head popped up through the hole. She shot it before it could climb out. Blood sprayed the stainless-steel wall and the head disappeared back down the hole. Krysty slammed the door, and as there was no lock on the outside, she threw her back against it and pushed with her legs to hold it shut.

Jak's Magnum blaster bellowed from the front of the bus. As Krysty looked up, he fired again. His first shot had debrained another hellhound; his second was fired almost point-blank into the chest of a leaping animal. The albino had no time to get out of the way. One hundred fifty pounds of dead dog hit him head-on. The momentum knocked him to the floor.

At that instant something rammed the bathroom door against her back, making it jump in the jamb. A dog was throwing itself at the other side over and over, using its body like a battering ram. It took everything she had to keep the door shut and the beast out of the compartment.

Jak was in an even worse predicament than she was. He had regained his feet, but in the process two more dogs had made it up the steps and into the wag. Though Krysty had bullets left, with the door ramming into her back, she couldn't trust her aim.

One hound had grabbed Jak by the pant cuff and was trying to pull him off his feet.

The other dog had its huge paws on his shoulders, trying to get a solid bite on his neck.

Yellow fangs tangled in the long white hair.

Chapter Twenty-One

Ryan ignored the rifle bullets screaming past him and returned aimed rapidfire with his SIG. Downrange, the line of 115-grain slugs sparked off the top of the corrugated culvert pipe, which jutted about ten feet from the side of the berm. The near-miss bullet strikes forced the defenders to cease fire and duck behind the steel culvert, which gave them some cover. Because the culvert stood a couple of feet above the ground, the Haldane sec force was only partially protected by it.

When J.B. cut loose with his Uzi machine pistol, he aimed low on purpose. With the first withering burst he chopped the legs out from under three of the enemy fighters. Amid clouds of bullet-raised dust, they writhed on the ground beneath the pipe. Ryan and J.B. sprayed the fallen with 9 mm rounds, making sure they didn't get up.

The three remaining sec men didn't stick around for the funeral. Two of them took off for the cover of the berm gate, firing their AKs blindly—and ineffectively—over their hips. The third trooper escaped by climbing into the open end of the pipe, headfirst.

Mildred's Czech wheelgun barked three times in rapid succession. She hit one of the running men in the chest, knocking him sideways into the berm. He slid down the slope on his back, limbs limp and rubbery, lower jaw agape. High-kicking, the other sec man reached the safety of the ville's wag gate, which was a semitrailer parked across the opening. He dived out of sight under the double rear wheels.

When the SIG's slide locked back, Ryan dropped the empty mag into his palm, pocketed it and took a fresh clip from his belt, slapping it home. He broke into a trot, heading for the culvert entrance to the westernmost machine-gun post.

The Haldane sec men who had climbed to the top of the berm to potshot at the cannon fodder now directed their blasterfire into the ville, at the Malosh fighters surging through the breached wall.

With the defenders' attention fixed on the main attack, the companions closed on the culvert without drawing fire. They approached it with caution, weapons up.

Nobody went near the opening.

At the opposite end of the culvert, on the other side of the berm, the heavy machine gun was raining bloody hell on the Malosh force in the gorge.

That had to stop.

J.B. reared back a leg and booted the side of the pipe.

Autofire roared like thunder from deep inside it. It was from small arms, not the M-60. A flurry of slugs whined from the end of the culvert, kicking up puffs of dust as they ricocheted wildly across the compound.

The gunpost's defenders were ready for them, and determined to hold them out.

Without grens to chuck up the pipe, the companions had to go to Plan B. Under the culvert three bullet-

riddled bodies lay in a bloody tangle. Caught up in the
mess were three Soviet-made assault rifles. Ryan pulled
one of the AKs out from under a dead man's arm. J.B.
used the toe of his boot to turn over a corpse and then
picked up the autorifle that had been under it. Without
bothering to wipe the blood off the wooden stocks, they
dropped the mags and checked the round counters. After
clearing the actions, they snapped the 30-round clips
back in place.

Ryan threw a leg over the pipe and slid over the top
to the far side. The scraping sound he made drew more
fire. From the increased volume of the racket, and un-
godly hail of lead skipping over the hammered ground,
there were now two AKs defending the entrance. And
they were in position to shred anyone who stepped in
front of the culvert.

Ryan and J.B. moved beside the mouth of the pipe,
just out of the line of fire. Dropping the selector lever
to automatic, the one-eyed man flipped the AK around,
holding it upside down, magazine and pistol-grip butts
toward him. He held on to the end of the clip with his
left hand; he held the pistol grip with his right hand with
his thumb inside the trigger guard, resting on the trigger.

When the mad shooting from inside the pipe
stopped, Ryan leaned forward. Still out of the line of
fire, he poked the muzzle's flash-hider into the mouth
of the culvert and mashed down the trigger. The AK
jittered wildly in his hands, spewing lead up the pipe.
He didn't try to control the weapon's aim point. He
emptied the mag in a single horrendous burst, then
tossed the blaster to the dirt, making room for J.B.

The Armorer followed his lead, staying far enough

back from the lip of the pipe to avoid return fire. As he was on the opposite side of the culvert, he had reversed Ryan's hand position on his autorifle. Left hand on the pistol grip. Right hand on the mag. As Ryan withdrew, he stuck the barrel and gas cylinder into the pipe and flattened the AK's trigger with his thumb. The vibration from the prolonged full-auto burst made his spectacles slip down the bridge of his nose. When the rifle came up empty, he, too, flipped it aside.

There was smoking brass all over the ground in front of the culvert. They had fired close to sixty rounds of full-metal jackets into the confined space of the converted SUV gun emplacement. It was a straight shot to the steel plate that covered the post's front windshield.

And the Haldane fighters caught in between were fish in a barrel.

Sweet silence came from the machine gun end of the pipe. It had ceased firing into the gorge.

"What do you think?" Mildred said. "Did we get 'em?"

"Could be playing possum in there," J.B. said.

"Let's make sure," Ryan said. He kicked over a sprawled body and scooped up the remaining AK by the buttstock. After giving the assault rifle a quick once-over, he stepped in front of the opening. Making no attempt to conceal himself, he fired into the culvert from the hip. In a matter of seconds, he poured another twenty-five rounds of predark lead into the emplacement. There was no answering autoclatter.

No answer of any kind.

The machine-gun post was dead.

Bullets whined at them from the berm's wag gate.

They whanged into the side of the steel pipe and slammed into rocks at the base of the perimeter wall, sending sparks and splinters flying. The muzzle-flashes came from the shadows under the trailer. The culvert's lone escapee had summoned others to defend the entrance.

Farther along the berm on the gorge side, Haldane's men were abandoning the crest and making for the backside of the Welcome Center.

The companions ran straight for the gate, returning fire.

As he sprinted, J.B. fanned his Uzi, stitching across the back of the trailer, blowing out all four tires on the rear axle. The trailer dropped hard onto its rims, sending up a cloud of dust. For a moment the shooting from the shadows stopped.

Ryan and Mildred cut left, swinging out wide to flank the sec men hiding underneath. As they changed course, blasterfire broadsided them from the corner of the Welcome Center. Bullets skipped and zipped to little effect. The hastily aimed blasts came from troopers who were beginning to panic at the rapid turn of events. But success was just a matter of time. Caught out in the flat, the companions' only chance was to reach the cover of the wag gate.

The shooters under the trailer had other ideas about that.

KRYSTY LINED UP THE SIGHTS of her .38 but as she tightened down on the trigger, the door bucked hard against her back, knocking off her aim. The dog in the Trailways toilet wasn't running out of steam.

Jak had his handblaster out, too, but he was too

occupied to use it. One of the hellhounds was on his back, its front paws on his shoulders. The other had hold of his pant leg and was dragging him backward, shaking its head, twisting its powerful body as it tried to flip him to the floor of the bus. Jak couldn't spin around and shoot either one of them without ending up on his face. It took everything he had just to keep his balance and keep the dog from clamping onto his neck.

Once those long fangs pierced his flesh, the battle was lost. The beast had a prominent sagittal crest, the muscle anchor for its massive jaws. If it couldn't snap his neck or crush his vertebrae, it would drag him down and strangle him, tiger style, by squeezing off his airway.

The tall redhead waited for the next slam against her back. Despite the fact that she was leaning back with her full weight, the door jumped open an inch or two, driven by 150 pounds of canine battering arm. Krysty felt the dog bounce off. She immediately turned and, pressing the muzzle against the door, fired through it three times in rapid succession, angling her shots down toward the toilet floor. The door dimpled and burned powder starbursts marred the brushed steel.

A shrill yelp came from the other side.

Krysty glanced at the children cowering behind the stove as she braced herself to fire. Then she was looking over the Smith's sights at Jak sliding helplessly backward.

She aimed at the dog trying to bite off his head and squeezed off a single shot. The slug smacked into the beast's spine, at base of its thick neck. The impact made a solid, meaty whack and sent up a puff of dirt, blood and hair. It was a chillshot. The dog's bowels emptied voluminously onto a cardboard mattress, its jaws relaxed, its rear legs crumpled, and slid off Jak's back into a twitching heap.

Partially freed, the albino twisted from his hips, the stringy, slobbery plaits of his hair slapping his shoulder, and fired down into the head of the dog that had hold of his pant leg. The point-blank .357 Magnum round left a smoking crater down to the hinge point of its jaws. Its brains and tongue were blown out through the front of its throat.

His leg splattered with cranial blowback, Jak swung his Python up to cover the bus entrance. Both he and Krysty waited for long seconds, anticipating another attack, but nothing came up the steps and nothing burst out of the dented toilet door.

Either that was all the dogs Meconium could gather, or they'd decided to try some easier prey.

"This is a death trap," Krysty said, pulling the boys from behind the stove. "Let's get out of here."

Jak didn't say anything. He was already heading down the steps.

When Krysty jumped down beside him, she saw the head swampie running down the lane, away from Welcome Center. Maybe he was hoping to link up with his fellow swampies. Safety in numbers.

The albino had his blaster up, tracking the slow-moving target, but he didn't shoot.

Swampies couldn't run for nukeshit. Their legs were too short and heavy. And male and female, they had monumental lard asses. Meconium's stumpy arms pumped, his barrel chest heaved, but he was going nowhere fast.

"Mine," Jak announced, holstering the Python.

The wild child took off after the swampie, running in long, loping strides, his white hair flying.

Krysty ran after him with the children in tow.

Meconium made it around the first bend before Jak caught up with him. The swampie glanced over his shoulder, hatchet in hand, seemingly weighing the odds if he stopped and fought back.

Jak dived at his ankles, tackling him from behind, pile driving his bearded face into the dirt.

Before Meconium could recover, the albino ripped the hatchet from his hand. Jak turned the swampie onto his back and straddled him. He didn't reach for his holstered Colt Python. When the swampie tried to buck him off, Jak raised the hatchet overhead and the mutie went suddenly still. It was a predark camp ax; the head had an edge on one side and it was flattened on the other for use as a hammer. Jak held the blade side cocked to strike and with his free hand he ripped off the red knit cap.

Krysty turned the boys' faces away from what was about to happen. "You don't need to see," she told them.

But she did.

Meconium was stubborn and defiant to the last. "This don't change a fuckin' thing," he snarled up at Jak, spitting flecks of white foam over his beard.

Jak stared down at him with unreadable bloodred eyes.

"Yer still a mutie…" Meconium howled.

The hatchet came down in a silver blur.

Meconium's skull split from hairline to nose bridge,

the hatchet blade half buried in his head. It had to have hurt like all rad blazes. The swampie let loose a piercing scream and arched his back, reaching out for the handle. Even with his short, powerful arms, he couldn't budge the ax from his skullbone. He screamed louder.

Jak picked up a heavy chunk of rock from the ground beside him and with a single, two-handed, overhead blow he drove in the wedge-shaped blade to the flare of the head's hammer end. Blood squirted from the swampie's ears, nose and mouth. His brain cut in two, Meconium's fingers slipped lifelessly from the handle.

"Not mutie," Jak said, getting the final word on the subject.

He left the hatchet stuck in the swampie's head as a drop-forged punctuation mark.

Chapter Twenty-Two

Despite the flurry of explosions on the far side of the berm, and a mad clatter of blasterfire inside the ville's walls, heavy slugs from the three facing machine-gun posts continued to whipsaw the gorge bottom, chewing rock and flesh alike.

Bezoar and Young Crad squatted in bloody water up to their waists, pinned down by the fusillade. The elder swineherd shivered uncontrollably from the cold and from shock, but his friend seemed inured to both. Dense layers of body fat and a cross-wired droolie brain protected Young Crad from the totality of the horror and the proximity of death.

Corpses caked in mud made of sandy dirt mixed with gore lay all around them. More dead floated facedown in the destroyed interstate's seep pools. Under hellacious fire, the wounded crawled across open ground to reach the cover of shallow ditches and piles of concrete, some dragging twenty-foot-long tails of uncoiled entrails behind them. As the dying cannon fodder curled into tight balls and bled out, they moaned piteously, begging for a mercy bullet.

If he'd had a blaster, Bezoar would have gladly given it to them, just to shut them up.

Some of the sacrificial lambs continued to return

fire from behind the larger chunks of concrete. Holding their weapons by the pistol grips, they reached high over their heads. Sticking the muzzles over the tops of blocks of the shattered roadway, they cut loose unaimed bursts in the general direction of the ridge.

Keeping Haldane's forces honest.

Ferdinando scampered up and down the firing line, jumping from ditch to ditch and mound to mound, carefully doling out a limited supply of full magazines. It was plenty light enough for Haldane's gunners to see the movement, and for them to track it. As the one-armed man hopped behind a tabletop of uptilted predark roadbed, slipping in beside the droolie already hiding there, concentrated machine-gun fire chewed the edges of the slab to dust. Blinded by flying concrete chips, the dimmie stumbled away from cover before Ferdinando could stop him. Caught in a 100-round, triple cross fire, he was literally blown apart.

It was hard for Bezoar to get his mind around the fact that what dropped to the ground—some here, some over there—had once been human.

Then the machine gun on the western gate stopped firing.

Cut off as if by a switch.

Control of the gorge, and of the access routes in and out of the ville depended on three fully operational blaster positions. One at each of the gates at either end. One in the middle. The gunpost on the eastern gate could only bring its sights to bear on the edge of Malosh's attack force, which left the emplacement amidships on the berm with the job of pinning them down. A job it couldn't handle. Without multiple lines of cross fire, it was impossible to contain the attacking force and to prevent them from taking the western gate.

Malosh swung back onto his horse. Spurring it, he rode at a gallop back the way they had come.

"We have them now!" he shouted at his fodder as his stallion leaped over their heads. "Come on!"

The ville's middle M-60 tried to hit him. But it couldn't.

Even with daylight fast upon them.

Even with a big, horse-and-rider target.

Despite himself, Bezoar was stirred by the sight of the black-masked Impaler fanned by hundreds of slugs but riding on unharmed.

Those with functioning blasters, those whose courage hadn't been broken, jumped from cover and ran after him.

"The west gate is falling!" Ferdinando cried to the others. "Get your asses up. Get moving."

No one obeyed. If anything, they all crouched lower.

The leader of the cannon fodder held an AK in his crippled hand. It wasn't so crippled that he couldn't pull a trigger. Ferdinando fired a short burst over the heads of the cowering conscriptees.

"Die here or die there," he said. "Get the fuck up."

Everyone who was still able roused him- or herself, crawling out of the puddles and trenches, slipping out from behind mounds of dirt. Young Crad helped Bezoar from the water, then retrieved his floating crutch.

The elder swineherd nearly fell on his face at the first step. His hip and knee joints had stiffened from the cold bath. And he was shivering so violently that he couldn't speak. He leaned on Young Crad, who half carried him over the demolished ground. Bullets continued to whine past them, but they were more widely spaced and less effective.

As he hobbled along, Bezoar saw a child curled up in a narrow space under a slab of concrete. The boy couldn't have been more than nine. He was alive. Their eyes met, but Bezoar said nothing. He looked away from the mirror of his own mortal fear. The boy wasn't the only one hiding in the blown-up section of highway. Other young children concealed themselves in small dark places, hoping to turn invisible until the battle was done.

The going was faster once they reached the turnoff and the more or less intact roadway.

Ferdinando shouted at the ragged file not to bunch together, because they made easier targets that way.

Bezoar looked up at the ville. The pitched battle for Sunspot ground on and on. Blasterfire raged; grens exploded. He was certain that he was going to die this day. Beside him, Young Crad had a smile on his face, no doubt thinking that soon he was going to be with his piggie dear. Then he began to whistle in his irritating way.

The elder swineherd didn't have the energy to tell the triple-stupe droolie to shut up.

Although heavy machine-gun fire still laced the air, none of the fodder bothered to duck their heads anymore. Ducking every few seconds didn't do any good; it just slowed you down. By the time you ducked, the slugs were already either past you or through you.

The farther they got from the blown-up section of highway, the less effective the machine-gun fire from the middle of the berm became. The kill zone was way too wide for one blaster to saturate with bullets. The best it could do was harass.

Ahead of the ragged company, Baron Malosh raced across the four-lane road, his horse's hooves striking sparks on the road metal. As the fodder followed, the machine gun got lucky. In the last few degrees of its firing arc, it managed to lay down a ten-ring hit.

The woman right in front of Bezoar staggered as the back of her head exploded in a puff of red. He and Young Crad were pelted by pieces of her skull with long strands of hair attached. The woman's legs buckled under her, and she promptly sat down on the road. Her upper body bent at the waist, leaning forward until her chin lay on the ground. As he limped past, Bezoar could see what was left of her brains through the crater in her head. It looked like bloody soup in there.

When they reached the bottom of the path, the middle machine gun could no longer turn far enough to hit them.

There were scattered shouts of triumph as they advanced up the grade. They were celebrating the momentary lull in the hellstorm.

Above them on the path, Bezoar could see the black rider galloping full-speed toward Sunspot's western gate. The Impaler had an AK-47 in either hand. Neither hand held the reins. Controlling the war horse with knee and boot pressure on its sides, Malosh rode straight for the double gates. The larger of the two was meant for wags. The side of a semitrailer blocked that opening. The foot-traffic gate consisted of a half-buried, yellow school bus.

The sight of their commander charging headlong into combat spurred on the fodder.

Even Bezoar's spirits were lifted as he imagined the terror in the hearts of the Haldane troopers manning those gates. The berm perimeter had already been broken, which meant enemies were coming at them from behind. Now more attackers were coming from the front.

If the gate guards had had an escape plan before the attack, it was out the window now. And they knew that Malosh never took prisoners.

It was either hold off the fodder or die.

As the baron charged the berm, a pair of AK-47 sights poked out over the bus's dashboard, through the glassless windshield, and opened fire on him.

Malosh dug his heels into the horse's sides, making it suddenly veer to the right. He rode for the school bus and the two shooters.

From Bezoar's point of view, it looked like a suicide run.

Certain death for animal and rider.

But because the baron was on horseback, and therefore elevated above the ground by at least ten feet, he could angle his fire over the end of the engine block. In truth, the school bus sentries had no more protection than he did. Malosh opened fire with both predark assault rifles. Controlling the muzzle climbs single-handed, he peppered the hood, fenders and grille with full-metal jacketed slugs. The rounds he sent through the open front windshield drove the sentries to their knees, forcing them to stop shooting back.

Malosh's horse didn't shy at the blasters going off over its head. It bore down on the gate at a full gallop.

Sensing their own impending doom, the two Haldane guards broke and ran, heading for the open rear doors of the bus.

Before they reached them, the baron closed the gap. As the stallion skidded to a stop in front of the bumper, he emptied the AKs through the windshield, cutting down both men from behind.

While Bezoar and the fifty or so other survivors of the gorge hurried up the path to join him, Malosh dismounted and tethered his horse to the bus's bumper. Taking fresh 30-round mags from his saddlebags, he reloaded the AKs, then packed his pockets with additional full clips.

Grens were going off inside the berm as the fodder reached the baron. Torrents of blasterfire poured from under the semitrailer. Most of it was aimed into not out of the berm.

A half dozen Haldane fighters scrambled out from under the wag gate, driven from the ville by Malosh shooters on the inside. Though they all held blasters, they didn't try to use them. They couldn't; they were out of ammo. Confronted by the baron and his too old, too young, too crippled fodder at the head of the path, they threw their guns down at once. They were the ones who looked scared now. Even though they were stronger, two-legged and two-armed.

Right off the bat, and without a direct order, some of the sponges cut loose with their battered assault rifles. Under the hail of bullets, three of the enemy were slammed, then pinned against the side of the berm, their bodies juddering from full-auto impacts.

"Save your bullets!" Ferdinando yelled at the shooters. "Use your blades and gun butts on the ones without blasters!"

It became a rather one-sided game of run down, beat down.

The fodder showed no mercy to their adversaries. No doubt some were thinking about friends who had been left on the ground in the gorge as they attacked the out-numbered troopers. Some were relishing the joy of dishing out punishment. They fell into a frenzy of mob chilling. Every one was caught up in the brutal tit-for-tat.

Young Crad swung up his massive forearm and clotheslined a running Haldane soldier.

Bezoar hopped in and started beating on the supine man with his crutch. The first blow broke the soldier's nose. After that, the victim raised his arms to fend off the strikes.

Young Crad seized the man from behind. He grabbed this chin in one hand and the ball of his shoulder in the other, a neck-breaker hold.

With blood running down over his lips and chin, the trooper struggled to stay alive, fighting the thick wrists, shifting his weight, bucking back against his adversary.

The stalemate went on for a few seconds.

Then in a blur Young Crad's powerful hands twisted and the man's neck made a wet snapping sound. When he let go of the man's jaw, his head lolled forward at an unnatural angle. Young Crad flung the chilled trooper aside.

At the top of the path, their fellow fodderites were chasing down and cornering the remaining escaping Haldane fighters. When they caught the men and knocked them off their feet, those without gunbutts or clubs used rocks and bootheels to finish the job.

The last of the troopers made a fight of it. He dashed around, ducking blows, punching, slashing with a razor-sharp sheath knife, doing everything he could to keep the attackers back.

When it was clear that the game was up, that he was about to overwhelmed and pounded to death, he took a running jump off the side of the ridge. His swan dive looked good for the first thirty feet or so, but it ended in an arm-waving, leg-kicking belly flop on the rocks another hundred feet below.

With Malosh in the lead, the cannon fodder scurried under the belly of the wag gate's semitrailer, entering Sunspot.

When Bezoar stuck his head around one of the flat-tened front tires, his jaw dropped.

Sunspot was an even worse shit pile than Redbone. The only dwellings were a bunch of wrecked wags and trailers lined up in a pounded dirt field. It wasn't a place worth dying for, but already more than a hundred people had done just that. There were bodies and parts of bodies strewed everywhere; and it was impossible to tell which side they had been on.

The fight wasn't over.

Under the Impaler force's onslaught, the remaining Haldane defenders were disappearing into the entrance of a predark concrete block building.

There to make their last stand.

Chapter Twenty-Three

Rustling sounds from just beyond the circle of Magus's wags made Baron Haldane prick up his ears. He strained to precisely locate their source, but couldn't. It was still too dark to see anything moving. He prayed that the noise was Bollinger returning from Sunspot with the full garrison on his heels. Then the sounds stopped. They weren't like the footfalls of men, he decided. They were more like soft scrapings, scratchings, even hissings. Not from the wind shaking the chaparral. There was no wind. The night was deathly still. After a pause, the sounds started up on the opposite side of the circle.

Haldane's sec man Cuzo pulled a rebuilt pair of predark infrared goggles down over his eyes and carefully scanned the surrounding darkness. "Whatever the hell it is," he said, "it sure ain't Bollinger. I can't see nothing out there. Not a rad-blasted thing."

"Something's sneaking around, though," said Bertram, another of Haldane's seven remaining sec men. "Mebbe it's rattlesnakes."

"There'd have to be an army of them to make that much noise," Haldane said.

"And they'd be crawling through the camp for sure, looking for heat or meat," Cuzo added.

"Where the hell *is* Bollinger?" Bertram said. "The bastard should've been back here four hours ago."

That wasn't news to Baron Haldane.

He was well aware of the round-trip time to Sunspot.

As the interminable, awful night had worn on and Bollinger had failed to show up with the garrison's troops, he had grown more and more concerned. There had been no sounds of blasterfire though, which meant that Malosh's army hadn't intercepted Bollinger and the others on their way to the ville. If they had been attacked en route, they would have gotten off at least a few shots. If they had been attacked on the way back, more than a few shots would have been exchanged.

It was just starting to get light when the first crackle of heavy blasterfire echoed down from Sunspot ridge.

"Dammit to hell!" Haldane swore. He recognized his own M-60s opening up. If his garrison had already been evacuated, Malosh would have taken the ville without a struggle. Bollinger and the others hadn't made it there, and they weren't going to make it back.

"Our guys are in for it," Cuzo said.

"Mebbe they can hold them off," Bertram said.

They listened in silence to the multiple machine-gun fire in the distance. It rattled nonstop. If there was answering fire, it was lost in the torrent coming from the ville.

"Our gun posts are pouring fire into the gorge," Cuzo said. "Old Malosh is getting the shit kicked out of him."

After a few minutes of one-sided combat, they saw a signal flare burst high over the ville. The red star slowly floated down and disappeared behind the berm walls.

"Shit," Bertram snarled.

"Baron Malosh has got something nasty up his sleeve, you can bet on that," Cuzo said.

Soft booms rolled down from the high ground, followed by additional overlays of machine-gun chatter.

"The gorge assault was a feint," Haldane said. "The main attack is coming from the north."

Then a bright flash bloomed in the sky above the ridge, backlighting the berm before winking out. A second later they heard the thunderclap of a much bigger explosion.

"The bastards just blew the berm," Cuzo said. "There's nothing stopping them now. It's gonna be a bloodbath."

"We should be up there with our people, dammit," one of the other sec men said.

Haldane looked over his shoulder at the shadowy Lyagushka artillery piece. It stood ready in the middle of the circle of wags, waiting for the warm-up act to end and the main event to commence. Magus's gunner had done his preliminary calculations the previous evening. He'd determined the distance to target and the necessary powder charge. He'd tilted the barrel up for a high arc lob that would drop the warheads over the wall and into Sunspot's midst. The Lyagushka was already loaded with a D-462 smoke round. More D-462 rounds and propellant charges were stacked on the left side of the gun; the chem projectiles were separately stacked on the right. To mark the impact of the smoke rounds, and pinpoint the target for the sarin projectiles, the gunner had to wait until full daylight, which was only ten minutes or so away.

The baron realized that probably he would never learn what had gone wrong the previous night. Bottom line, one way or another, was that his entire garrison was going to die. Which meant that Haldane wouldn't have enough men to overwhelm Magus's road trash and rescue Thorne.

It was the worst of all possible outcomes.

Haldane felt a crushing sadness. He knew his soldiers in Sunspot would fight to the death. They could expect no mercy from Baron Malosh. Haldane had failed them. He had failed their families. He should have pulled the garrison out earlier.

Victory, if and when it came, was going to be hollow.

And it was going to taste of ashes.

At that moment it occurred to him that Magus, himself, might have had something to do with Bollinger's failure to safely reach Sunspot. Steel Eyes could have easily sent a few his own men out to waylay and chill the warning team. By making sure the garrison didn't escape the ville, Magus could extract the most suffering and pain from the circumstances under his control. By playing his cards right, he could get rid of Malosh and Haldane, and most of their standing armies in one fell swoop. He wouldn't need to use chem weapons against Nuevaville, then. He could lurch in and take over the entire barony, or loot it and burn it to the ground.

"Are you okay, Baron?" Bertram asked with concern. "Because you don't look okay."

"We're in a bad spot," he said.

"You can't blame yourself for what's happening up in Sunspot," Cuzo said. "You tried your best to get our troops out. It was up to Bollinger and he blew the mission."

"Our guys might still turn Malosh back," Bertram said. "Drive him out of the ville."

That was most doubtful, Haldane knew.

"And if they don't," Cuzo said, "there's nothing you could have done about it. Malosh still would've broken through the berm. You know he's going to chill all our people. He never leaves survivors."

Like Haldane, the sec men were heartsick over losing their comrades. But there was more tough news.

"I'm not going to give up my son to Magus," the baron told them. "I've got to save him. Without reinforcements from the ville that's going to be a lot harder."

Cuzo and Bertram and the other five sec men exchanged grim looks. They knew they were going to have a lopsided fight on their hands. That didn't deter them, though. They were seasoned, dedicated fighters, long in the service of their elected leader.

"We'll do whatever you tell us, Baron," Cuzo said.

"No way are we gonna let that clanking bag of bolts hurt your boy," Bertram promised.

"I know you won't," Haldane said. "I'd better go check on Thorne."

He turned away from his sec men and walked along the perimeter of the circled wags. A 150 feet farther on, next to the landship, a high-backed captain's chair had been set out on the desert hardpan, facing the battle that raged on the ridge.

It was plenty light enough to see what was sitting in it.

And what it was was more silver than pink, more metal than flesh.

As the baron approached Magus's throne chair, a pair of road trash stepped forward, blocking his path and taking aim at his chest with their spanking-new H&K machine pistols.

"No, no, it's all right," Magus told them. "I have nothing to fear from Baron Haldane. Do I?"

The question was addressed to Haldane. If he said, "No," it was an admission of defeat. He chose not to answer it.

"From the fireworks up there, it looks like Malosh is getting the upper hand," Magus said. "Little does he know that it will be his final victory. Everything is working out exactly as planned."

Haldane wondered what Steel Eyes' plan really was, and how he fit into it. Eventually he would find out. With luck, before it was too late.

"You're getting a bargain, I hope you know," Magus said. "This is all working out so perfectly I should have charged you more for my services. Mebbe triple. But a deal is a deal."

"What are you getting out of this?" Haldane demanded. "You don't need the jack."

"Everyone is measured in this life by their deeds."

"Your deeds are already well-known throughout Deathlands."

"That's true enough. Then let's say I possess a certain technology and an overwhelming desire to see it put into action. What good is the power to destroy if it is never exercised? Empty threats do not accomplish anything. Resolve must be shown. Besides, I feel morally compelled to help my friends and punish my enemies."

In any other situation, Haldane would've laughed out loud. Magus defined his "friends" by their ability to outbid his "enemies."

"I hope you are not starting to regret the bargain we've made," Magus said. "It is a great pity that your troops didn't make it out before Malosh arrived. But there is no turning back now."

Steel Eyes had no conception of pity. And coming from that hideous mouth, the word had an obscene ring to it.

"Like you said," Haldane replied, "the deal is done. No turning back. Now I'm going to see how my son is doing, if you don't mind."

"Why would I mind? Remember, don't cross the line. If you do, you know what will happen." Magus showed the baron his right hand. Clutched in the half-human fingers was a dark object the shape of a playing card, but about a quarter-inch thick.

The remote detonator.

Visible in the early morning light, out on the flatland mebbe eighty yards from the captain's chair was a beige box with a handle on top.

At least Thorne wasn't locked up somewhere inside the landship, Haldane told himself as he set off across the dry earth. But it was small comfort. There were no doors, no locks between the boy and rescue; but there was a small electronic device and a wad of gray plastic explosive.

When he got closer to the beige box, he could see a curved line scratched in the dirt. On Magus's orders a crude, twenty-foot-diameter circle had been drawn around the pet carrier. Inside the perimeter was no-man's land. If he stepped onto it, Magus would detonate the explosive, perhaps chilling both father and son, most certainly chilling son. The booby-trapped cage was far enough from the camp so the blast wouldn't injure Magus, his wags or his men.

The baron rounded the curve of the circle until he faced the metal-barred door. He couldn't see inside the cramped box.

"Thorne? Son?" he said.

"Dad?"

"I'm here."

"I'm cold, Dad."

Haldane heard the scratching sounds behind him. Before he could turn his head, he caught something moving out of the corner of his eye. He pivoted and swung up the Remington 1100, but whatever it was was already gone, vanished over a hummock in the sand like a shadow cast by a scudding cloud. He had the impression of a blackish body. Mebbe two feet long. Something scooting along close to the ground.

His son couldn't have seen it from the cage. Mebbe he hadn't, either, Haldane thought. Mebbe he had imagined it.

"Everything's going to be all right, Thorne," he said. "You've got to stay strong a little longer."

"What's the shooting for?"

"It's a long way off. It'll be over soon."

"Will I get out of here then?"

"Yes, son. Then we'll go back home to Nuevaville."

"I'm scared, Dad."

"I won't let anything happen to you."

"Promise?"

"I promise."

Haldane hunkered down on one knee, staring at the cage, forcing himself to swallow his fury. So far, he hadn't been able to protect his only son, to keep him from being humiliated and terrified. Magus was capable of much worse, he knew. The lives of others meant absolutely nothing to him. Human beings were playthings to be toyed with and squashed. They were his spare-parts repositories. The baron had fooled himself into thinking that he could outwit Magus. He had fooled himself into thinking that his barony's desperate situation required that he surrender his own hard-earned sense of right and wrong. A series of unfortunate, perhaps even tragic, rationalizations on his part had led directly to this catastrophe.

If Haldane felt guilt over the deaths of his brave men and the risk to his innocent son, he had few qualms over the fate of the residents of Sunspot. As a group the ville folk had always been trouble to him. Always difficult to deal with. No matter what Malosh and his army had done to them during occupation, they had refused to see Haldane and his troopers as their liberators. They had chilled his men whenever they could. They had withheld food. They had stolen gear, weapons, ammo. And they had lied about all of the above. Now they were about to be wiped off the face of the earth. If the people of Sunspot had been better subjects, more loyal to him, more honest, his feelings toward them might have been different. But as things stood, he saw their extermination as good riddance.

Behind him, another machine gun dropped out of the conflict. Two guns crackled instead of four. There was no doubt about it, Haldane's forces were losing the battle. Magus planned wait until the shooting stopped before he launched the gas attack. By that time, every member of the garrison would have been chilled.

It never occurred to the baron to call off the sarin bombardment. For one thing, he knew Magus wouldn't have honored such a request. For another, if he had done so, his troops would have died in vain. And the Malosh problem would have still existed.

Everything that the baron held dear lay in the hands of Magus. The future of his son. The future of his people.

And Magus couldn't be trusted.

Haldane had a plan, but it was born of desperation.

As soon as the gas rounds were away, Magus had to die.

Haldane had already decided that he would do the honors on Steel Eyes, personally, while his sec men held off the road trash. Before Magus could detonate the plastic explosive, he'd blow the titanium hip and shoulder joints apart with his 12-gauge shotgun, turning the half man, half machine into a quadraplegic. Then he'd drive a wag back and forth over the head until the body stopped thrashing.

Chapter Twenty-Four

As Ryan and Mildred charged the side of the wag gate trailer, they fired at the defenders crouching behind the wheels and bellying down beneath the undercarriage. Bullets from the SIG and the ZKR sprayed across the double front wheels, blowing out the tires. As they flattened, that end of trailer dropped violently onto its rims.

No way could they stop to take more careful aim.

Answering starburst muzzle-flashes winked at them from the deep shade and the solid cover of the trailer's steel wheels. Slugs freight-trained past their ears and kicked up the dirt in front of them. They were taking heavy fire from autorifles positioned at the corners of the Welcome Center, as well.

But they didn't change course, and they didn't slow down.

That would have been suicide.

The chaos of battle swirled around them like a touched-down tornado. People and dogs running in all directions. Blasterfire rattling on every side. Grens popping off, shooting out clouds of boiling smoke. In the blur of surrounding movement it was impossible to tell friend from foe. There were a hundred simultaneous threats. Ryan and Mildred had on their battle blinders, which reduced the world to a finite goal in tight focus. There was cover and safety under the trailer, if they could drive out the current occupants. With everything they had, they went for it.

Two of the wag gate's defenders broke under the pressure. They squirted out from under the front of the trailer and sprinted along the berm in the direction of the Welcome Center.

Ryan and Mildred let them go. They were no longer an immediate threat. And there were still Haldane fighters shooting from under the semi.

With his fedora jammed way down on his head and a wild look in his spectacle-magnified eyes, J.B. came at the trailer from the rear. Having emptied his Uzi, he switched to the M-4000 on the run and fired from the hip. The pump gun bucked hard in his hands. He cycled out the empty hull, and fired again. Cycled and fired. Cycled and fired. His shot patterns spread wide under the trailer, raising clouds of dust. The Haldane fighters hiding behind the wheels to avoid Mildred's and Ryan's blasterfire couldn't hide from his volleys of Number Two pellets.

Shrieking with pain, the troopers stopped shooting.

The clatter of their blasters was replaced by concentrated autofire at the foot gate fifty feet farther on. Bullets from outside the berm skipped through the yellow wag's open rear doors and plowed into the ground. In hail of lead, a pair of bodies fell halfway out of the school bus, headfirst, arms hanging down, blood pouring from open mouths.

Ryan skidded to a stop beside the trailer's wheel. Ducking, he peered around the ruined tires. Over the sights of the SIG, he saw the last of the wag guards sprinting away from the trailer and down the path that led to the Interstate.

In their haste, the wag gate troopers had left empty assault rifles and spent mags on the ground. They had also left their blood.

J.B. scrambled under the trailer's rear bumper, crawling on all fours, keeping his head low to keep from bumping it on the undercarriage.

Mildred scooted in behind Ryan as he moved to the path side of the trailer. One look told him that Malosh had brought the cannon fodder into play.

"Bastards ran," Mildred said, puffing hard as she reloaded her Czech wheel gun.

"Not far enough," Ryan said. He replaced the mag in his SIG.

Blasterfire chattered outside the berm. It continued until someone shouted to call it off.

Ryan couldn't see who had been shot, but he could guess.

Then the rest of the wag guards dashed into view, chased by a howling mob. Haldane's men tried to fight back, tried to run, but for once the oldies and the crippies had the advantage. For once they had hold of the clean end of the stick. The defenders could still move faster than they could, but they had no place to go. The mob closed in with cudgels, rocks and boot heels. Haldane's troopers disappeared in mass of moving bodies, bobbing heads and stomping feet.

Ryan and Mildred advanced to the front of the trailer while J.B. finished reloading his weapons.

On the one-eyed man's signal they moved out from

under the gate, running along the inside of the berm, to the protection of the back end of the school bus.

Bullets from the Welcome Center slammed the opposite side of the bus and sparked off the berm's rocks. The dead arms drooping from the bus's rear opening shuddered as bullets thumped and gnawed the bodies inside.

It was the only direction fire was coming from.

The machine guns had stopped shooting, presumably because the remaining gun posts at the center and east end of berm had been abandoned. The survivors of Haldane's force had pulled back, retreating to make their stand inside the most solid structure in the ville.

The cannon fodder spilled out from under the wag gate, red-faced and triumphant from their stomp fest. Behind the first wave, a tall figure in black appeared. Baron Malosh held an AK-47 in either hand. At his command, the bullet sponges crossed the stretch of open ground, limping and hopping for the first row of Sunspot's shelters. Slugs from the corners of the Welcome Center chopped down the fodder on either side of the baron. Sawed by blasterfire, the droolies and cripples were spun down hard to their knees, or hurled aside. The Impaler reached cover untouched by lead. Not all of his companions were so lucky. Easily one-third of the expendable had been expended. They lay facedown in the dirt behind him.

Ryan scanned the battlefield. Some of the hellhounds were running loose, in three- or four-dog packs. Others were dead, either shot or blown apart by gren blasts. There were wounded ones, too. Along the edge of the ville garden a dog with a broken spine pulled itself along with its front legs; its back legs dragged uselessly behind. Malosh's norm fighters had moved around the other side of the ville, along edge of berm, coming at the Welcome Center through the rows of makeshift shelters. Swampies waited with them at the edge of the shacks. No ville folk were visible. Ryan figured they were hiding in their shacks, trying to keep from being chilled in a cross fire.

The Impaler and his men led the attack in two prongs, a pincer movement closing in on Welcome Center, raining twin streams of small-arms fire on the building.

Haldane fighters shot back from behind the garden's concrete compost bins, trying to protect the retreat of their comrades.

Grens arced through the air, lobbed from behind an immobile Winnebago into the middle of the garden. They thunderclapped, sending shrap, soil and greenery flying in all directions. When the Comp B smoke cleared, the rings of leveled foliage revealed corpses sprawled facedown between the rows. Some were torn apart. Either before the fact by dogs or by the string of gren explosions.

Following up on the frag grens, Malosh and his fighters poured concentrated fire on the Welcome Center, chipping out chunks of the concrete blocks and the planters out front, driving the defenders back behind their shooting positions.

With no cover between the bus and the center's entryway, Ryan, Mildred and J.B. couldn't advance on the target. They held their fire and watched the battle unfold.

Backed by the full-auto assault, Malosh's norms

rushed for a corner of the garden, firing as they went. Haldane's men abandoned the compost bins, pulling back to the concrete planters.

The attackers pressed on, dashing through the garden rows to the just vacated compost bins. From that position, the Impaler's men started chucking more grens, blind tossing them over the roof and corner of the Welcome Center. The first couple bounced on the concrete path and rolled away toward the berm, exploding with solid whacks but without consequence.

The third gren landed smack in the middle of one of the long concrete planters. The four fighters hiding behind it turned to run for the protection of the Welcome Center entryway. The gren blew up before they got there. The rocking explosion lifted and slammed three of them against the concrete block wall. The fourth man was bowled over from behind by a yard-long chunk of flying concrete.

The deadly blast triggered the defenders' final retreat. As the last of Haldane's soldiers disappeared inside the doorway, Malosh and his combined forces charged the building, shouting and hollering.

Ryan searched the rampaging mob for Krysty and Jak. In vain. There was no sign of Doc, either.

AS KRYSTY AND JAK USHERED the boys down the lane, screams from behind made them turn to look over their shoulders.

Two swampie females were kneeling in the road beside the corpse of Meconium, grieving their head mutie's loss with balled fists and shrieks of outrage.

Mebbe Meconium had been their father, Krysty thought. Or their brother. Or the father of their children.

Or all of the above.

The thing about swampies, they stuck together. Inside and outside of the bedroom, which was one reason why Malosh hadn't given them blasters. The cussed little bastards were likely to turn them on the first nonswampie they came across.

When Krysty saw the females whip a pair of found AK-47s out from under the folds of their loose-waisted, ground-dragging skirts, she had no doubt who they were intending to shoot.

The other thing about swampies was that they lived for revenge.

"Gonna get you for what you done to him, Snowball!" one of the females cried as she clumsily shouldered the predark assault rifle.

The second she pulled the trigger it became obvious that she hadn't been trained in the art of firing a full-auto blaster. The furious, staccato kick of the predark rifle clearly took her by surprise, and as the muzzle climbed higher and higher with every discharging round, despite the considerable moorings of her big feet and her massive behind, she went down on her butt, firing straight up in the air.

Before she could recover, Jak calmly shot her through the face.

The Magnum round jerked her head back and sent her long hair flying forward. A glistening puff of red burst from the rear of her skull. Cranial shrap and blenderized brains scattered behind her, and she flopped onto her back, a bag of cooling flesh.

Her sister swampie somehow managed to find her own blaster's selector switch. Squinting down the AK's sights, she fired a single shot at Krysty. The rifle's recoil jolted her upper body backward. She shot again before the recoil wave subsided.

And again.

The slugs banged into the corrugated steel wall of a cargo container. Each one higher and wider of their target.

Krysty aimed and fired her revolver twice, hitting the swampie in the chest and stomach, doubling her over. The swampie dropped the AK and, holding in her guts with one hand, whipped out a nick-bladed filleting knife with the other. "I'm gonna stick you good with this," she promised, wheezing with pain. "Then I'm gonna twist it around."

Boom!

Jak's Magnum blaster knocked the swampie ragdoll sideways, cartwheeled her and slammed her into the ground. In the process, her long skirts were thrown up over her head.

"Now there's an unhappy sight," Krysty said.

Jak frowned and pointedly looked away.

The dead swampie female shunned underwear.

The two boys were riveted by the splayed, dimpled thighs and vast buttocks. With that central plume of porcupine-stiff hair, it was something out of a carny show.

Krysty grabbed them by the shoulders and shook them to break the terrible spell.

"We have to keep moving, or we're all gonna get

chilled," she told them. "Is there some place safe we can leave you?"

The boys stared at each other, gravely weighing whether they should give up such an important secret to virtual strangers. In this case, the strangers had saved their lives more than once.

"This way," one of them said.

Krysty and Jak followed as they took off up the lane. The boys stopped at a rust-orange cargo container and pushed open a crookedly hanging door, which was nothing more than a rectangle of metal cut from the wall and hinged with concentric loops of baling wire.

Inside, the light came from a series of holes hacked high in the back wall and a torch burning in a crude stanchion. The pallets on floor were jammed edge to edge. There was no telling how many people slept in the enclosure. It smelled of torch smoke and layers of unwashed humanity.

A curtain of black plastic covered part of one end of the narrow metal room. The children headed straight for it. Pulling back the plastic, they revealed what looked like an indoor toilet. A three-holer seat made of a wooden plank formed the top of the holding box below. A plastic bucket hanging from the wall was half filled with corn cobs.

The boys gripped either end of the plank seat and started to lift it to one side.

"Wait!" Krysty said. "What are you doing?"

"It's okay," one of the boys assured her. "It's not real."

Jak snatched the torch off the wall. Leaning forward,

he sniffed the air above the three holer. "Not shitter," was his assessment.

"What's down there, then?" Krysty asked the boys.

"It's an entrance to the tunnels."

"Tunnels?"

"Well, there're more like caves, really," the boy said. "They're natural. We didn't dig them out. They run all under the ground of the ville. There must be miles and miles of them all down through the ridge. That's where everybody from the ville is hiding. It's where we always go when the coldhearts come. When the fighting's over we come out."

"You two can come down with us, too," other boy said. "It's okay. You'll be safe there."

"We can't do that," Krysty said. "We're looking for a friend."

Jak swept the torch back over the commode. "Ha!" he exclaimed, his ruby eyes glittering in the light.

"You found him, my dear," said a soft, disembodied voice.

She peered down into the crapper and saw a familiar face framed by the center seat hole. His LeMat in hand, Doc Tanner smiled up at her with his excellent teeth.

Chapter Twenty-Five

Ryan, Mildred and J.B. joined the throng storming the windowless flank of the Welcome Center. From the ground to fifteen feet up its sides, it was pocked with overlaid bullet craters. The corners of the building had been gnawed into saw teeth by slugs and grens. The bigger holes had been crudely patched with mortar.

Inside the berm, fighting had virtually ceased, although here and there isolated and terrified Haldane men were being chased down and slaughtered by dogs and swampies.

All of Haldane's other survivors had withdrawn through the Welcome Center's locked and blocked front entrance. Heavy, four-by-eight steel plates covered the inside of the double entry doors. The facing windows were all blocked, as well, either by more steel plates or by plywood baffles. There were no gunports cut for the defenders to shoot through. Perhaps because such ports were used to fire in as well as out. Perhaps because the game plan of Haldane's troopers was to withstand a siege.

As there was no immediate threat from the trapped enemy, Baron Malosh let his own fighters have a bit of a rest. The norms sat in the shade of the building, drinking water, nursing minor wounds and sprains, and attending to their weapons. Some of the swampies caught and leashed their remaining dogs, others moved around the compound, robbing valuables and weapons from the dead.

During the lull, Ryan, Mildred and J.B. looked for their missing companions among the crowd.

"Don't see them," Mildred said.

"Me, neither," J.B. said.

Ryan glanced back at the bodies strewed on the ground, the tendons in his jaws flexing.

"Don't go there, Ryan," Mildred said.

"Yeah, but mebbe they're wounded," he told her. "Or trapped. Anything's possible. We've got to search every stinkin' trailer."

Ryan set off for the nearest row of shacks. His friends had to hurry to keep up.

"Where are the ville folk?" Mildred said.

"Probably under their mattresses, pissing themselves," J.B. said.

A burst of blasterfire at their backs made them stop and turn, weapons in hand. Baron Malosh had fired one of his AKs in the air. Now he was pointing both weapons at them.

"Where do you think you're going?" the Impaler said.

"We got missing people," Ryan told him.

"Take another step and you'll be missing, too. Nobody leaves the battlefield until I say so. There's still work to do."

Mildred and J.B. knew what to do if Ryan made a move on the baron. They'd used the same technique before with success, and they practiced it to keep their skills honed. As he dropped into a shooting crouch, they would dive away from him in opposite directions, tuck, roll and come up firing. The diverging, rapid movement would leave Malosh hunting targets for the split second that Ryan needed to put a slug in his head, with follow-ups from Mildred and J.B. stitching his chest. But before Ryan could act the muzzles of Malosh's officers' autorifles bracketed them, as well. And there were too many opposing blasters for the strategy to work.

"Fine," Ryan said. Although fine it was not.

As they walked past him, Baron Malosh turned to his officers, "Blow the plates on the front doors," he told them. "Use grens. I don't want to destroy the building unless I have to."

Ryan understood that control of the ville had passed back and forth several times, and that the defenders and attackers had had plenty of opportunities to try different strategies on each other. Both armies knew every inch of the ground, had fought over it, and lost soldiers and treasure in the process. The result was a gradual destruction of the site over time. Increased fortification demanded more aggressive attacks, which brought on changes in the defenses. This constant modification and testing of same had only served to create a more efficient meat grinder.

Why was the building still standing? he asked himself.

The answer was simple. It was too valuable to both sides for either to completely raze it.

While the officers organized the task their baron had set for them, the three companions conferred.

"What are we going to do about finding Krysty, Jak and Doc?" Mildred asked.

"Can't fight the whole nukin' army," J.B. said. "Old Malosh has got his eye on us now. He's not going to let us slip away before he takes the Welcome Center."

"I only see one way out," Ryan said. "We have to get the battle won. Once that's done, we can locate Krysty and Jak. They've got be inside the berm. We'll split up and search the place as fast as we can."

"What about Doc?" Mildred asked.

"We don't even know if Doc is here," Ryan said. "Mebbe he never made it this far. If he isn't here, he's out on the interstate somewhere. After we regroup, we'll head out through the west gate and backtrack his route."

"And if we don't find him there?" Mildred said.

"We'll find him," Ryan assured her.

The discussion ended when the officers came barreling out of the entryway shouting, "Take cover!" Everyone scurried to duck around the corner of the building.

All four grens blew.

The force of the blast surged outward and upward, bringing down the doorway's lintel and a section of the covered walkway. Pieces of concrete sailed through the air and slammed against the side of the berm.

Though flashburned, the steel doors still stood. They had held up to the assault.

"Not enough C-4," was J.B.'s evaluation.

Baron Malosh agreed with the Armorer. "Use satchels!" he snarled at his officers. "Get those doors open!"

The men disappeared into the lingering smoke carrying canvas bags of explosive charges. They reappeared moments later without the charges and running for their lives.

Determined to succeed the second time around, they had gone a bit too far. The explosion blew the steel reinforcing plates loose from their moorings, all right; but with an earsplitting thundercrack and a mass of expelled smoke and dust, it also took out the rest of the covered walkway and shook the whole building to its foundation. Zigzagging cracks appeared in the lines of concrete blocks. The force of the explosion caved in the building's entrance all the way to the roof, twisting apart the join of the steel barriers like a giant can opener.

If Malosh was unhappy about the collateral damage, his nose-to-chin leather mask kept it hidden. "Clear the rubble, pull those plates out of the way," he ordered the assembled fodder.

At the direction of their one-armed captain, the oldies and the cripples moved to the piles of tumbled-down and fractured concrete blocks and started shifting them to the sides of the ruined entrance.

As they opened a path to the gap in the plates a flurry of gunshots rang out. The bullets dropped four of the fodder at once, blowing them off their feet and onto their backs on the heaps of broken blocks. They wailed and writhed while their fellow bullet sponges dived for cover.

"Put up some fire," Baron Malosh said, impatiently waving his armed norms forward.

Ryan, J.B. and Mildred moved ahead with the others, taking up shooting positions behind piles of rubble. Bullets zipped out of the three-foot gap in the plates, slapping into the concrete debris in front of them.

The intense incoming fire forced the companions to

keep their heads down. Even if they could have raised their heads, they couldn't have seen the shooters. Trapped smoke and dust, residue from the satchel charge explosions, poured out from between the plates.

Unable to take aim, the companions shot over and around the rubble, laying down random return fire. The other norms did the same. Their bullets spanked and sparked off the steel plates, flying between them into the bowels of building.

They put up enough covering fire for one of the officers to reach the protection of the left-hand plate. He primed a gren and chucked it through the gap. Four seconds later a hollow blast echoed through the building and brought down more of the facade.

Malosh signaled for more grens.

The officer chucked in another two. After the concussions faded, there was no more shooting from inside the Welcome Center.

The Impaler's force sent up a cheer.

"We've got 'em, now!" Malosh shouted. "Follow me." With AKs poised in either hand, he charged through the narrow gap, running low and fast. His officers shoved the norm fighters after him.

Ryan and the others swung in behind them, into the mass of acrid smoke and hot dust. Coughing hard, their eyes streaming tears, they crouched inside the hallway, blasters up with nothing to shoot at.

Gradually the smoke lifted and the dust dropped out of the air, revealing a reception area packed with cardboard mattresses, some feebly burning. Scorch marks blackened the walls. About half the torches in the room were still lit; the rest had been blown out. There were three dead Haldane fighters on the far side of the garrison's communal bedroom. Caught from behind by the gren blasts, they all lay facing a hallway that led deeper into the building.

Malosh stopped in front of the bullet-riddled information desk. He gestured toward the deserted hallway. It was about twelve feet wide, and there were three closed doors on each side. In the dim torchlight Ryan could see there was another door facing them at the end of the corridor.

"Clear every room in the hall," the baron told his officers.

Instead of doing the job themselves, the officers pushed some of the norms in front of them. The conscripted clearing team included Ryan, Mildred and J.B.

Ryan noted the hinges were on the hallway side, so the doors opened out. Turning the first knob and finding the door unlocked, he pulled it wide open. J.B. darted into the room, his Uzi ready to rip. Mildred entered after him. The windowless room was empty. From the shelves that lined the walls, it had once been used for storage. Some of the shelves had been tipped over onto the floor by the explosions.

The companions moved back into the hallway. The second door on their side hid a utility closet, also bare to the walls. Either the garrison had no supplies, which was unlikely, or they had moved them all somewhere else in the Welcome Center.

The three norms checking the other side of the corridor weren't working so efficiently. They were a door behind as Ryan, Mildred and J.B. cleared their last room.

When the Malosh fighter opened the door, he and the

man who lunged over the threshold with his assault rifle got a big surprise.

A final surprise.

The hallway rocked with a deafening blast. Two men were hurled away from the doorway in a flash of light. They slammed into and bounced off the opposite wall. One of them was nearly cut in two, a three-inch-wide seam whipsawed through his midsection. The other lost his right arm to the shoulder and his torso was laid open from armpit to hip.

Above the crumpled men, a line of ball bearings studded the bloody sheet rock.

"Claymore mine," J.B. said. "The bastards booby trapped the rad-blasted hall."

As he spoke, fifteen feet away, the door at the end of the corridor swung inward. Mildred, who was covering it with her wheelgun, opened fire at once. Ryan pivoted and cut loose with the SIG. J.B. added some Uzi full-auto chatter to the mix.

Under the horrendous, close-range fusillade, the bottom half of the hollow-core door turned to splinters. It continued to swing open for another twenty degrees of arc, then stopped abruptly.

Ryan could see at least two prostrate bodies on the other side. He booted it all the way open. There were actually three, heaped on a landing at the top of a flight of stairs leading down.

After the last door in the corridor had been checked, the baron advanced to the end of the hall. "Out of the way," he said.

Ryan stepped clear, letting the masked man move onto the landing.

"Drag these bodies out of here," Malosh said.

Ryan and J.B. bent, grabbed limp arms and pulled the corpses into the nearest room.

By the time they were done, the officers had moved the entire norm force into the hallway.

"Haldane's men are holed up in the basement," Malosh told them. "We've got to clean them out."

The fearless baron was the first down the stairs.

Ryan was fourth; J.B. and Mildred were the fifth and sixth, respectively.

In the flickering torchlight, Ryan counted ten metal-edged steps before they came to another landing, then the stairs turned at a right angle and descended again.

The ceiling of the Welcome Center's basement was covered with pipes and ducts of all sizes, strung with cobwebs. A polished concrete floor reflected the light of dozens of wall-mounted torches. The wide room was furnished with machines inoperative since nukeday—electric power, water pumps, air conditioning, furnace—some obviously plundered for scrap. All the torches hung along the right-hand concrete block wall. The row of lights pointed the way to another corridor entrance; at its end were two doors. Like the ground-floor entrance, both were sheathed in heavy steel plate.

Only these had gun ports at waist height.

Ryan could see a blaster muzzle poking from each, leaving little doubt where the bulk of the Haldane force lay.

"Put out the torches," Malosh said as his conscripts scattered out of the line of fire.

As the lights in their part of the room were extinguished, the baron ordered the last of his fodder to come forward.

"I want you to douse the torches in that hallway up there," he told the one-armed captain of the doomed. "Make it to those doors and push grens through the firing ports."

The fodder captain didn't argue about the feasibility of the mission. In the weak light, he accepted some grens from an officer, then addressed his motley crew. "It's up to us to finish this," he told the twenty-five or so cripples and ville idiots still sucking air. "First, we're going to put out the rest of the torches. If they can't see us, they can't hit us." He showed them the cluster of frag grens. "Then we knock the bastards out."

Ryan had a hard time understanding the man's enthusiasm for the job he'd been handed. Mebbe he was tired of the crippie life?

The one-armed captain counted off a dozen of the fodder, then led them in a mad rush to the mouth of the hallway.

Haldane's machine gunners let them get inside the entrance of the twelve-foot-wide corridor. Then both blasters roared, sweeping the narrow passage with full-auto streams of lead.

A shooting gallery.

Bullets sliced through the fodder. The one-armed man took a burst through the chest as he reached for a torch, and he went down hard. Somehow the other sponges managed to put out all but two of the torches, nearest the doors. In the process all twenty-five were chilled. The last three of the fodder were so close to the machine-gun barrels that they were literally shot to pieces.

When the ricochets stopped zinging around the dark basement, Malosh turned to an officer. "Go back to the entrance," he said. "Get the swampies to drag down one of those steel plates."

It took a while for the muties to accomplish that. Ryan could hear them banging and cursing as they struggled on the stairs. You didn't have to be a white-coat to predict what Malosh intended to do with the plate. The only question was who was going to get the job?

A question that was answered after the swampies lost control of the massive plate and it crashed to the bottom of the steps.

The Impaler picked out a hefty-looking norm, then selected J.B. and Ryan. "Use the plate as a shield," he ordered them. "It's plenty thick enough to stop machine-gun bullets. Carry it in front of you to the end of the hall. Angle it so one of you can plant a satchel charge against the doors, set the fuse, then back out."

Sounded easy.

It wasn't.

When the trio tried to raise the four-by-eight sheet of armor plate from the floor, Ryan knew why the muties had been cursing. Armor of sufficient thickness and temper to deflect heavy duty bullets wasn't light. The rad-blasted thing weighed more than three hundred pounds. If it was awkward to lift, it was even harder to carry.

To protect their feet and legs from blasterfire, they let the bottom edge scrape along the concrete, and held the top tipped back on their shoulders as they crouched and pushed.

The metal made a screeching sound as it slid across the floor.

When they reached the mouth of the corridor, the machine guns cut loose and the deluge of .308-caliber rounds drowned out the screeching. The din was ear-splitting. The vibration felt like a hundred maniacs beating on the other side of the plate with ball-peen hammers. Ricochets sprayed the ceiling and shot back into the steel doors. Under the concentrated bullet impacts, the armor plate started to heat up. They inched forward for five more yards, then hit an obstacle. The fodder bodies were in the way. They had to lift the bottom of the plate over the corpses to get past.

The machine guns continued to fire, perhaps in desperation, even though the rounds weren't penetrating the steel.

Choking on the dense gunsmoke, Ryan, J.B., and the hefty norm turned the plate at a forty-five-degree angle to the doors and advanced closer, shoving one end against the edge of the left-hand door. Working behind the low cover, which was supported by J.B. and the hefty norm, Ryan quickly planted and primed the satchel charge.

There was no room for error as they retraced their steps under ravening fire. They had to move quickly, but if they let the plate slip, they'd be chopped down. Pulling the plate turned out to be much more difficult than pushing it. Especially when they had to accommodate the corpses on the floor. The way they were hustling Ryan thought they could clear the short hallway before the bag blew.

He was wrong.

Ryan didn't actually hear the explosion. Nor could

he distinguish between the blinding flash outside and inside his head. As the blast's pressure wave flattened the plate that protected them, the world went white.

Then cold.

Then hot.

Then dark.

Ryan felt nothing as he hit the floor and the heavy plate fell on top of him. He was unconscious.

THE ONE-EYED MAN came to as the crushing weight was lifted off his chest. He looked up to see Mildred leaning over him with concern on her face. Torches along the corridor had been relit.

The woman's lips moved, but Ryan's ears were ringing so badly couldn't hear what she was saying.

Beside him, J.B. was sitting up, shaking his head as he tried to clear it. His glasses and fedora were coated with fine white dust.

The hefty norm hadn't been so lucky. Because he had been holding the right-hand end of the plate, he'd had no wall to protect his exposed flank. Mebbe he'd let the plate had slid down an inch or two at just the wrong moment, as well. Chilled stone-dead by the concussion, he lay on his side while blood dripped from his plaster-dusted ears, eyes, nose and mouth.

The metal doors to Haldane's underground stronghold were buckled and bent inward. No blasterfire came from inside the room; only smoke and dust.

Leaning on Mildred for support, Ryan and J.B. moved away from the breached entrance.

If there were any Haldane defenders who wanted to surrender, the baron didn't give them the chance.

He wasn't known as Malosh the Merciful.

At his signal, his men tossed handfuls of grens through the torn-apart doors, into the smoke.

A string of explosions violently shook the floor. Orange flame belched from the entrance; shrapnel whined through the basement. Ryan could barely hear the blasts. It felt like his ears were stuffed with cotton.

Malosh and his fighters waited until all the smoke cleared before they moved into the room. This gave Ryan and J.B. enough time to recover their hearing. The three companions followed the other norms over the threshold, into an abattoir.

The cellar room was littered with bodies and severed body parts. Belonging to mebbe fifty men, Ryan guessed. The walls and ceiling were decorated in a two-tone palette of black scorch and red gore.

The Haldane garrison was history.

As Ryan surveyed the ruination, he caught a movement in a corner in a pile of bodies. A wounded man raised his head from the heap, his face sheeted with blood.

"We didn't chill all the bastards," one of the norms said.

"Spiking time!" another shouted with glee.

As they closed in on the Haldane trooper, someone cried, "Look out! He's got a blaster!"

The Malosh fighters backed away, reaching for their own weapons.

As it turned out they had nothing to worry about.

The lone survivor parted his bloody teeth and shoved the muzzle of his blaster into his mouth. Without a word, he pulled the trigger, painting the wall behind him with his own brains. Gunsmoke billowed from his gaping mouth.

Ryan, J.B. and Mildred joined the troops pouring out of the Welcome Center. The battle was over. Sunspot had fallen to Malosh. The companions didn't share the fighters' jubilation; their only concern was finding their missing friends, and doing it as quickly as possible.

Which turned out to be much simpler than any of them had anticipated.

As they stepped away from the building, J.B. pointed toward the ville's residential area and exclaimed, "Lookee there!"

"Lookee where?" Ryan said as he stared at the mass of ville folk that suddenly popped out from between the shanty lanes and started heading for the Welcome Center. Then he saw a trio of familiar faces. Krysty, Jak and Doc walked across the devastated compound toward them.

All under their own power and seemingly in good health.

All still armed.

Ryan felt a wave of profound relief. In truth, he had been a lot more worried about them than he had let on to Mildred and J.B.

The tall, smiling redhead came into Ryan's arms and he embraced her for a long moment.

The embrace ended abruptly when blasterfire chattered behind them.

"Would you look at that masked asshole," J.B. said.

"Asshole," Jak agreed.

Baron Malosh was celebrating his big win by riding his horse around the inside perimeter of the berm, shooting his twin AKs in the air.

Ryan checked the gate exits and saw that the victory lap hadn't been the baron's first act. Malosh had already assigned a number of armed guards to the exits so the conscripts couldn't desert. The only way out of Sunspot appeared to be climbing over the berm, which in broad daylight would draw attention and bullets.

"Are you all right, Doc?" Mildred asked, giving the scarecrow Tanner a quick hug.

"I am perfectly fine, my dear Dr. Wyeth," Doc replied.

Ryan noticed a blond ville woman standing behind the time traveler. Her expression changed when Mildred touched Doc. It went from friendly to irritated in a split second. He also noted her strange, beautiful violet-colored eyes.

In the middle of the compound, the swampies were looting the bodies of foes and friends alike. As they gathered up dropped weapons and ammo, they rifled the pockets of the dead, looking for small, easily conceal-able items of value.

Other muties and the surviving cannon fodder were cleaning up the Welcome Center. It appeared that Malosh intended on reoccupying it as soon as possible. The limp bodies of the Haldane defenders were lugged out by their hands and feet. The body parts were carried piled on tarps. The human litter of battle was dumped in the middle of the compound, waiting either crema-tion or burial. Some of the muties had started a bonfire to burn up the cardboard mattresses and bloody rags.

"Dear friends, I would like you to meet Isabel," Doc said, urging the blond woman forward. "She is the leader of Sunspot ville."

The companions nodded to her.

She nodded back.

"Isabel and the ville folk," Doc went on in a more hushed tone, "are planning to hit Malosh."

"You'll never beat him," Mildred told the woman. "He's got too many troops. It'd be suicide to even try."

Isabel put a hand on Doc's arm and looked into Mildred's eyes. A proprietary hand, it seemed to Ryan. "We plan to wait until Malosh and most of his soldiers leave for the attack on Nuevaville," she said. "The odds are in our favor then."

"Timing is everything," Doc said.

"You might be able to win a temporary victory against a reduced Malosh force," Ryan said. "But what do you really gain in the long run? Can you hold the ville when Malosh comes back, pissed off as hell, with the rest of his fighters? Can you hold it when Haldane comes back? One or the other of them will crush you, that's guaranteed."

Isabel was unconvinced by his argument. "We've been caching arms and ammunition for months now. We intend to use it at the very first opportunity. We don't have any choice anymore. We have to fight. These bastard barons are grinding us into dust."

"Either way you're going to die," Krysty said.

"If you had to choose a way to go," Isabel asked her, "would you take starvation or a bullet?"

"Bullet," the redhead replied without hesitation.

"Then you know how we ville folk feel."

"You could leave," Doc told her. "You are most welcome to come along with us. Deathlands is an immense place. Its settlements are widely separated. It's easy to evade pursuit in the hellscape. All that's required is a week or two of nonstop walking. It's also easy to start another life somewhere new. Somewhere better."

"I won't desert my people," Isabel said. "And we can't all come with you. The barons want us here, as their field hands. If we try to run, they'll just hunt us down and drag us back. The fight is here."

"Perhaps we could join you, then?" Doc said.

"You have no stake in this. Sunspot's our ville. We've bought it with our blood and sweat and lives."

Doc was about to say more when he was interrupted by a joyous shout from atop the berm.

"Yee-hah!" one of the norm fighters hollered. Straddling the berm's crest, he waved his arms over his head. "Everybody! Come up here! You've gotta see this!"

Chapter Twenty-Six

A bit of free, light entertainment was hard to come by in the hellscape.

And it was an especially welcome release after a morning of pitched combat and mortal danger.

"Mutie fight! Mutie fight!" the man on the berm bellowed through cupped hands.

All of Baron Malosh's fighters, save those manning the wag and foot gates, surged for the ville's gorge-facing wall.

Though she was loath to admit it, the call to spectate touched even Mildred. And for reasons she knew were suspect. Her curiosity about what was chilling what had nothing to do with the spirit of twentieth-century scientific inquiry in which she had been trained. In her previous existence, prior to being put into cryosleep, she had always disliked and avoided brutal sports. She had considered them senseless and of value only to those who promoted them. Her years in the hellscape had changed her in many ways, some subtle, some not. The constant fight for survival reduced everything to the lowest common denominator. Even the concept of suitable entertainment. When Ryan said, "Might as well have a look-see," she joined the other companions as they rushed up the side of the berm.

Standing on the crest of the barrier, she looked down on the gorge and the blown-up section of Interstate 10. Immediately, she saw movement in the canyon bottom. Rapid movement. In the clouds of raised dust, something large and dark was frantically running and jumping in great bounds.

It appeared to have too many legs by at least a couple of pair.

"What the hell is that?" J.B. asked.

Which was Mildred's question, too.

"We call it the grave digger," Isabel told them, as if that explained anything at all.

Doc quickly filled in some of the blanks. "In point of fact," he said, "that creature is more of an exhumer. I came across it on my way up here last night. Although I couldn't see it clearly in the dark. From the evidence along the highway, it appears to feed upon the bodies buried in the gorge. Hence, the name grave digger."

Mildred was amazed by the mutie's two seemingly contradictory attributes. The shaggy monster was incredibly fast and spry; it made consecutive, twenty-foot standing broad jumps, yet it was very large. She could only estimate its size in relation to other objects in the gorge. The width of the four-lane interstate; the bodies of the fallen fodder. From this she guessed it was at least eight feet across the body. It had very long, jointed legs; by straightening them it could raise its belly six feet from the ground. Despite its size, it had to be very light, otherwise it couldn't have propelled its mass over such extreme distances and with such alacrity.

Was it a spider? A panther?

It leaped atop a block of concrete and for a second they could all see it in more detail.

"Where's its head?" Krysty said.

It was true. There was no head in evidence. The hairy body appeared to be nearly circular. And the four sets of legs allowed it to jump in any direction and hit the ground running.

"It could be a trannie," Mildred said. Trannie was short for transgenic bioweapon. Also known in the ultra-secret whitecoat ranks as chimera. Trannies were living beings constructed from a mishmash of other species' genetics. It was yet another example of the lunacy and arrogance of predark scientists. They had mixed snippets of DNA from different, naturally occurring species to produce new and unique living creatures for specific functional and research purposes. The technology explosion near the end of the twentieth century had allowed scientists to create bacteria that ate oil spills and other toxics, and that manufactured tiny electronic components in invisible assembly lines. Living industrial machines on a microscopic scale.

If small was good, big was better.

And the military applications were obvious.

The goal of the military researchers was to mass produce custom-designed warrior breeds. Some of these constructs turned out to be so dangerous that the only way to control them was to include a death gene in their chromosomes, a time bomb that limited their life span and their reproductive capability. In many cases, the time bomb hadn't gone off. And the trannies had multiplied. The companions had crossed paths with such critters several times before. And the outcome had always been hellish and touch-and-go in the extreme.

"It eats the wounded, too," Isabel added. "It prefers not to fight for its dinner. It showed up down there about a year ago. Nobody knows where it came from, but there's only the one of them as far as we can tell. It only feeds at night. We've never seen it after sunrise. When there's fighting and dying it's always hanging around. It stays hidden during the day. Something's chased it out of its hidey-hole."

Because of the distance, the terrain, the speed and the dust, it was difficult for Mildred to see exactly what that something was. Although she could tell there were lots of them and they were much, much smaller than the thing they were chasing.

A roar of catcalls and bloodthirsty cheers from the Malosh fighters lined up along the berm top sent chills up her spine. The soldiers were taking bets on which mutie would win the battle in the gorge.

Baron Malosh had joined the fun. He stood watching the show with his men. His expression was hidden by the leather mask he wore.

"The little muties are baby scagworms," Doc said. "There are so many of them in this area that the Sunspot folk have started eating them regularly. They taste rather like lobster with a hint of pork chop. I highly recommend them."

Mildred remembered the scagworms from previous encounters. They were an insectoid mutie species, possibly another flawed batch of trannies with a nonfunctioning death gene. They were almost unstoppable because of their speed, mobility and armor plate. And they came factory-equipped with an insane and bottomless hunger.

The grave digger darted about in the gorge bottom like it had eyes in the back of whatever passed for its head. Again and again, it avoided the relentless predators with prodigious bounds and blindingly quick reversals of direction. Even so, the odds weren't in its favor.

As the great beast leaped over a water-filled trench, scagworms dashed up an overhanging tilted slab of concrete and jumped. When the grave digger landed, the worms came down on its back.

Biting.

The men who had bet on the scagworms cheered while the worms sheared off great clumps of the grave digger's fur with their jaws.

Whirling, the spiderlike monster shook off two of the black shapes. It scraped off two more with deft blows from its front legs. Then it jumped away before the rest of the pack could close in for the chill.

The worms riding on its back attacked its rear pair of legs at their join with the body. The power of the transverse jaws was immediately evident. In seconds they clipped those legs off cleanly, but in the process were thrown from the grave digger's back. A creamy white fluid, perhaps blood, gushed from the still moving stumps.

The bucked-off scagworms fell upon the long limbs they had severed, cracking them like crab legs and digging out the meat.

The digger still had six legs to run on, and wasn't noticeably slowed by the amputations. Twenty or thirty worms were in hot pursuit. Shiny black in the sun, they looked like fat, stubby snakes as they slithered over the broken ground in its wake.

Mildred watched the jittering, jerky, frenetic chase in fascination. It looked like a sped-up motion picture. Prey and predators splashed through pools and jumped over blocks of concrete. The worms showed no sign of real organization; they proceeded in straight lines over and through the obstacle course. Like radar-guided missiles. And it was every missile for itself. Instead of trying to encircle or trap their prey, instead of trying to bring it down, the worms were content to tear off manageable-size chunks for individual consumption.

Both species ignored the fodder bodies at their feet. Mildred couldn't decide whether the worms were fighting over control of the turf and its spoils, or whether they just considered the grave digger dinner.

If the larger mutie was trying to defend its claim on the Sunspot body farm, the loss of its limbs changed its mind. It reversed course yet again, making for the relatively intact roadway leading out of the gorge. Mildred was astonished at the speed it made on flatter ground. She couldn't even see its legs, they were moving so fast.

The grave digger quickly put distance between it and the low shapes in pursuit. It raced out of the mouth of the gorge and continued down the ruined highway, heading due west. As the distance increased between predator and prey, the horde of black specks gave up the chase. Their intended target left the interstate and disappeared over a rise in the desert scrub.

Along the berm top, the losers in the fighters' betting pool cursed and kicked the dirt. The winners laughed and grinned as small quantities of jack and jolt changed hands.

If the scagworms were trannies, what the hell were

they made of? Mildred asked herself. Instead of being a simple cross between two divergent species, they were more like a genetic stew. Of millipede. Giant cockroach. Rhinoceros beetle. Mebbe with a helping of anaconda on the side. Unlike the scagworms that had probably been protected in deeply buried, hardsited redoubt labs, the creatures that had provided snips of its component DNA hadn't survived nukeday and the prolonged stresses of skydark.

Because of her training in predark science Mildred understood full well the danger of invasive species.

New life-form.

New attributes.

Bad news for existing organisms.

Even naturally occurring organisms had the potential for great harm. Killer bees, fire ants, zebra mussels had all taken their toll before Armageddon. In this case, the predator was much larger, and its limitations, if any, were unknown, and may well have been genetically engineered away. There was no information on the worm's life history, nothing about maximum population densities or range size requirements. If what Sunspot had experienced so far was just the first wave of a much bigger invasion, a spear point driven into the belly of what once had been New Mexico, there was no telling how long it would last or how far it would penetrate.

Adaptation had no conscience and no foresight. It existed outside the individual organism. It was a mechanism of nature without the power of self-understanding or self-analysis. In the end, all that could be done was to cede territory to it, to set up boundaries and to try to maintain them.

"Look, they're coming back," Isabel said, pointing at the undulating black shapes flowing into the gorge. "Manna from heaven."

Mildred turned on the ville's head woman. "Are you out of your frigging mind?" she said. "Don't you see what's happening here?"

"What's happening is that God has finally answered our prayers," Isabel told her. "We will have plenty of food again."

Hunter-gatherer wasteland becomes a hunter-gatherer paradise.

Hunter-gatherers had no obligation to look further than their next meal.

Sunspot ville was living proof that humanity hadn't advanced an iota in the last fifteen thousand years.

"How can you be so stupid?" Mildred said.

"Easy, Mildred," Ryan cautioned.

"Easy what? She sees the hand of God and I see extermination for every living thing within a thousand miles. What we're looking at is a force of nature that can't be anticipated or controlled. You won't be eating the bugs, for long, lady. They'll be eating you! Look down there!"

Back down on the field of death, the scagworms slithered into view. They began feeding at once. Not just on the bodies of the fodder. They also hunted down the living who hid among the rubble. The unarmed deserters, some mere children, screamed for help as they took to their heels. But there was no way for anyone on the berm to render help. The fastest, the youngest of fodder ran from the blown-up section of interstate, trying to escape the gorge.

"You ate scagworm flesh?" Mildred demanded of Doc.

The old man heard the question but didn't respond. Perhaps because he was too busy fighting to keep down his dinner.

"It tasted like pork, huh?" Mildred said. "Maybe there's a simple explanation for that. It's called cannibalism, once removed."

As they watched, the children and other deserters were chased down from behind and dragged to the ground. Five to ten worms set upon each victim, slashing great gashes in the torso then disappearing headfirst into the wounds. The deserters' bodies jerked and flailed as they were tunneled and cored. The scagworms went in shiny black, but they emerged red and dripping

To Mildred, the mindless slaughter exemplified everything that was wrong with this world.

"Dammit to hell!" she cried.

She turned and half ran, half slid down the side of the berm. Blaster in hand, she barged past the fighters standing next to the gorge's center gunpost entrance. She speed-crawled on hands and knees through the culvert, into the front seat of the half-buried Cadillac Escalade.

Seized by blind fury Mildred yanked the charging handle of the post's M-60, dropped the sights and cut loose on the scagworms. She walked fire over the feeding muties, chewing up the rotten tarmac, blasting the worms to bits, shattering their carapaces. She managed to nail about half of the bastards before the rest slithered back to the blown-up section of road and solid cover.

Mildred eased off on the M-60's trigger, her head

wreathed in gunsmoke, spent brass piled around her feet. Breathing hard, heart pounding, she realized that someone was behind her in the SUV.

"Feel better now?" Ryan asked.

Chapter Twenty-Seven

The gruesome show in the gorge over, Doc descended the berm with Isabel. She seemed withdrawn, subdued, pensive.

"Mildred made some cogent points about the danger, I thought," he told her.

"You mean, your loose cannon girlfriend?"

"Mildred is hardly a romantic interest of mine. And I do believe an invasion by a hostile species like the scagworms could mean disaster for this ville."

"I wouldn't call what is happening an 'invasion.'"

"But you said the number of scagworms has steadily and rapidly increased of late."

"Yes."

"I have witnessed their lethality, myself, in more than one arena. How can you deny the danger you and your people are in?"

"I don't deny it. Sunspot folk are accustomed to danger. We've lived with it for many years, thanks to the barons. And we have learned how to handle the worms. And they can be handled, I assure you. We are top dog in the food chain in this corner of Deathlands."

"Unless you count Malosh and Haldane."

"We will defeat them, watch and see."

"I trust you aren't counting on the scagworms to help you do that. If you are, I must admit I am stunned."

"And why shouldn't we count on it?" Isabel snapped, her lovely eyes flashing. "The barons and their troops have no experience dealing with them. They don't know anything about their defenses, their habits or breeding cycle. If the scagworms attack and chill the barons and their fighters, the people of Sunspot no longer have a problem."

"My dear, you can't possibly think you can domesticate a three-hundred-pound homicidal insectoid," Doc replied. "These worm creatures won't be made into pets or penned like livestock. They are nothing but killer instinct. It is hardwired into their nervous systems."

Isabel turned her face away. Doc gently took hold of her chin and made her look into his eyes.

"Listen to me," he said. "Even a tiger has some of the same urges as a human being. A tiger protects its offspring, it provides for them, and it teaches them the rudiments of making a living. Just as we try to do. These common urges create an empathetic bond between our two species. Mammalian species. We humans have nothing in common with scagworms. Their instincts are alien to us, and they are utterly incomprehensible. Worm sows teach their offspring nothing, nor do they protect them. And as a reward, the offspring eat their mothers alive."

"We can herd the worms and we can hunt them," the ville's head woman insisted.

"Isabel, you are missing the point. Scagworms are carnivores, first and foremost. Yes, they will feed on one another when prey is scarce. But they will also eat everything else in their path. They will sweep over Sunspot like the nuke wind. You'll never be able to contain them."

"I don't believe there are that many more of them coming," she said. "There's no proof that the numbers won't level out, or even fall off. That the high point of the population isn't already past. Scagworms haven't been around long enough for us to know whether they will all stay here or move on. Or whether just a few will stay.

"We have suffered for so long, Doc. Because you weren't here, you can't understand or even imagine our situation. Our hopelessness. We are owed this chance. This is the light at the end of the tunnel."

"Indeed, I know you have been hard set upon by fate, and you are correct, I cannot put myself in your place. But you cannot put yourself in mine, either. I have good reason to respect Mildred's scientific opinion. She knows whereof she speaks."

"Perhaps that's true, but I know what I feel in my heart. And I know what I must do."

"Ah, yes," Doc said sadly. "Must do. Two of the most regrettable words in the English language."

"It seems we have come to a parting of the ways."

Doc reached out and softly stroked her cheek with the back of his hand. "You set fire to my ancient heart, madam," he said. "I had forgotten how warmly it could burn."

"Not so ancient, then."

"My dear, if you only knew."

"Some things are not meant to be."

Doc nodded. After a pause he said, "I wonder if my

companions and I might use your caves to take our leave of Sunspot?"

"When will you go?"

"Shortly, I fear."

"Kiss me goodbye, then."

Doc leaned down and she raised her face to meet his. Their lips touched tenderly. Again the sensation was exquisite and riveting.

"I could have loved you, Isabel," Doc said as he pulled back.

"And I could have loved you."

WHEN DOC RETURNED to the companions, Krysty was telling the others about what she'd learned of the ridge's cave system.

"What do you think, Doc?" Ryan said. "You were down there, too. Can we retreat through the caves and reach the desert floor?"

"It is possible if we have a knowledgeable guide," Doc said. "Impossible if we do not. The caves are natural fissures in the rock. Many of them branch off or narrow down to dead ends. Some of them terminate in sheer drops of untold depth. The geology of the ridge is very unstable, as well. I saw a man most horribly crushed by falling rock."

"Where are we going to get a guide?" Mildred said.

"Guides," Krysty corrected her. "Follow me."

The companions trooped after Krysty as she headed away from the Welcome Center.

"Do you know what she's up to, Jak?" Ryan asked.

"Wait, see," the albino replied.

No one stopped or challenged them as they crossed

to the lanes of shanties. As long as the conscripts remained inside the berm, they were free to move around as they wished.

Krysty walked up to a pair of blond boys, perhaps twins, certainly brothers, who were sitting back-to-back on a tireless truck wheel lying on its side in the dirt. The boys stared wide-eyed at Ryan and J.B., whose crusty, grizzled, blood-spattered masculine charm had a powerful appeal to ten-year-old aspiring road warriors.

"Will you help us through the caves?" Krysty asked them. "Do you know the way to the bottom of the ridge?"

"We know the way," one of the boys admitted.

"What do you want in return for guiding us there?" Krysty said.

"You saved us twice," the other boy said. "We don't want anything from you."

"We've got to be careful, though," the first boy said. "We're not supposed to take strangers down there. If anyone sees us, we'll be punished and you'll be stopped."

"We don't want that to happen," Ryan told them. "Where's the tunnel entrance?"

"Over in that cargo container, the third from the end."

"Go ahead of us," Ryan said. "We'll follow you by twos."

But before they could move, volleys of blasterfire erupted from the gates and the top of the berm, directed into the gorge.

"Rad blazes, they're comin'!" shouted a man on the berm's crest. "Get the baron. The bastards are comin'!"

"Stay here, close to the cave entrance," Ryan told the others. "Let's go have a look-see, J.B."

The two of them ran back to the berm and scrambled up to its crest.

"Nukin' hell!" J.B. exclaimed as he surveyed the gorge.

It was just as Mildred had predicted.

The main thrust of the scagworm invasion hadn't arrived yet, but that arrival was only minutes away. Ryan and J.B. could see them coming from the south across the desert, up the interstate and into the gorge. There were tens of thousands of them, perhaps hundreds of thousands of them. They were moving so quickly their numbers were impossible to estimate. There were so many of them they turned the sand black; and the front edge of the wave was already slithering up the side of the gorge.

Blasterfire crackled along the top of the berm.

"Stop shooting!" baron cried as he, too, mounted the summit. "You're just wasting bullets. Wait until they get closer before you fire. Then blow their fucking heads off."

Under other circumstances, it was sound advice.

Under these circumstances, it was easier said than done.

Ryan knew firsthand how hard the scagworms were to hit with small-arms fire. And how hard they were to chill even when hit.

"Get up here!" Baron Malosh shouted at the mass of his troops milling around the Welcome Center. He waved them forward to defend the berm alongside him.

Ryan and J.B. did just the opposite. As the soldiers rushed up the slope, they rushed down. They ran across the compound, going against the flow of fighters hurrying into action.

The flow had dwindled to nothing by the time they reached the companions and the two boys.

"It's the scagworms," Ryan told Mildred, Krysty, Doc and Jak. "Thousands of them are coming up the gorge. Malosh's troopers will never beat them back. They're going to overrun the berm. We've got to get out of here before they do that."

As they turned down the lane, they came face-to-face with the ville's head woman. Isabel was carrying a folding stock Kalashnikov. Extra mags stuck out of her pants' pockets. She wasn't alone. There were at least forty other armed ville folk behind her. The rest of the Sunspot population had once again vanished.

"What do you think you're doing?" Doc said. "You can't fight off the worms. There are too many of them."

"Who said anything about fighting worms?" Isabel replied as she walked past him. "We're seizing the moment. It's Malosh and his men we're after. And this is our chance to get them."

"You're making a big mistake," Ryan said to her back.

Too late.

Kneeling at the end of the lane, Isabel and her followers opened fire on the troopers strung out along the berm top. Their assault rifles clattered and bullet impacts swept across the line of fighters. Ten or so died in that first burst, shot in the back. The survivors, Malosh included, clambered to the gorge side of the berm crest and returned withering fire.

Before the companions' eyes three of the ville folk, two men and a woman, were chopped down at the mouth of the lane by multiple bullet strikes. Isabel and the others quickly moved to the cover of a Winnebago's rear end and continued to fire.

Ryan stepped up behind the ville head woman.

"Face it, you've shot your wad," he told Isabel as she reloaded her AK. "You're not going to get them all. You've got to pull back to the caves. Let the scagworms have them."

"Are you going to talk or shoot?" she said.

When Ryan looked up, he saw the Impaler pop up over the top of the berm. Firing his AKs two-handed, the baron stormed down the slope, leading his troops toward the Welcome Center.

"Stop them!" Ryan shouted to the others as he brought up his SIG. He took a fixed aimpoint and punched out a string of rapid-fire single shots, letting the troopers run into his kill zone. He sent a couple of the fighters sprawling, but Malosh, his number-one target, was already behind the cover of the predark building.

The companions added their fire to the mix, leaving bodies dotting the side of the berm. Most of Malosh's troopers made it to safety.

"Now there's nothing between us and the nukin' worms," J.B. said ruefully.

"They'll be coming over the battlements in a minute or two," Ryan said. "Then it'll be too late to do anything."

"Isabel," Doc said urgently, "it's time to find cover. We can't do anything more here, except die."

"All right, all right," the blond woman conceded as she stood. "Everybody pull back. We'll join the others in the caves."

As they all turned for the cargo container that hid the entrance to the tunnels they heard something in the distance. A whining sound. Coming from high in the sky. Growing louder and louder.

"Fireblast!" J.B. cried. "That's incoming!"

There wasn't enough time to take shelter. Ryan shielded Krysty and the boys with his body, anticipating a violent explosion and flying metal. The explosion was all flash and no shrap. More of a wet pop than a thunderclap. When Ryan looked over his shoulder he saw a thick pillar of white smoke rising from the middle of the garden, rising straight up in the air.

"That's a ranging round!" he said. "It's got to be Haldane. He's shelling the ville! Go! Go! Go!"

With Isabel in the lead, they all raced for the cave entrance.

Chapter Twenty-Eight

On the eastern side of Magus's artillery encampment, away from the master and the main body of his road trash, two low-level minions hunkered in the shade of a Winnebago's flank, waiting for the shelling of Sunspot to begin. They had gotten as far from Steel Eyes' pounding boom box as they could. Magus was playing some kind of godawful predark racket. Squawking horns. Screeching fiddles. Thundering drums. A selected accompaniment to mass slaughter. It made their skins crawl. And they didn't dare get caught with cotton wads stuffed in their ears.

Magus took that as an insult to his musical taste.

Insults to his taste, or anything else for that matter, were repaid by insults to living bodies. Vitals removed. Guts strung like garlands over the tops of the sage-brush.

One of the minions wore a headband made from a long strip of plastic trash bag. His face was rimed with dirt mixed with body oils; it made his lips look extra red and his eyeballs extra white.

The other man was equally filthy, as if he'd been slathered with lard, then rolled head to foot in coal dust. He sported a dense black beard that came down to the middle of his broad chest.

In contrast to their shabby duds and absent personal hygiene, both men carried brand-new, full-auto blasters on canvas shoulder slings.

"This job is a piece of cake," Headband said.

"Yeah, I wish they were all this easy," Beard said. "Chilling at long distance is sweet. Only hassle is the looting."

"What looting?"

"That's what I'm talking about. There ain't any of that good old hands-on with this one. We get paid out of the price Haldane is giving Magus. No extra. Me, I like a treasure hunt. Adds some spice to the day."

"Folks up there on the ridge gonna get a big surprise," Headband said with a grin.

"So will the buzzards who try to eat 'em."

Headband wiped his mouth on the back of his hand. The hand stayed dirty, and his mouth was no cleaner, either. "Damn, I wish I had me a gallon jug of beer. None of that week-old green shit, either. Gives me the runs something fierce."

"Yeah, some six-week brew would be good right now. Even warm. Can't seem to wash the grit out of my back teeth with plain water."

"You gonna stick around for Steel Eyes' next job?"

"Dunno," Beard said. "Been thinking about spending some of the jack I got put away, mebbe take a little vacation from the mercie trade for a while."

"You mean, two weeks in a trailer-house gaudy?"

"More like a month. Take me that long to catch up on my screwing. You heard about what the next job is yet?"

"No. And I know better than to get nosy. Nosy can get you chilled in a hurry around here."

"Don't I know it."

"What was that?" Headband said, stiffening. His eyes narrowed to slits.

"What was what?" Beard asked.

"I saw something move over there." Headband raised his H&K, using it to point away from the circle of wags. About twenty yards distant, out on the desert, there was a fresh hole in the dirt.

"What was it?"

"Didn't see it that clear. Just caught the butt end of it as it slipped down the hole. Looked mighty big and meaty. Mebbe a nice fat jackrabbit. You a little hungry?

"Always."

"Let's go get us a snack."

The pair of road trash spread out and approached the hole gingerly from two sides. Headband paused en route and used his sheath knife to hack off a long branch from a creosote bush. He quickly trimmed off the side stems, creating a pointy stick. Creeping forward, he dropped to his knees in front of the hole and shoved the stick in, poking it around.

Beard had his machine pistol ready to fire, his stout legs braced. Headband was trying to encourage whatever it was to pop out of an escape hole so he could blast it with his H&K.

Nothing doing.

"It ain't coming out," Beard said after a minute or two. "Mebbe it ain't a bunny."

"What do you mean?" Headband said, drawing back the stick.

"Shit, it could be anything hiding in there. You didn't see it, you said."

"You sound scared. You scared?"

Beard didn't like the question, or its implication. "Gimme that stick," he snarled, and snatched it away.

"Don't worry, I'll cover you," Headband said sarcastically.

Beard hunkered down on the ground on his belly and rammed in not just the stick, but his arm all the way to the shoulder. Driving with his legs, he straining as far forward as he could get.

"I feel something…"

"Get it."

"I'm trying."

"Don't let it give you the slip."

"I think I got it. Yeah, I got it. It's tugging on the end of the stick. Man, the sucker's strong!"

"Hee, hee, ha." Headband chuckled.

Beard carefully started backing up, scooting on his knees, pulling his arm and the stick out of the hole.

What was clamped onto the end of the probe was no rabbit.

It had a black, eyeless, domelike head and a black, segmented shell. Halfway out of the hole, its transverse jaws snapped open, releasing the stick. They looked like ebony meat hooks.

"Chill it!" the kneeling and totally vulnerable man cried.

Before Headband could bring the muzzle of his machine pistol to bear, the creature moved in a sinuous blur, its hundreds of legs churning. It shot out of the hole and ran up under the man's coarse black chin whiskers.

Beard jolted backward. A gargling sound came from

his gaping mouth and the thing's tail end thrashed against his chest.

"I think it's got you, droolie," Headband said, "instead of the other way around." Then he started laughing and couldn't stop himself. The sight of the squirming fat tail of the black critter hanging out from under the guy's beard, and the guy trying to pull it off his neck was most comical.

Headband was too preoccupied watching his road buddy roll and thrash in the dirt, unable to dislodge the two-foot-long attacker, to keep his eyes on the hole.

A second black mutie scuttled out of the opening, ran across the sand, up his right leg to his hip. He felt rippling, scratchy bug feet on his chest a second before it sank its pincer jaws into the front of his throat. Their power was astounding. The twin prongs locked down in a vise grip, shutting off his laughter, and turning his breathing into a faint shrill whistle.

As the black worm squirmed from side to side, its jaws dug deeper and gripped even tighter, and hot blood sheeted over his chest.

Headband fought for his life, his eyes bugging out from the pressure of trapped blood inside his head. He let his machine pistol drop on its sling. The creature was too close for him to try to shoot it. Reaching to his belt, he managed to unsheathe a long knife. Grabbing a handful of bug ass, he stabbed at the back of the shell. The knife point, though needle-sharp, slid off; it wouldn't penetrate. Headband dropped to his knees and stabbed again. Failed again. The blade wouldn't even penetrate the dark band of cartilage between the armored segments. Because of his angle of attack, he just couldn't stab hard enough to get the job done.

He became more and more frantic, realizing that his time and his air were running out. He made a mighty stab and the point slipped off the shell. The long blade speared into his chest to the hilt. While he clutched the knife handle, eyes wide with surprise, the creature continued to squirm and thrash, slicing its jaws in deeper, as if trying to behead him.

Even though help was only a few dozen yards away, with their airways cut off, neither of the road trash could scream.

Not that screaming would have helped.

Nothing short of a gunshot could have been heard over the roar of Wagner emanating from Magus's boom box.

OUT OF SIGHT BETWEEN the parked wags, his arms folded across his chest, Baron Haldane watched the two men's futile struggles with fierce satisfaction on his face.

"Shouldn't we do something?" Bertram asked him, without suggesting what that something might be. Even the seasoned sec man blanched at the brutality and savagery of the attack.

"Let them die," Haldane said. The insect muties had saved him the trouble of chilling them.

And when the road trash stopped jerking under their own power, the worms slithered into their bodies, biting holes in their soft bellies, flopping back and forth until their tails disappeared inside. Then the stilled flesh moved again, shuddering, pumped by internal puppet masters.

"That's what we've been hearing creeping around here all night," Cuzo said. "What the hell are they?"

"Fucking deadly, that's what," Bertram replied.

"Stabbers sure don't chill them," Cuzo said. "We know that for a certain fact."

"Mebbe blasters don't, either."

"Don't be a triple-stupe," the baron said.

"Fucking A," Bertram countered, looking warily at the surrounding desert, "those rad-blasted things could be anywhere."

"They could be tunneling under our feet," Cuzo said.

"They can't eat through Humvees," Haldane said. "Safeties off. Keep your eyes peeled."

"What about those bodies?" Bertram asked.

"Leave them where they are," Haldane said. "Unless you want to risk getting a dose of what those two got."

"They might get seen by Magus's men."

"So what? We didn't chill them."

"They might attract more of those things," Bertram continued.

"The more the better," Haldane said. "They can do the mopping up for us."

The baron stepped out from cover and walked away from the corpses, toward the loud music. Thorne was still out in the open, under the full sun. He knew had to be broiling inside that tiny plastic cage. Haldane could see the remote detonator's red arming light. It was blinking.

The doomie oracle hadn't said that his son would be put in danger. Had it slipped his mind? Or had he just not seen it coming? Either way, another chilling was on tap when Haldane got back to Nuevaville. Mebbe he'd toss the whole lot of them over the cliff.

His plan for rescuing his son was to hit Steel Eyes and his men with an all-out assault as soon as the last of the chemical weapon rounds was fired. Before that happened, he and his sec men had to put some of Magus's wags out of commission.

From what he'd seen of the remote detonator and the firing device, he figured they had to be radio-controlled. Which meant the only way to block the omnidirectional signal was to surround the pet carrier in a thick lead box. Which of course he had no access to. Shooting the firing device out of Magus's hand was a dicey proposition, even at close range. And the half man still might be able to detonate the bomb before he was hit. The guards surrounding Steel Eyes would expect an attack on foot, and would be prepared to thwart it. Without the element of surprise, there was no way to free Thorne.

His plan involved not only what he hoped was surprise, but a critical supposition about why Magus had ordered his men to draw a wide perimeter around the cage. If the explosive device on the carrier had had a motion sensor on it, there was no need for the circle in the dirt. Just touching it would have set it off. If the bomb didn't have a motion sensor, then it could be removed.

Even if Haldane was right, he knew the odds for success were piss poor. But failure had its compensations. If father and son were both blown up in the attempt, at least Thorne wouldn't be vivisected, and the baron wouldn't have to live with the fact that he could do nothing to stop it.

Magus came into view, lounging in his throne chair. Boom box by his feet. He raised his hand and made a circular motion to the gunner waiting beside the cannon in the middle of the ring of wags.

Let's roll.

Steel Eyes reached up and turned off his auditory sensors.

"Stand clear!" the gunner barked. Sticking a finger in the ear facing the gun, he yanked the lanyard with his other hand.

Blam!

The Lyagushka jolted on its carriage, its barrel belching smoke.

The ranging round arced away, sizzling and squealing as it cored the fresh morning air.

With the gathered road trash cheering and jumping up and down, Magus turned his ears back on, then cranked up the awful music. Valkyries shrieked at top volume.

Haldane couldn't follow the round as it streaked downrange; it flew too fast and too high.

Seconds later, a puff of white erupted over Sunspot's ridge, plainly visible in the bright sunlight. The shell had landed inside the berm; its smoke swept east, into the canyon. The breeze over the target was blowing from left to right, thanks to the funneling effect of gorge.

"Nice shooting!" Magus shouted over the musical clamor. "Let's see if you can lay another one in the ten-ring."

As the gunner and his crew started to reload, Haldane and his seven sec men retreated along the outside of the ring of wags; when they were out of sight, they broke and ran. The goal was to decommission all but three of the fastest vehicles. They ignored the Winnebago

Braves and the milspec six-by-sixes, which didn't have the top-end speed to keep up with Humvees. They moved quickly to their preassigned targets.

Easing a Hummer's front passenger door open, Cuzo slipped inside, across the seats. He reached under the dashboard for the ignition wires. Yanking down a bundle of brightly colored spaghetti, he slashed through it with his sheath knife several times, cutting it into short, useless pieces. Elapsed time, twenty-five seconds.

As Haldane stood guard for Cuzo, the landship's blond-dreadlocked caretaker stepped out of nowhere, appearing right in his face. Before the man could yell a warning, the baron jammed the muzzle of his Remington sawed-off hard against his chest. The sound of the contact gunshot was drowned out by the earthshaking boom of the second smoke round's launching.

The force of the shot lifted the sec man off his feet and hurled him backward. He hit the ground limp and lifeless; four inches of his spine had been blown out his back.

The yank-and-slash sabotage of three Humvees took a little more than two minutes, and was accomplished without raising an alarm. Haldane crouched on the passenger side of one of the still-operational SUVs while Cuzo crawled in behind the steering wheel.

In the middle of the wag circle, the gunner was finishing his final calculations. He made a show of kissing the nose of the sarin projectile before it was rammed into the Lyagushka's breech.

Through the Humvee's grimy side window windshield, the baron saw Cuzo reach for the ignition switch.

Chapter Twenty-Nine

Baron Malosh stiffened when he heard the noise coming from the south. He couldn't believe his ears. It got louder and louder until it drowned out the seesawing autofire, until it was screaming down on Sunspot like a meteor.

The screaming ended with a sudden bright flash and a hollow whump in the middle of the garden. Limp foliage and clods of dirt flew in all directions. From the blast crater a broad pillar of smoke drifted upward, angling over the east end of the berm, spiraling into the blue sky.

A targeting round.

Malosh was momentarily stunned. The use of pre-dark artillery in the hellscape was as rare as the proverbial thirteen-year-old virgin. Even though such weapons existed in the arsenals cached in hidden stockpiles, no more than a handful of Deathlanders understood how to use them. Like so many other elements of whitecoat science, ballistics was a semi-lost art. Artillery wasn't favored in post-Apocalypse warfare because the stationary targets, isolated villes, weren't so well defended that they required bombardment. And at the first sign of a shelling, the human targets could usually run away.

In this case, that wasn't possible.

There was no time to run. Nowhere to run.

As the second smoke round exploded, hitting the top of the berm near the western gate, the baron knew the ville had been effectively bracketed. Moreover, he and his fighters were sandwiched between cannon fire and the waves of chill-crazed muties slithering up the side of the gorge.

The artillery was Haldane. It had to be.

The bastard had trapped him good.

"Get inside!" he roared at his men as he grabbed the reins of his stallion.

The fighters followed him and the horse into the Welcome Center. Malosh figured that the basement was deep enough and strong enough to withstand high-explosive shelling. In addition, the Welcome Center's entrances and exits could be either blocked or defended against all comers. The building's narrow entrance would force the attacking worms into tight bunches, which were made to order for autofire to grind into pulp.

"Get the fodder out of here!" he shouted to his fighters as they swept into the building.

There was room for a horse, but not fodder.

The troopers started shoving the terrified unarmed men and women out the front doors. The sponges had already cleared out most of the Haldane garrison's corpses; the place still reeked of burned Comp B and spilled guts.

Malosh didn't try to lead his horse down the steep staircase. He left it in the reception area. Before he headed for the basement, he ordered five of his men to remain at the front doors.

"Whatever you do, keep the worms out," he told them. "Defend the entrance."

As he dashed down the hall toward the stairway, the fighters opened fire.

WHEN THE FIRST smoke round exploded, Young Crad and Bezoar lay prostrate behind the tarp-load of body parts they had been carrying. They were pinned down by the intense cross fire between the ville folk and Malosh's forces. Neither of the swineherds understood the significance of the plume of white smoke. But they couldn't miss its consequence. The wild blasterfight abruptly stopped and the ville folk headed for cover.

Bezoar started to get up, but Young Crad snatched hold of his arm and held him down. "Not safe."

"We gotta find someplace to hide," Bezoar said, shaking off his hand.

"Hide from what?" Young Crad said.

Then they heard the second shell plummeting down on them.

"Oh, shit," the elder swineherd moaned.

The round exploded on the berm top to their left, near the gate. Thick white smoke boiled up from the hole. The breeze sent wisps of it rolling over them.

Bezoar pushed to his feet. As he turned toward the Welcome Center he saw Malosh, his horse and his troopers retreating through the ruined entryway, then there was movement along the entire gorge side of the berm. Black, shiny creatures topped the crest, climbing over one another's backs in their eagerness.

"Oh, no," Young Crad gasped.

"You know what they are?"

"Bad. Oh, lordy. Bad."

That was already evident. The tide of scagworms tore into the dead fighters sprawled along the inside of the slope. There were lots of bodies and they were still warm. Thus occupied, the mutie predators didn't bother to chase down the living. Yet.

"Come on!" Bezoar cried, grabbing his young friend by the hand. They hiphopped across the compound to the corner of the Welcome Center, then turned into the building's entrance where five AKs awaited them.

"Let us in! Please!" the elder swineherd begged his fellow Malosh conscriptees.

For his trouble, Bezoar was shot twice in the gut. He fell back into Young Crad's arms, moaning and clutching his stomach. As Crad pulled him out of the line of fire, the entrance guards all cut loose, sending a withering message to anyone else thinking of rushing the stronghold.

The young swineherd leaned his friend back against the side of the building. When he looked up, he saw that the scagworms were animating the berm top's corpses. In their feeding frenzy, they made arms quiver, chests heave. Headless bodies appeared to be crawling down the slope.

Bezoar squeezed Young Crad's hand triple-hard. Under his grizzly beard, his face was dead pale.

A third meteor descended on Sunspot.

The shell landed in the western corner of the compound. It exploded with the same muffled whump, but the burst of smoke was different. It was much more dense, and not white, but sickly yellow-green. Pushed by the prevailing breeze, it rained a superfine, sticky mist over everything.

The fodder and the swampies caught out of doors froze in place as the mist enveloped them.

Those closest to the groundburst clutched their throats, staggered a step or two, then toppled onto their faces in the dirt. Their legs kicked spastically, going nowhere. The swampies farther away clawed at their eyes, choking on their own vomit. The hellhounds fell to the ground, frothing at the mouth and nose, and biting through their own limbs. Even the mutie worms weren't immune. They lashed and squirmed in place, digging their own shallow graves in the compound's packed earth.

If Young Crad was baffled by the mass die-off, Bezoar understood what was happening. That the yellow-green smoke was toxic.

"Don't breathe in, just run!" were the elder swine-herd's final words of advice.

When the callused fingers relaxed their grip on his hand, Young Crad knew his friend was gone. And that he was alone. Utterly alone. He sucked down the deepest, biggest breath he could manage and took off along the berm, running as fast as he could for the west gate. The sticky mist swirled around him, dotted his pumping arms and sweating face. He blinked it out of his eyes.

Don't breathe! Don't breathe! he told himself, even though his lungs had already started to burn.

Halfway to the gate, his vision began to blur. His eyes and nose streamed tears and mucous. His throat felt like it was closing up. He wanted to cough, but he gritted his teeth and swallowed. Three steps later he couldn't hold it back. He hacked and gasped, spewing copious fluids. Then his stomach lurched and he projectile vomited. Staggering forward like a marathon runner stretching for the finish tape, he reached the rear bumper of the foot gate.

As his fingers touched it, he collapsed.

IN THE TORCHLIT BASEMENT stronghold of the Welcome Center, Baron Malosh listened as another dull explosion burst overhead. He was tensed, waiting for the earth-shaking rumble of HE, but it never came.

Two more soft, widely separated booms followed.

Then nothing.

After a while, his men started giving him puzzled looks.

"Just wait. Wait," he told them.

It was very quiet in the cellar. Quiet on the floor above, as well. The men guarding the entrance had stopped shooting.

Malosh got his first inkling of the nature of the attack when the people around him began to fall ill. They first complained of headache, eye pain, constricted breathing. When they began to wheeze, he knew.

They had been gassed.

The chemical weapons were heavier than air. The invisible gases were designed to sink to the lowest point, to wipe out anyone hiding in a below-ground shelter. In this case, that was the basement.

The troopers getting sick the quickest were those whose skins were the most exposed. Men without shirts or hats.

Malosh was well covered except for the upper half of his face, so less of his surface area was exposed to neurotoxins. To stay below ground was certain death.

Clamping a gloved hand over the mesh of his mask, he bolted from the stronghold and ran up the steps to the ground floor. Some of the less effected troopers tried to follow him. They fell along the way as their legs gave out, on the basement floor or on the stairs.

The baron found his treasured horse in convulsions on the reception room floor; the entrance guards were likewise down, shitting and pissing themselves. They had received a higher immediate dose. Malosh burst out of the doorway, his hand still covering the mask hole.

Sunlight filtered through gauzy yellow-green clouds. Poison gas still hissed and boiled from the impact craters in the compound.

The baron shielded his eyes from the falling mist with his other hand. He ran headlong into the breeze, stumbling over the corpses of humans, muties and scag-worms. He knew he'd been dosed, though perhaps less than fatally. His head had started to throb, the pain centered in the middle of his eyes. He had to get upwind of the toxins to have any hope of surviving. He couldn't scale the berm because his legs were already starting to feel weak. The closest exit was the foot gate.

He reached it without drawing another breath, but as he stepped over the body lying in front of the back bumper, something seized his left ankle in an iron grip. He looked down and saw the body wasn't dead. One of his own fodder, a barrel-chested droolie, had him by the foot.

Malosh didn't ask to be let go. He didn't order the dying man to release him. He started mule-kicking the stupe in the face, breaking out his teeth with the heel of his boot. He managed a half dozen stomps before his kicks weakened and his knees bucked. He sat hard beside the bloody-faced fodder.

Even though the dying fingers let go of his ankle, he couldn't get up from the ground.

He had to breathe, and did so, but little or no air came through his constricted airway. Above the edge of the leather mask, his face was slowly turning blue.

Malosh ripped off the mask, gasping.

Under it there was no hideous battle scar.

No putrid decay from rad cancer.

No mutated mandibles.

Framed by the pasty patch of skin from nose to chin were a pair of baby lips. A tiny rosebud of a mouth. Feminine, infantile, and ridiculous in his wide face and masculine jaw. Most unbaronlike. Who would take orders from a mouth like that? A mouth perpetually pursed to suckle at its mother's bulging teat? Who would march at its command into the jaws of death? Not even an idiot. Malosh had concealed his genetic flaw with black leather and brutal skewerings. They were diversions, slight of hand.

There was no one left alive to see the truth.

No one left to snicker and laugh. To mock him.

Nor would there ever be.

As he died sitting in his own shit, the circle of death came full. Every structure, every inch of the grounds was painted in yellow-green toxin. In the finest of fine mists, it had penetrated deep into the Welcome Center, filling the basement with a lethal concentration of fumes. There lay a jumble of corpses, their faces blue and bloodied in their struggles with death and with one another.

In the end those closest to the shellburst got off the

easiest. They were poleaxed by the poison. Those who soaked it up more slowly suffered all the torments of hell.

The sarin gas barrage attacked and chilled every living thing within the perimeter of Sunspot ville. It did so by inhibiting the production of an enzyme vital to all neural systems. Without this enzyme, nerve function ceased. Smooth muscles stopped reacting.

The oncoming wave of scagworms turned back from the flanks of the berm as members of their species slid dead on their backs down the slope, spreading death by contact. Sensing their mortal danger, the worms on the gorge below cut a wide path around Sunspot.

Even the ville's ubiquitous horseflies were dead; they fell from the air bouncing on the ground like tiny black BBs.

Everything that Sunspot had ever been, everything that it had ever hoped to be was left to rot.

Forever.

Chapter Thirty

Ryan was the last through the door hacked into the side of the cargo container. It took a second for his eye to adjust to the dim light. At the far end of the steel box, a woodstove on a platform had been swung aside, revealing a hole in the floor. The two boys disappeared down it, followed by Isabel, Doc, Krysty, Jak and Mildred. J.B. squashed down his hat and jumped in after Mildred.

Ryan looked down into the opening and saw the floor of the tunnel about four feet below, lit by flickering torches. He hopped through the hole, turned and pulled the stove platform back over the hole to cover their retreat.

After a four- or five-foot crawl, the floor of the passage dropped away from the ceiling, and he could stand upright. There was no wood- or metal-beam bracing of the tunnel walls or roof. The passage was a fissure cracked in the naked rock. Ahead he could see J.B. vanishing around a turn. As he started after him, he heard the dull pop of a second smoke round, and he knew that Haldane had the range.

The tunnel angled down.

But not down far enough to suit Ryan.

It opened onto a low-ceilinged chamber where the

entire ville appeared to be waiting. Thanks to torches set in the stone walls, he could see weapons, ammo canisters and shoulder-to-shoulder men, women and children.

"You can't stay here," Ryan told them. "If the ground overhead takes a direct hit of high explosive, this room will cave in."

"We're just fine here," Isabel said. "There's twenty feet of solid rock above us."

"And it's all going to come down on your heads," Ryan insisted. "You have to evacuate the tunnels. Get out at the bottom of the ridge, and let Haldane finish off Malosh."

"We're not leaving," Isabel said. "We need to be here when Haldane tries to retake the ville. We've got a big surprise for him."

The ville folk nodded in the flickering light, their assault rifles in hand.

"What about the worms?" Doc said.

"I told you we know how to handle them."

Then they heard another soft boom from above.

"Is that a third smoke round?" Mildred said, grimacing. "Why would they need a third?"

"Mebbe the breeze is shifting topside, and they had to bust another smoke bomb to nail down the zero," J.B. said.

"Come with us now," Doc entreated the head woman. He tried to take her hands in his, but she stepped back out of his reach. "Please, Isabel. Before it is too late."

"Goodbye again, Theo," she said.

Doc shook his head, a profound sadness in his eyes.

"Do what you want, but we're leaving," Ryan told the ville folk. "Just point us in the right direction."

"You'll get lost for sure," one of the blond boys said. "You need somebody to show you the way out. We'll do it. We said we'd do it."

"No, you won't," a woman stated emphatically.

Ryan assumed she was their mother or a close blood relative. She had the same color eyes and hair.

"You stay here where you'll be safe," she told the boys, "and I'll take them myself."

The woman slung an AK, grabbed a torch and led them out a side passage. Jak and Ryan took torches, as well.

The chosen tunnel began to descend at a steep angle almost immediately. In places it narrowed so much they had to turn sideways to squeeze past the opposing walls. As they reached a hairpin turn an even softer boom came from above.

"What's going on up there? That's still not HE," Mildred said.

"Keep moving," Ryan said.

Ahead, the corridor ceiling necked down. They had to crawl on hands and knees to pass through the gap. It was hot in the passage and getting hotter the deeper they went. Sweat peeled down the sides of Ryan's face and trickled along his scalp. The air was noticeably stale.

The reason for this soon became clear. Thirty feet farther on, the passage was completely blocked off by a floor-to-ceiling pile of rocks.

Their guide immediately started pulling stones off the pile and tossing them aside. "We've got to reopen the tunnel wide enough to squeeze through," she said.

"Why is it sealed off?" Krysty said.

"Scagworms were using it to get at our livestock," she said.

The companions pitched in, and in a matter of minutes they had opened a two-and-a-half-foot-diameter hole at the top of the pile, near the tunnel roof. At once they could feel a breeze on their faces.

"Gaia, that's fresh air," Krysty said.

"We should be close to the exit at the bottom of the ridge, then," Mildred said.

The guide climbed up the pile and squirmed through the opening, torch first.

One by one, the companions followed.

On the other side of the barrier, the arm's-width passage descended in a steep, straight incline. The flow of air was much stronger. Almost a wind.

"Hold it," their guide said. "Listen…"

When they stopped, over the hiss of their torches they could hear sounds from the tunnel below.

Scrabbling sounds.

The sounds of tens of thousands of crisp claw feet scraping over bare rock, and coming fast.

"Pull back!" the guide cried, turning uphill.

"No, we'd never make it," Ryan told her as he stuck his torch in a crack. "They'd pull us down from behind. We've got to hold them off here, or die trying. Jak, plant your torch. Everybody, weapons up. This isn't gonna be pretty."

"I'm going back to the ville," the guide said, pushing past Ryan and heading up the tunnel. "I'm sealing up the hole after I get through it. If you want to go ahead, you're on your own."

The scrabbling sound grew louder and louder, and as it did there were other, intermittent noises, like bolt cutters snapping shut.

J.B. stepped in front of the others, his Uzi held level in both hands. The passage was so narrow that only one person could fire at a time.

When the scagworms came, they didn't just run along the tunnel floor. They scampered across the walls and ceiling, too.

J.B. opened fire the second he saw their shiny helmet heads. The roar of his machine pistol was deafening in the cave. Gooshey guts, like hot vanilla pudding, splattered the walls and misted his glasses as the worms distintegrated under the 9 mm hail. Their bodies dropped from the ceiling and walls, tumbling onto their dead fellows on the cave floor.

J.B. emptied his Uzi in short order. He let it fall on its neck lanyard and swung up his 12-gauge pump. Serious boom time. He fired and cycled, fired and cycled, blowing the scagworms apart.

When that blaster came up empty, too, he spun away, letting Ryan take the lead. The worms seemed endless, J.B. hadn't made a dent in them. Ryan didn't think, he shot. He picked off the four-inch-wide targets as fast as they appeared. Even so, their bodies were falling closer and closer to him. In the flickering light, the heaps of dying scagworms writhed and thrashed.

When Ryan's slide locked back, he stepped aside for Doc, who raised his LeMat and discharged the shotgun barrel. The flash lit up the tunnel for thirty feet. Switching to his revolver cylinder, Doc popped off the weapon's .44-caliber lead balls.

Not one scagworm got past him, but there were more where they came from.

"We've got to move back," Ryan said as J.B. returned to the fray with his reloaded Uzi.

The air was no longer fresh. It was thick with gun-smoke and the stench of aerosolized scagworm.

The creatures were falling at J.B.'s feet when his machine pistol ran out of bullets.

Before Ryan could take up the chilling slack, a single scagworm raced along the wall past J.B.'s head. It jumped to the floor behind him and scampered on.

Doc promptly skewered the tip of its ass to the ground with the rapier blade of his swordstick. Hissing and snapping its jaws, the agile worm tried to turn and bite off his leg.

Jak put the muzzle of his Python to its eyeless head and fired. Problem solved.

Ryan still had six rounds in his SIG when the worm wave suddenly faltered and stopped.

"Looks like we won," J.B. said, peering through spectacles coated with white spray.

"Let's get the hell out of here," he said. "Watch your step."

They trotted downhill, crunching and sliding on the spilled pudding and slick-armored backs. On the far side of the patch of dead, the footing was better. They made quick time to the circle of light at the end of the tunnel.

After Jak and Ryan made sure there were no worms lurking just outside, the companions left the cave and headed upwind as fast as they could run, moving west of the ville, away from the spear point of the insectoid invasion, parallel to Interstate 10. The way west was free from human coldhearts, as well, because all of Malosh's fighters were up in Sunspot.

There was still no HE thunder from above.

No blasterfire anymore, either.

Ryan didn't like it. He didn't like it one bit.

Baron Haldane wouldn't have called off the bombardment after locking in the range. And he wouldn't have laid down a bunch of smoke rounds just for the hell of it.

Mebbe the worms got them all? he thought as he ran.

What had actually happened was something much, much worse.

When the companions were far enough from ridge to get a view of the summit, they could see thick plumes of yellow-green smoke angling upward, stretching five or six hundred feet in the air.

They stopped to catch their breath and to stare.

"That's not from a ranging round," J.B. said.

"What is it, then?" Krysty said.

High above the ville, a sparse flock of buzzards descended, spiraling down to the feast. Long before they reached the top of the column of sickly smoke, they crumpled in midair, every one of them, and fell like stones from the sky.

"Good God!" Mildred said.

Chapter Thirty-One

As the third and final sarin round whistled away toward the distant hilltop, Magus slapped the arms of his throne chair and smiled.

It wasn't a pretty sight.

Only one side of his mouth turned up, and it locked there, twitching as guy wire spools slipped and caught, slipped and caught.

Baron Haldane tapped the Hummer's side window and Cuzo started the engine. As he popped it into gear and swerved out of the wag circle, Haldane ran low and out of sight on the passenger side.

Cuzo shifted into second and flattened the accelerator against the firewall, taking dead aim at the captain's chair and the half-human thing that sat on it.

As Magus turned in his chair to look, his alert bodyguards stepped right into the Humvee's path, opening fire with their machine pistols. Baron Haldane was already sprinting away from the wag, making a beeline for the booby-trapped pet carrier.

Cuzo ducked below the dash as 9 mm slugs stitched across front window, blowing glass shards over his back. He plowed into one of the sec men, flipping his body up and over the SUV's roof. The other bodyguard barely managed to scramble out of the way, on all fours.

Before he could recover and resume shooting, Cuzo tapped his brakes, stuck his AK out the driver window and put thirty holes in his road trash ass.

In the meantime Magus was backing up around his captain's chair, all herky-jerky, and calling for help from the rest of his crew. He still had the detonator clutched in his hand, but he wasn't looking over at the pet carrier. He was too occupied by the startling, seemingly suicidal, vehicular assault.

Haldane dashed across the death circle, knelt in front of the carrier and ripped the explosive package off the door. He snap-tossed it as far away as he could.

Magus realized what was happening and jammed his thumb down on the trigger, but it was too late.

The bomb exploded harmlessly in the air.

Cuzo cranked the steering wheel hard over and floored the gas pedal again. Fishtailing the wag, he took aim at Haldane and the carrier. As he did so, two other stolen Humvees roared out of the circle, catching broadside blasterfire as they passed the road trash. From the back seats of the Humvees, two of Haldane's men returned fire but were overwhelmed and undone by hundreds of incoming slugs. Magus's full-auto firing squad blew in the side windows and chewed up the sheet-metal doors on the drivers' sides. One of the Humvees immediately coasted to a stop, the inside of its surviving windows tinted red from cranial back splatter. The other Humvee kept going, but no one was driving. It ran head-on into a sandy bluff.

The road trash turned their fire on the rear of Cuzo's Humvee, then suddenly directed their aim down at the ground in front of them.

Two-foot-long critters were popping up from the soil all around them, even from between their boots, like black maggots squirming out of a long-dead, hollowed-out rat. They swarmed from the shadows under the parked wags, turning the ground black and shiny.

It was as though somebody had rung the dinner bell.

There was only one item on the menu. It was road trash, and it was going fast.

Attacked from all sides at once, Magus's sec men stood back to back and fired full-auto. Even at 500 rounds a minute, they couldn't keep up with the worms. There were too many of them popping up, and they moved too quickly and too erratically over open ground. When they paused to reload, one by one the road trash were overwhelmed. Ebony jaws snapping, the worms ran up their legs and ripped into them. Literally. The worms tore holes in the living torsos and wriggled inside the tropical warmth and humidity. The plundered men screamed like little girls. Around the broken circle, wag doors slammed as the luckier ones ducked behind solid cover.

The worms were coming for Haldane, too. He held his fire and blew them apart at close range, defending his caged son with double-aught buck.

Cuzo drove over dozens of the mutie insects, crushing them. He skidded the Humvee to a stop in front of Haldane. The baron hoisted the pet carrier by its top handle and swung it onto the back seat. Over the wag's roof he saw Magus momentarily holding his own while five or six black worms bit into the metal struts on his legs. Steel Eyes held worms in his bare hands. His half-mechanical fingers crushed their domed heads like raw eggs.

Cuzo had the Humvee rolling again before the baron could get both feet in the cab.

Haldane saw the blood all over the wag's interior. The steering wheel was slick with it. "Are you hit?"

"Shit, yes. Look at the floorboards."

"Let me drive."

"No time to make a switch. We've got to put some distance between us and them." Cuzo shifted into a higher gear and the wag surged faster, bounding over low boulders and shallow ruts. The wind shrieked through the bullet holes in the windshield.

"You're going the wrong way," the baron told him. "Nuevaville is behind us."

"I'm gonna cut around to the northwest," Cuzo said. "Swing wide of the Sunspot ridge and miss those nasty black critters."

Haldane stuck his head out of the passenger-side window and looked behind them. It was hard to see because of the way the Humvee was bouncing around. When he pulled back inside he said, "Don't think anyone is coming after us yet. No dust clouds but ours. You want me to drive so you can see to that wound you got?"

"I think it's stopped bleeding some," Cuzo said. "Hurts like a mutie bitch, though. I'll give you the wheel after we cross old Interstate 10. I can see it about three miles ahead. We should be well in the clear by then."

Haldane twisted around to the back seat. He rattled the padlock on the pet carrier door. It seemed plenty solid; it had a case-hardened frame. Even if he'd had the proper tools, he'd have had a tough time getting it open with the lurching, bucking motion of the wag.

"I'm sorry, I can't get the door open for you, son,"

he said to the small face behind the steel grate. "It's going to have to wait until we stop for a minute. Then I'll shoot the damn lock off, I promise."

"I'm okay, Dad," Thorne said bravely. "Don't worry about me. I can wait all day if I have to."

"It's not far," the baron assured him.

Through the dusty, cracked windshield, Interstate 10 became an ever more distinct ribbon across their path.

Cuzo kept the pedal to the metal, even as they neared the edge of the ruined roadway. The desert ahead looked fairly flat, except for occasional hidden dips that made Haldane's skull bump into the headliner and his backside crash into the seat cushion. Without warning, a huge creature popped up from one of those depressions, popped up right in front of them. Its hairy jointed legs looked like tree trunks.

When Cuzo swerved to avoid a fatal collision with the thing, the Humvee went airborne. It seemed to float for sickening seconds before it crashed nose-first into a shallow gully.

The impact slammed Thorne into the door of his cage. He blacked out, for how long he couldn't tell. When he awoke, he had a bad headache and there was blood in his mouth. Through the bars, he could see the two front seats and they were both empty. The windshield was gone, except for a sawtooth edge along the bottom of the channel.

"Dad? Dad?" the boy cried.

Then he heard wet, crunching sounds.

Very close.

Chapter Thirty-Two

"Why would Haldane fire poison gas on his own troops?" J.B. asked as the companions walked away from the smoking ridgetop, heading toward the ruined highway.

"The price of final victory is steep," Ryan replied. "He managed to chill his arch rival and his whole army."

"Not only that," Mildred said. "The bastard slaughtered every living soul in Sunspot. Chem gas is heavy. It seeps underground. The ville folk are all dead, too. You can bet on that."

"If she had only listened to me…" Doc muttered, leaning heavily on his swordstick.

"You couldn't have forced her to come with us," Krysty said. "She made her choice. It was the wrong one."

"That absolves me of nothing," Doc said miserably. "I failed her by not making a better case. And I failed myself."

"You're not responsible for what happened to her," Krysty said. "Baron Haldane is responsible."

"Why does that not make me feel better?"

"Because you really cared, that's why."

"Haldane didn't have to use gas to win the war," Mildred said. "The invading scagworms would have finished off Malosh and his army. If the worms take root here, this strip of land isn't going to be habitable for a long, long time. Maybe not ever again."

"So he bloodied his hands for nothing," Ryan said.

"Looks like," Mildred said.

"Wags," Jak announced over his shoulder. He pointed at the horizon. "There…"

The morning sun illuminated beige clouds of dust. Big wags, daisy-chaining. The multivehicle convoy was moving slowly south, away from Sunspot.

"Haldane is making his getaway," Krysty said.

"Nuevaville is the other direction," Ryan said.

"Another wag," Jak said, pointing west and slightly south.

"I don't see anything," Mildred said.

"If he says there's a wag, there's a wag," Ryan said. "Let's go check it out."

"Follow," the albino said.

The companions smelled the wreck long before they saw it. Spilled antifreeze, cloyingly sweet, rode on the eastward breeze. After they had crossed the interstate and climbed over hump of shoulder, the Humvee's uptilted rear end came into view.

Spreading out, they advanced on the wag.

The Humvee had taken a header into the bottom of the gully. The front windshield was broken out, the hood popped and buckled. Steam billowed up from the engine compartment. There were no signs of life. But plenty of signs of death. The hood was streaked and smeared with fresh blood.

"Dad?" a child's voice said desperately.

The companions quickly circled the wag.

When Ryan looked in the back seat, he saw the plastic box. It was just big enough to hold a small child. He wrenched open the side door and turned the carrier on the seat. "Damn," he said when the little face looked back at him from behind the bars.

He swung the carrier out of the Humvee and put it on the ground. "Cover your ears and turn your head away from the bars," he told the boy. Then he put the muzzle of the SIG against the lock and fired a single shot. The hasp snapped open. Ryan tossed the broken lock aside.

Mildred bent and helped the child out of the cage. He was shaking all over, wringing wet, and there was blood on his bruised chin.

"Where's my dad?" the boy said.

"Who's your dad?" Mildred asked.

"Baron Haldane. I'm Thorne Haldane."

"He was with you?" Ryan said.

"He was in the front seat, with Cuzo. We crashed and I got knocked out."

Mildred tried to give him a sip of water from her canteen. He shook his head and waved her off. "Where's my dad?" he said. "Is he chilled?" Then he started to cry.

Ryan looked at the gore smeared on the hood and all the churned-up dirt in the gully bottom. Lots of feet had been moving around the wreck. Heavy ones. Cawdor knew what had made the tracks. He and the companions had seen the beast from the battlements of Sunspot, fleeing from a pack of scagworms. It had to be the grave digger.

"Don't worry, Thorne," Ryan said. "We'll see you get home safe."

"It took my dad, didn't it?" the boy said, gulping air between sobs. "Didn't it? The mutie thing. I saw it right before we crashed. I heard it outside when I woke up."

"I'm sorry, there's no sign of your father, Thorne," Ryan said. "No sign of the other man, either."

J.B. stepped forward, "All that's left is this…"

"That's my dad's!" the boy cried.

Ryan took the sawed-off Remington 1100 from J.B. He jacked out the live rounds and handed the weapon to the boy.

Thorne cradled the blaster hard against his chest, tears streaming down his cheeks.

"We've got some heavy walking ahead of us," Ryan told him. "If you get tired, you let me know. I'll carry your blaster for you until you get home."

* * * * *

ROOM 59

Welcome to Room 59, a top secret,
international intelligence agency
sanctioned to terminate global threats
that governments can't touch.
Its high-level spymasters operate
in a virtual environment
and are seasoned in the dangerous game
of espionage and counterterrorism.

A Room 59 mission puts everything on the line;
emotions run high, and so does the body count.

Take a sneak preview of
THE POWERS THAT BE
by Cliff Ryder.

Available January 8,
wherever books are sold.

"Shot fired aft! Shot fired aft!" Jonas broadcast to all positions. "P-Six, report! P-Five, cover aft deck. Everyone else, remain at your positions."

Pistol in hand, he left the saloon and ran to the sundeck rail. Although the back of the yacht had been designed in a cutaway style, with every higher level set farther ahead than the one below it, the staggered tops effectively cut his vision. But if he couldn't see them, they couldn't see him either. He scooted down the ladder to the second level, leading with his gun the entire way. Pausing by the right spiral stairway, he tapped his receiver. Just as he was about to speak, he heard the distinctive *chuff* of a silenced weapon, followed by breaking glass. Immediately the loud, twin barks of a Glock answered.

"This is P-Five. Have encountered at least three hostiles on the aft deck, right side. Can't raise P-Six—" Two more shots sounded. "Hostiles may attempt to gain access through starboard side of ship, repeat, hostiles may attempt access through starboard side of ship—" The transmission was cut off again by the sustained burst of a silenced submachine gun stitching holes in the ship wall. "Request backup immediately," P-Five said.

Jonas was impressed by the calm tone of the speaker—it had to be the former Las Vegas cop, Martinson. He was about to see if he could move to assist when he spotted the muzzle of another subgun, perhaps an HK MP-5K, poke up through the open stairwell. It was immediately followed by the hands holding it, then the upper body of a black-clad infiltrator. Jonas ducked behind the solid stairway railing, biding his time. For a moment there was only silence, broken by the soft lap of the waves on the hull, and a faint whiff of gunpowder on the breeze.

Although Jonas hadn't been in a firefight in years, his combat reflexes took over, manipulating time so that every second seemed to slow, allowing him to see and react faster than normal. He heard the impact of the intruder's neoprene boot on the deck, and pushed himself out, falling on his back as he came around the curved railing. His target had been leading with the MP-5K held high, and before he could bring it down, Jonas lined up his low-light sights on the man's abdomen and squeezed the trigger twice. The 9 mm bullets punched in under the bottom edge of his vest, mangling his stomach and intestines, and dropping him with a strangled grunt to the deck. As soon as he hit, Jonas capped the man with a third shot to his face.

"This is Lead One. I have secured the second aft deck. P-Two and P-Three—"

He was cut off again as more shots sounded, this time from the front of the yacht. Jonas looked back. *A second team?*

And then he realized what the plan was, and how they had been suckered. "All positions, all positions, they mean to take the ship! Repeat, hostiles intend to take the ship! Lead Two, secure the bridge. P-Three, remain where you are, and target any hostiles crossing your area. Will clear from this end and meet you in the middle."

A chorus of affirmatives answered him, but Jonas was already moving. He stripped the dead man of his MP-5K and slipped three thirty-round magazines into his pockets. As he stood, a small tube came spinning up the stairway, leaving a small trail of smoke as it bounced onto the deck.

Dropping the submachine gun, Jonas hurled himself around the other side of the stairway railing, clapping his hands over his ears, squeezing his eyes shut and opening his mouth as he landed painfully on his right elbow. The flash-bang grenade went off with a deafening sound and a white burst of light that Jonas sensed even through his closed eyelids. He heard more pistol shots below, followed by the canvas-ripping sounds of the silenced MP-5Ks firing back. That kid is going to get his ass shot off if I don't get down there, he thought.

Jonas shook his head and pushed himself up, grabbing the submachine gun and checking its load. He knew the stairs had to be covered, so that way would be suicide. But there was a narrow space, perhaps a yard wide, between the back of the stairwell and the railing of the ship's main level. If he could get down there that way, he could possibly take them by surprise, and he'd also have the stairway as cover. It might be crazy, but it was the last thing they'd be expecting.

He crawled around the stairway again and grabbed the dead body, now smoking from the grenade. The man had two XM-84 flash-bangs on him.

Jonas grabbed one and set it for the shortest fuse time—one second. It should go off right as it hits the deck, he thought. He still heard the silenced guns firing below him, so somehow the two trainees had kept the second team from advancing. He crawled to the edge of the platform, checked that his drop zone was clear, then pulled the pin and let the grenade go, pulling back and assuming the *fire in the hole* position again.

The flash-bang detonated, letting loose its 120-decibel explosion and one-million-candlepower flash. As soon as the shock died away, Jonas rolled to the side of the boat just as a stream of bullets ripped through the floor where he had been. He jumped over the stairway, using one hand to keep in touch with his cover so he didn't jump too far out and miss the boat entirely. The moment he sailed into the air, he saw a huge problem—one of the assault team had had the same idea of using the stairway for cover, and had moved right under him.

Unable to stop, Jonas stuck his feet straight down and tried to aim for the man's head. The hijacker glanced up, so surprised by what he saw that for a moment he forgot he had a gun in his hand. He had just started to bring it up when Jonas's deck shoes crunched into his face. The force on the man's head pushed him to the deck as Jonas drove his entire body down on him. The mercenary collapsed to the floor, unmoving. Jonas didn't check him, but stepped on his gun hand, snapping his wrist as he steadied his own MP-5K, tracking anything moving on the aft deck.

The second team member rolled on the deck, clutching his bleeding ears, his tearing eyes screwed tightly shut. Jonas cleared the rest of the area, then came out and slapped the frame of his subgun against the man's skull, knocking him unconscious. He then cleared the rest of the area, stepping over Hartung's corpse as he did so. Only when he was sure there were no hostiles lying in wait did he activate his transceiver.

"P-Five, this is Lead. Lock word is tango. Have secured the aft deck. Report."

"This is P-Five, key word is salsa. I took a couple in the vest, maybe cracked a rib, but I'm all right. What should we do?"

"Take P-Six's area and defend it. Hole up in the rear saloon, and keep watch as best as you can. As soon as we've secured the ship, someone will come and relieve you."

"Got it. I'll be going forward by the left side, so please don't shoot me."

"If you're not wearing black, you'll be okay."

Jonas heard steps coming and raised the subgun, just in case a hostile was using the ex-cop as a hostage to get to him. When he saw the stocky Native American come around the corner, Glock first, Jonas held up his hand before the other man could draw a bead on him.

Martinson nodded, and Jonas pointed to the motionless man in front of him and the other guy bleeding in the corner of the deck. "Search these two and secure them, then hole up. I'm heading forward. Anyone comes back that doesn't give you the key word, kill them."

"Right. And sir—be careful."

"Always." Jonas left the soon-to-be-full operative to clear the deck and headed topside, figuring he'd take the high ground advantage. Scattered shots came from the bow, and he planned to get the drop on the other team—hell, it had worked once already. "P-One through P-Four, Lock word is tango. Report."

"P-One here, we've got two hostiles pinned at the bow, behind the watercraft. Attempts to dislodge have met with heavy resistance, including flash-bangs. P-Two is down with superficial injuries. We're under cover on the starboard side, trying to keep them in place."

"Affirmative. P-Three?"

"I'm moving up on the port side to cut off their escape route."

"P-Four? Come in, P-Four?" There was no answer. "P-Four, if you can't speak, key your phone." Nothing. *Shit.* "All right. P-One, hold tight, P-Three, advance to the corner and keep them busy. I'll be there in a second. Lead Two, if you are in position, key twice."

There was a pause, then Jonas heard two beeps. *Good.* Jonas climbed onto the roof of the yacht, crept past the radar and radio antennas, then crossed the roof of the bridge, walking lightly. As he came upon the forward observation room, he saw a black shadow crawling up onto the roof below him. Jonas hit the deck and drew a bead on the man. Before he could fire, however, three shots sounded from below him, slamming into the man's side. He jerked as the bullets hit him, then rolled off the observation roof.

That gave Jonas an idea. "P-Two and Three, fire in the hole." He set the timer on his last XM-84 and skittered it across the roof of the observation deck, the flash-bang disappearing from sight and exploding, lighting the night in a brilliant flash.

"Advance now!" Jonas jumped down to the observation roof and ran forward, training his pistol on the two prostrate, moaning men as the two trainees also came from both corners and covered them, kicking their weapons away. Jonas walked to the edge of the roof and let himself down, then checked the prone body lying underneath the shattered windows. He glanced up to see the two men, their wrists and ankles neatly zip-tied, back-to-back in the middle of the bow area.

"Lead Two, this is Lead. Bow is secure. Tally is six hostiles, two dead, four captured. Our side has one KIA, two WIA, one MIA."

"Acknowledged. Bridge is secure."

Jonas got the two trainees' attention. "P-One, make sure P-Two is stable, then head back and reinforce P-Five, and make sure you give him the key word. P-Three, you're with me."

Leading the way, Jonas and the trainee swept and cleared the entire ship, room by room. Along the way, they found the body of the young woman who had been at position four, taken out with a clean head shot. Jonas checked her vitals anyway, even though he knew it was a lost cause, then covered her face with a towel and kept moving. Only when he was satisfied that no one else was aboard did he contact everyone. "The ship is clear, repeat, the ship is clear. Karen, let's head in, we've got wounded to take care of."

"What happens afterward?" she asked on a separate channel.

"I'm going to visit Mr. Castilo and ask him a few questions."

"Do you want to interrogate any of the captives?"

Jonas considered that for only a moment. "Negative. All of them are either deaf from the flash-bangs or concussed or both, and besides, I doubt they know anything about what's really going down today anyway. No, I need to go to the source."

"I'll contact Primary and update—"

"I'm the agent in charge, I'll do it," Jonas said. He sent a call to headquarters on a second line. "No doubt Judy will flip over this. Do you still have a fix on that Stinger crate?"

"Yes, it's heading south-southwest, probably to Paradise," Karen replied.

"Naturally. See if you can get this behemoth to go any faster, will you? I just got a really bad feeling that this thing is going down faster than we thought." He gripped the handrail and waited for the connection, willing the yacht to speed them to their destination more quickly, all the while trying to reconcile the fact that his son was involved in a plot that could very well tear a country apart.

* * * * *

Look for THE POWERS THAT BE
by Cliff Ryder in January 2008
from Room 59™.
Available wherever books are sold.

ROOM 59

CRISIS: A massive armed insurgency—
ninety miles off America's coast.

MISSION: CUBA

A Cuban revolution threatens to force the U.S.
into a dangerous game of global brinksmanship,
thrusting spymaster Jonas Schrader into an
emotional war zone—exacting the highest price
for a mission completed.

Look for

THE
powers
THAT be

by cliff RYDER

GOLD
EAGLE ®

Available January wherever you buy books.

GRM591

TAKE 'EM FREE

2 action-packed novels plus a mystery bonus

NO RISK
NO OBLIGATION TO BUY

ROGUE Angel™

Look for

AleX Archer
SERPENT'S KISS

While working on a dig on the southern coast of India, Annja finds several artifacts that may have originated from a mythical lost city. Then Annja is kidnapped by a modern-day pirate seeking the lost city. But she quickly sides with him and his thieves to ward off an even greater evil—the people deep in the Nilgiris Mountains, who aren't quite human...and they don't like strangers.

Available January wherever you buy books.

GOLD EAGLE®

GRA10

James Axler
Outlanders®

GRAILSTONE GAMBIT

Across mystical Celtic lands a devious enemy has resurfaced, a new messiah of the Druidic religion. Ushering in a new age of magic, terror and human sacrifice, the interloper seeks an ancient relic that will resurrect the dead. To rescue a culture from barbarism, the Cerberus warriors stand with a warrior queen in a final challenge to turn the tide of ancient madness that threatens to engulf the entire world.

Available February wherever you buy books.